W9-DBX-447

OFF MAGAZINE STREET

a novel by Ronald Everett Capps

OFF MAGAZINE STREET

a novel by Ronald Everett Capps

MacAdam/Cage

MacAdam/Cage
155 Sansome Street, Suite 550
San Francisco, CA 94104
www.macadamcage.com

Copyright © 2004 by Ronald Everett Capps
ALL RIGHTS RESERVED.

Library of Congress Cataloging-in-Publication Data

Capps, Ronald Everett.
    Off Magazine Street / by Ronald Everett Capps.
        p. cm.
    ISBN 1-931561-74-5 (alk. paper)
    1. Universities and colleges—Admission—Fiction. 2. Moth-
ers—Death—Fiction. 3. Father figures—Fiction. 4. Teenage
girls—Fiction. 5. Alcoholics—Fiction. 6. Authors—Fiction. 7.
Orphans—Fiction. I.Title.

    PS3603.A67O35 2004
    813'.6–dc22

                                            2004015288

Paperback Edition: January 2005
    ISBN 1-59692-132-3

                Manufactured in the United States of America.
10 9 8 7 6 5 4 3 2 1

Book and jacket design by Dorothy Carico Smith.

Publisher's Note: This is a work of fiction. Names, characters,
places, and incidents either are the product of the author's
imagination or are used fictitiously. Any resemblance to actual
events, locales, or persons, living or dead, is entirely coincidental.

*For Linda and Grayson
and the Belleville Avenue Quartet*

ONE

Standing with his back to the kitchen sink, lighting a cigarette from the stove that would be turned off that day, a man glanced about his house trailer. He had loaded an old Pontiac with all he planned to take. He stepped to the refrigerator, empty except for a pint bottle of Popov vodka, a woman's shoe, an orange juice can and a paperback copy of *A Portrait of the Artist as a Young Man*. Pouring what was left of the orange juice into the nearly empty vodka bottle, he went to the bathroom, tossed his spent cigarette into the commode and looked at himself in the mirror. Byron Burns was forty-nine years old, underweight, his auburn hair beginning to fade. He leaned toward the mirror to run his fingers through his hair. His face tended toward emaciation. Byron rolled the sleeves of his wrinkled white dress shirt to his elbows. The hue of his eyes changed with the colors of the shirts he wore. His eyes dominated his face—vulnerable—giving away his shifting feelings to anyone who knew him well enough to read them.

After a glance at his loose-fitting khakis, not terribly wrinkled, he took a final walk through the trailer to make sure he had not left anything he might later need. A few things lay on the coffee table that, for the past few years, had been his medicine cabinet, bar, bookshelf and ashtray. An empty bottle of Tums, some old cough medicine, a writing tablet with one sheet remaining and a spent ballpoint pen.

He looked round his bedroom, empty except for the bed and several inexpensive prints by van Gogh and Picasso, and a painting a woman had given him years back. Byron had decided to leave the artwork in hopes of influencing a potential trailer buyer's decision. The place had always looked desolate, too cold in winter, too hot in summer, never warm. He had mostly nursed hangovers there and occasionally bedded a one—or two—night stand.

Byron Burns grew up as one of the local fair-haired boys in the small, prosperous town of Eanes, Alabama. His mother had died when he was still an infant. His father, successful property owner and merchant, died three years ago. The children had all done well, except for Byron, the black sheep of the family. He had a brother who lived in Eanes, a lawyer and family man who belonged to the country club and the Presbyterian church, another brother who was an attorney in Atlanta, and a sister who taught school. Her two boys, who played football at the socially superior of the two high schools in town, were the pride of the community.

Byron had played quarterback on that school's

football team and had been expected to outshine his brothers in life. But Byron started down the wrong path during his days at the University of Alabama. A lust for wine, women, song and good writing had been his undoing—that, and Bobby Long, another Eanes fair-haired boy, seven years to the month older than Byron.

"The boy took to drinking and reading too many books," said his father, whose influence got Byron a teaching position back in Eanes after he had been let go from other positions he held briefly. He taught school in his hometown for several years before a scandal forced him to resign. That was when his father bought the fish market, a last-ditch effort at redemption. After neglecting the fish market for several years—sleeping in the afternoon, chasing women and other debaucheries—Byron leased it and took a job on a tugboat running freight up and down the Alabama River.

Byron Burns closed the door to the trailer, left the key in the door and drove away in the old Pontiac, the backseat cluttered with clothes and piles of books. Literary anthologies, classics, a Tao-te-Ching and others that had been significant for him over the years. He took a considerable swig from the bottle of Popov vodka and laid it back on the seat. On the way out of town, he turned on the local AM station where a Pente-costal pastor was proclaiming a familiar message.

***

"Lo and behold," the black woman said as the man passed his tray to her in the cafeteria of the veterans' hospital in Biloxi, Mississippi. The man leaned down and forward to speak to her beyond the stack of dirty breakfast trays.

"You had your chance, Callie," the man said with a grin that crooked his mouth.

The woman laughed in a guttural way. "Bobby, I always said you didn't belong here."

Bobby Long grinned and brushed his brown hair back with the tips of his fingers. With a flirtatious grin he said, "Are you certain you don't want to meet me in the cooler before I go?"

The woman laughed again, so loudly that several of the old soldiers still eating their breakfasts turned to see what had happened.

"Bobby," she said, letting the laughter die out of her voice.

"What, pretty Creole lady?" He never allowed her to get too serious with him.

"Don't come back here, you hear me? You ain't no alcoholic."

"Yassum," said Bobby Long as he reached through the window and squeezed the woman's hand. "And you, Callie, my love, keep your legs together."

He stepped outside to the veranda, a flip-flop shower shoe on the foot with a swollen, blackened big toe and one brown brogan on the other. Bobby walked to his barracks, took the elevator, and breathed, for what he knew would be the last time, the old-age stench of spent warriors. In the bay he sat on the bunk that had been the closest thing to a home he had known for the past two years. He was fifty-four years old, not quite the five feet ten inches he had been when younger and not bent at the shoulders. He had always been slender, without the extra weight he now carried in his stomach and shoulders. Dark skin stretched over high cheekbones, the left side sunken from an injury years ago. No one noticed the disfigurement unless he brought attention to it with one of several contradictory explanations as to how it happened. He had been downright handsome when he was younger, with a disarming grin that had allowed him to charm his way into many places and many arms that might have been more fortunately avoided.

Toward the back of the bay a solitary old man lay on his bunk listening to a radio. Bobby Long took a worn leather handbag from the locker at the head of his bunk and finished stuffing it with the rest of all that he owned—a pair of cowboy boots, a picture of two small boys, his toothbrush, a plastic shaving kit, three well-worn paperback short story anthologies and a flip-flop shower shoe.

He slammed the locker closed and walked toward the old man.

"Colonel," he said with an outstretched hand. The

old man sat up on the side of his bunk, coughed several times before offering his hand in return. He looked Bobby in the face. "You don't have a damn bit of business leaving this place."

Bobby grinned directly into the old soldier's eyes. "And you, Colonel, don't have a damn bit of business staying in this place."

"Three squares," said the old man.

Bobby held his grin and leaned his head, "What about pussy?"

"Shoo!" said the Colonel and looked away.

Bobby slapped him on the shoulder, grinning. "See you, Colonel."

As he went back up the bay, the old soldier called out, "Bobby."

"Yes sir?" Bobby answered without looking back.

"You're a good man."

Bobby Long felt his knees give before he walked on back to his bunk, picked up his bag and started for the elevator.

At the front desk he signed the discharge sheet, walked outside and considered looking back. He didn't. He moved in the direction of the slope that led down to the edge of the bayou—what the patients called the back bay. It was a well-kept sweep of lawn, with grand old live oak trees—a nice place to sit and reflect on things that might or might not matter to old soldiers. Young people water-skied on the far side of the bayou and thought nothing about decay and time.

Halfway down the hill, Bobby Long stepped behind one of the old oaks, brushed away some leaves between protruding roots and retrieved a bottle inside a paper sack. He sat down on the ground, twisted the cap off the bottle and took a drink, then leaned his back against the tree. It had been years since Bobby Long had shuddered or shaken after a drink. Another swallow, and the pain in his left cheek began to go away. He stuffed the bottle into his leather bag and stood up.

* * *

The fat woman, Lorraine, sat in front of a little black-and-white TV shoveling oatmeal into her mouth. Over the rim of the bowl she watched Larry, Moe and Curly running from a gorilla. All her belongings lay on the floor beside her, packed into two Winn Dixie grocery sacks, an overnight case, and a bright pink purse. She was waiting for a taxi. The little apartment, one in a row of several behind the main hospital, had been her home for the past six years—the HOME OF GRACE, a facility for the mentally impaired outside Panama City, Florida.

Finished with the oatmeal, she heaved herself out of the chair and went to the kitchen to rinse the bowl. She wore a shapeless green print dress, a man's gray sweater bought from a yard sale and red sneakers with green socks. Coarse bleached hair topped her round orange-pink face, the fat enveloping all but thin slits exposing the twinkle in her eyes.

Something was unsettling this morning. The wait, the bus trip, the anticipation of getting lost, the old fear of the unknown returning. She had been diagnosed as manic-depressive, a victim of childhood and adult abuse. Her symptoms included paranoia, obsessive-compulsive tendencies and borderline personality traits. Her obesity had given rise to several physical ailments, including a bad heart.

When the taxi arrived, the driver helped her with her bags and waited patiently for her to squeeze into the backseat.

Later, at the Trailways station, she untied a dirty handkerchief, emptied the knot of the coins it contained and bought a sack of potato chips from a vending machine. She lumbered over to a bench, sat down and ate. Once she tried to cross her legs, but got no closer than resting one foot over the other. Several times she tugged at her underwear through her dress. Her panties kept rolling over at the waistband. Finally she allowed a roll of fat to push them down to where they felt the most comfortable and went on ramming her puffy hands into the bag of potato chips. For no apparent reason she started to laugh, a cackle that shut the slits of her eyes. Crumbs littered her enormous breasts.

* * *

In an apartment in South Florida, in a rundown neighborhood, a girl was stretched out on a sofa staring at a television set without much interest. She was sixteen years old. Wearing nothing but thin white panties and a T-shirt, she lit a cigarette from the one she had burned to the filter, then ground the filter into an ashtray beside her. The apartment was sparsely furnished with no apparent thought given to arrangement of the furniture. Clothes lay strewn about, along with beer cans, empty fast-food cartons and magazines. The stench of stale sweat, cigarette smoke, gasoline and motor oil permeated the rooms.

The girl's, Hanna's, sandy blond hair hung limply to her shoulders. Her stark green eyes peered complacently out over a scattering of light freckles across her nose. Full lips closed over clenched teeth. Her breasts were visible under her T-shirt, and blond hairlets sprouted on her thighs where her razor had stopped.

The young mechanic's helper who more or less kept her up would be home soon, likely throwing his sweaty baseball cap at her crotch, scratching his stomach and saying something crude to her before going to the refrigerator. Later, they would probably go out to a beer joint where she would watch him play video games. Returning to the apartment, she would let him wallow on her in order to pay her share of the rent and meager upkeep.

After he had gone to sleep she would lie in the dark pretending she was something other than what she was—maybe an X-ray technician dressed in a clean white uniform or a secretary sitting behind a desk in a nice office where she would appear to be far more than she felt that she was—able, perhaps, to make a few choices in her life. Certainly, no one could accuse her of extravagant dreams.

The young girl had grown up with her grandmother, since her mother had rarely been in her life. Her mother had been in and out of a variety of lowdown men and mental health facilities most of her child's life. The girl's grandmother had little interest or control over her after pre-adolescence. The girl had learned a lot about self-sufficiency by then and spent as much time out of school as in. If she was in any way talented, it was in the art of survival. Her dreams had been her best friend until more recently when she had begun to accept the plain truth. She had begun to see herself as she imagined her mother to be.

On a cold, early evening, a long old Pontiac parked alongside a curb on lower St. Charles Avenue in New Orleans, Louisiana. After arguing about the legality of parking there, refilling plastic cups with vodka and coloring from a can of orange juice, two men stepped from the car and met on the sidewalk in front of the Hummingbird Café. As a streetcar approached, the men shivered, lit cigarettes against a gust of wind, and one said, "Streetcar named…" as they watched the dark green and red native of the city rumble uptown. One of the men, wearing a black shoe and a shower sandal against a white sock, sipping his drink, said, "This is it." Inside the steamed-over windows of the café, people were eating and drinking hot coffee. One of the men stepped over to a door beside the café that read "Hotel" in tacked-on metal letters from a hardware store. "Are you sure it is still a hotel?" the other man asked.

Just inside the door, stairs led upward toward pink light. "You don't think they've turned it into a whorehouse, do you?"

At the top of the stairs a faded burgundy carpet with a worn path led round a corner the men followed down a long hallway. The walls were nearly the color of the carpet, with a gold-colored baroque pattern between green doors along the way. "Looks like a brothel to me," said the man whose sandal slapped the floor as they reached a small lobby where a fat man sat behind a desk reading *The New Orleans Times-Picayune* and chewing on the stub of a cigar.

"Good evening," the man with the flip-flop shower shoe said with a crooked mouth grin. The fat man acknowledged them, moving his paper away from his face. "My name is Bobby Long, this is my friend Byron Burns. How are the Saints doing?"

The fat man only responded by moving his newspaper farther from his face, shoving a register with a fountain pen toward them. "Two double beds," said Bobby Long.

"No two double rooms," grumbled the fat man. "All rooms have one double bed. Front rooms seventy a night, backrooms, sixty."

"Boy, you want to sleep with me?" said Bobby, turning to Byron.

"Well, hell, we've done it before," said Byron, lighting a cigarette.

Bobby chuckled, then asked the fat man, "How much would it be for a week?"

"Front rooms three fifty. Back's three."

Bobby and Byron discussed the matter for several moments, as Bobby fumbled with a wad of crumpled money from his pocket. "Byron, all I have here is...uh, sixty-nine, seventy dollars."

"Now why doesn't that surprise me?" Byron said.

Bobby grinned and chuckled mournfully. "I'll pay you back when my check comes."

Reluctantly, Byron took out his wallet. "Give me what you have," he said. "Goddamnit."

Chuckling, Bobby said, "I'd do it for you, boy."

Thumbing through Bobby's crumpled bills, Byron said, "Sixty-seven."

"Then I miscounted," said Bobby with a grin, before turning to the fat man in explanation. "He always does this to me."

THREE

"Boo!" said Bobby when he put his hands over the woman's eyes. The fat woman's bag of popcorn scattered over the floor and her lap when she jumped.

"Lord God Almighty, Bobby, I could have had a heart attack."

"You keep eating all the time and you most certainly will. Byron, she eats all the time," Bobby said with a grin.

"Hello, Lorraine," said Byron. "How was your trip?" He had met the fat woman once before, when Bobby brought her to his house trailer. On that occasion Bobby had asked him what he thought about his new girlfriend. Byron was complimentary.

"I met this nice lady…" Lorraine said before she noticed Bobby's foot. "Bobby, what in the world happened to your big toe?"

"It's some kind of infection," Bobby said. "You met this nice lady…"

"Lord, it's more than an infection. It looks like it's about to rot off. Are you doctoring it with anything?

Look how black it is. Does it hurt?"

"He's treating it with uric acid," Byron told her.

"Uric acid? What's that?"

"Pee," said Byron.

"Pee? Bobby!" said Lorraine.

"Goodness, woman, haven't you ever heard of the medicinal benefits of pee?"

Lorraine cackled.

"You met this nice woman…"

Composing herself, still staring at Bobby's toe, Lorraine said, "She was from North Carolina. I felt sorry for her. She was going to Texas to bury her daddy."

"Did she feel sorry for you? Did you tell her you were a mental patient?"

"No," said Lorraine, thinking she should have.

"Well, that's alright," said Bobby. "But Byron knows you are, and don't start trying to pretend like you aren't. He'll see right through you. Byron, sometimes she tries to act normal. Lorraine, you have popcorn particles on your chin." Lightly brushing her chin with a grin, he said, "Now, where are your bags? You didn't forget and leave them on the bus, did you?"

Lorraine indicated the paper sacks and overnight case, and Bobby leaned his head sympathetically. "Lorraine, you look like a bag woman. Couldn't you find anything else to put your things in? Bless your big old heart. Byron, she has a heart almost as big as her titties."

Byron chuckled.

"Lorraine, do you want me to buy you another bag of popcorn before we go?"

Lorraine said, "No," then, "I like your flip-flop."

* * *

Carrying Lorraine's bags, they walked until eventually reaching a streetcar stop several blocks away, as Bobby, mostly, told her about New Orleans, the men glancing round whenever they spotted a woman, like the one across the street in high heels and tight chartreuse pants.

"Lorraine used to look like that," said Bobby, "before she lost her mind. Then she started eating everything she could get her hands on and watching television all the time."

"Lord, Bobby, you hadn't changed a bit," said Lorraine with a cackle.

At the streetcar stop, Lorraine sat down on a bench, sighed heavily, spreading her huge legs to relieve the chafing brought on by the walk. Bobby took a bottle from inside his coat pocket, had himself a drink, then sat beside her. "Byron found us a good place. It has only one bed, though. We've decided you can sleep on the floor."

"That'll be alright," said Lorraine.

Bobby and Byron laughed. "He's joking, Lorraine," said Byron. "Any way that suits you will be fine with us."

"I don't mind sleeping on the floor," Lorraine told them.

"Oh, woman, don't be so good. We are gentlemen! You know that!" This made Lorraine laugh. "Well, it's true. Byron and I just might be the last two gentlemen left."

They caught a streetcar back to St. Charles and stopped in the Hummingbird Café, where Lorraine ate a large stack of pancakes and ham.

On the sidewalk, before taking her inside the hotel, Bobby and Byron stopped to watch a woman across the street who reminded Bobby of Audrey Hepburn.

"Lord, you two," said Lorraine with a mild cackle.

After showing her the room, explaining the pitfalls and inconveniences of the hotel, the men went out for cigarettes, a new bottle of Popov and orange juice. When they had gone, Lorraine pulled out one of the chest of drawers, emptying it of rodent, or roach, pellets. She was glad to be alone, although she hoped the men would not be gone too long. Already, they had entertained her with some of their foolishness. They could be so nasty, especially Bobby. Lorraine did not mind. She and Bobby had met years ago when she was in the same hospital he had admitted himself into after one of his too-intense bouts with alcohol and debauchery. She was not as overweight then. They had slept together while there, and now and then over the years afterwards, years when Bobby had access to plenty of women. That was just before he entered the veterans' hospital in Mississippi. He had always been honest with Lorraine, not denying his fondness for other women. But they had a relationship of a kind. In one breath he could criticize her and compliment her. He wanted to know about her, how she felt, what she thought. When he had been too drunk to drive, she had driven him round Panama City to buy whiskey, out to the beach to sit in a bar, while Bobby tried to pick up younger and more attractive women, seldom succeeding after he overindulged and grew too blatant. Once, though, she had driven him around while he had sex with another woman—one not all that much more appealing than herself. And they had gone to yard sales where Lorraine would buy cheap trinkets and vases and used clothes. While she browsed, Bobby would talk to the people about anything that came to mind. He would apologize for her, telling most anybody that she was a mental patient and he had to look out for her. She had not minded, though. It had become a funny thing between them, and besides, he was good to her. Sometimes, when he was drunk enough, he had told her he loved her, and she had believed it only because she wanted to. She had seen him cry, but only after he reached a certain state of inebriation, when he would talk about his children who would no longer have anything to do with him.

Lorraine folded her three pairs of huge, stretched and stained panties, placing them in a drawer, along with two bras. She dumped the rest of her belongings on the floor and started to sort them out and fold them. They would come back drunk and loud. Bobby would want her to show her breasts to Byron and she would if that was what they wanted. Then Bobby may or may not want to sleep with her, or they might share her. Lorraine didn't mind. Warm drunk men who did not know what they were doing were better than no men at all. And she would laugh with them whenever Bobby started to complain about her fat being in the way. He meant no harm. He could laugh at himself, too. Lorraine sat on the side of the bed and opened the overnight case and reached for the package of Oreos and pushed one in her mouth as she held another ready. She would not eat them all tonight, not all of them. After putting the remainder of her things away, she took off her dress and put on her worn quilted pink house robe. She fell asleep on the bed with thoughts and imaginings of her only child.

* * *

Lorraine had never been to the French Quarter, so Sunday morning they took a streetcar downtown. Bobby wore his Panama hat, along with one of Byron's white shirts, a dark gray suit vest, one shoe and a flip-flop. Lorraine wore her gray sweater and a shapeless print dress with her sneakers. Bobby told her she looked like a pioneer woman. "A fat pioneer woman with sneakers."

When they stepped out the hotel door, Byron, wearing only a light blue cotton dress shirt and tobacco-colored corduroys, decided along with Bobby to go back to the room for coats.

On the streetcar, Bobby spoke to a young girl with her mother. He wanted to know if she had ever heard of banana fish. They reached Canal Street before he finished explaining the technique of catching them. And when they got off, the girl jumped across the aisle to lean out a window and watch the strange man move across the street. Lorraine dropped several steps behind the two men as they walked down Bourbon Street. She had to take in the details of the place. "Poor thing," said Bobby, "she lives such a deprived life. Come on, Lorraine."

The shops were beginning to open up on the street. Musicians were tuning up their saxophones and clarinets. The first place they stopped was an open-front bar. They sat at a table next to the street and ordered drinks—the men did. Lorraine wanted a bowl of red beans and rice. They were across the street from the Royal Sonesta Hotel.

"Remember that?" Bobby asked Byron.

"Oh yes," said Byron.

Bobby grabbed Lorraine's hand. "Woman, Byron and I brought two of the prettiest girls in the state of

Georgia there once, coeds from the university."

"And fuck 'em, I reckon," said Lorraine with a cackle.

"And fucked them," said Bobby.

Lorraine's beans and rice came and the two men called for another couple of drinks. When they came, Bobby said to the waiter, "Young man, this woman is a mental patient." The waiter smiled timidly. "She doesn't mind. She's a good woman. She just eats too much, and her mind leaves her sometimes." Bobby spoke softer. "I watched her watching you walk away awhile ago. She was admiring your backside. She does that often when I take her places. She doesn't mean any harm. Look at her. She will never have a young man again." The waiter did not know if he should laugh or not. "That's alright," said Bobby, "she has us. We take care of her. This is my friend here. I'm Bobby Long and this is my friend Byron Burns. And this crazy woman is Lorraine." Lorraine never lost the rhythm of her spoon. "We have just moved to New Orleans. Are you from New Orleans?" The young man told them he was from Massachusetts, that he was a student at Tulane.

"A very good school," said Bobby, and seeing the waiter was growing impatient, added, "You have been kind to listen to us. May we buy you a drink?" The waiter smiled and explained that it would not be a good idea and excused himself.

"Fine young man," said Bobby. "Lorraine, would

you like for Byron and I to buy you a young man like that for a couple of hours?"

Lorraine giggled. "That'll be alright."

After Lorraine finished scraping her bowl, they left the bar, strolled about the French Quarter, stopping to look in windows when Bobby wanted to exaggerate a point and when he felt like speaking to someone. Byron spoke mostly to counter or add to tales Bobby told Lorraine about some of their past escapades.

"Lord, ya'll talk about women like they were farm animals or something."

"Oh, Lorraine, we don't mean any harm," said Bobby. "Why I doubt if anybody on this earth loves women anymore than Byron and I...Chickens either." He leaned closer to Lorraine. "Lorraine, ask Byron if he's ever fucked a chicken."

Lorraine cackled.

"Ask him."

"Byron?" said Lorraine.

"Tell her, Byron."

"I haven't, but Bobby says he has."

Lorraine cackled too loud and Bobby said, "Woman, they're going to run you out of this place. And when they do and the cops pick you up, I'm going to pretend like I don't know you."

They reached Jackson Square where the painters and musicians were set up for the day. Bobby spoke to a woman painting a child's portrait. When Bobby asked her name she said, "Miriam."

"Miriam," said Bobby. "That was my grandmother's name." Byron stepped back smiling as he watched a young woman in jeans pass by.

"Miriam, these are my friends: This is Lorraine. And this is Byron. Byron is a writer. He's writing a novel, about me."

"Humm," said the woman as she glanced at the little model, who said, "What's wrong with your foot?"

"My foot? My big toe, you mean," Bobby said to the child. "Well, little miss, it's an intricate story. I was bitten by a manatee."

"It looks like its gonna rot off," said the girl, whose mother jerked her shoulder. "What's a manatee?" the child then asked. Her mother whispered in her ear.

"A manatee is…"

Bobby was finishing a tale about an attack in the waters of the Gulf of Mexico when Lorraine, after disappearing, returned with a well-bitten-into muffuletta. Byron had been enjoying the parade of women.

When Bobby finished saying good-bye to his newfound friends, Lorraine wanted to see the Mississippi River. Along the way, Bobby stopped a young couple to tell them how pretty they looked together. "She has a daughter about your age," Bobby, pointing to Lorraine, told the girl. The teenaged girl smiled as she leaned her head on the boy's shoulder. Bobby tilted his head, grinned, as he looked straight into the faces of the couple. "Stay young as long as you can, your youth is a fleeting thing. And then look what you can look forward to." He added with a chuckle, stepping back alongside Byron and Lorraine. The boy laughed and the girl smiled. "Are you two having sex with one another?" Bobby then asked. The girl jerked her head from the boy's shoulder and they looked at one another in disbelief. " Oh, it's alright if you are. Sex is nice. Ask Lorraine here."

The girl took her boyfriend's hand and proceeded to drag him away.

"Just be kind to one another," Bobby added as the couple started to run among the crowd on the sidewalk.

"Bobby," said Lorraine, "You nearly scared those children to death."

"I did not. They appreciate people telling them things. People don't tell one another enough."

As they moved toward the steps that led to the river, Bobby said, "Byron, Lorraine has a daughter about that age. She's…what, Lorraine, fifteen?"

"Sixteen," said Lorraine.

"Pretty as a button," Bobby said. "Lorraine thinks she's probably a slut."

"When have you met her?"

"I haven't. Lorraine showed me a picture of her. She was younger. She's probably now either stacked or fat like her mother." Bobby chuckled. "I told Lorraine I would marry her if I could sleep with her daughter."

"Sweet sixteen," said Byron as they approached the bank of the Mississippi.

* * *

When they got back to the hotel, Bobby needed to lie down for a while. Byron went down to Tiny's Bar, the bar beneath their room, and Lorraine went out to a nearby convenience store. When she returned with chips, Oreos and a Slim Jim, the men were playing cards. "Gin!" shouted Bobby. "That's seven thousand you owe me, boy."

"Seven thousand dollars?" asked Lorraine.

"Yes," said Bobby. "Lorraine, Byron probably owes me a hundred thousand dollars. But he never pays me."

"You had better hope we never start keeping a tally," said Byron with an agonizing frown.

"Heartburn?" asked Bobby. "Drink some more vodka."

"Lord," said Lorraine.

"Woman, you're one to talk. Look at you. It's a wonder you have a heart, eating all that junk. One day you're going to topple over in a heap. Byron, look at her, like a giant walrus. Show us your breasts, Lorraine. Byron and I will show you ours."

Lorraine cackled and shoved an Oreo in her mouth. "Ya'll seen my breasts."

"But they're pretty. Byron hasn't seen them as

many times as I have. Pull off all your clothes."

Again, Lorraine cackled.

"Byron, look what we've sunken to. Woman, we ought to throw you off that bed."

"Throw me," Lorraine mumbled with a mouthful of cookies.

"Throw you, hell. We couldn't even push you. Lorraine, quit acting so sure of yourself and show us your titties."

"Lorraine, do you want to play strip poker?" Byron asked.

"We don't need to do that," said Bobby. "Lorraine will drop her britches anytime I ask her to. Drop your britches, Lorraine."

Lorraine giggled but did not move from the bed. "I don't know how to play poker. Can ya'll play strip rummy?"

"Rummy. Old Maids. You name it," said Byron.

Lorraine struggled off the bed, not able to sit on the floor; she dragged up the desk chair.

After refilling two cups with vodka and dabs of orange juice, Bobby sat back on the floor. "Now, if you lose, woman, the first thing coming off is that harness you call a brassiere."

FOUR

They started renting the room by the month. There was a Laundromat down the street off St. Charles. Lorraine occasionally washed out her underthings in the lavatory, and they could go for a week or more with the same sheets. Shirts and trousers often doubled as towels.

Lorraine added to the income with her disability check, Bobby had applied for food stamps, and Byron's share came from what was left from selling his fish market, cash he had deposited in a bank back in Eanes.

Not wanting to ask the men for money, Lorraine waited until her check arrived before calling her daughter. Her daughter seemed aloof and impatient. Several times during the strained conversation, the girl giggled and twice yelled, "Stop it!" to someone on her end of the line. When Lorraine asked what was wrong, her daughter said, "Nothing."

"What did you call for?" the girl wanted to know.

"I just called to tell you I was staying in New Orleans and to give you my address and a telephone number where you could get me."

Suddenly the girl yelled, "You fuckin' shit ass!" Lorraine believed she was talking to someone on her end of the line.

When she returned to the room, the men were playing gin rummy. They were drunk and loud; the place was full of smoke, prompting her to take a grocery sack of dirty clothes to the Laundromat. When she returned late in the afternoon, Bobby sitting on the floor and Byron on the bed were poorly harmonizing "Barbara Allen."

"Woman, where have you been? Byron and I were starting to worry about you."

"Washing clothes. I told ya'll when I left."

"Lorraine," said Bobby, grinning suspiciously, "It didn't take that long to wash clothes. Now where have you been? We thought you might have ran off with a wino or something."

"I met a woman."

"A woman?"

"This Indian woman. She took me to her house over yonder, and we talked."

"What does she look like, Lorraine?" asked Byron.

"Tall."

"I like tall women," said Bobby.

"Real dark."

"Fat?" Bobby asked.

"No. Just big. I don't know." Lorraine seemed uninterested.

"There she goes, Byron, off in her own world."

"What was she built like?" Byron wanted to know.

"If you mean did she have big titties, they looked like it."

"Well, let's go meet her," said Bobby. "Lorraine, let's invite her over."

"I just met her."

"Well, just meet her again. Is she married?"

"No."

"Is she living with somebody?"

"By herself. You ought to see her place. Indian stuff everywhere. She has this big picture of Geronimo over her couch."

"I'm not interested in Geronimo," said Bobby. "Do you think she will fuck?"

Lorraine chuckled. "Ya'll will have to ask her about that."

"Did you tell her about us?"

"No."

"No? Woman, what's wrong with you? What did you talk about?"

"Nothing. Just things. She was real nice."

"Lorraine," said Bobby leaning toward her and being meticulous with his words, "would you say she was fuckable?"

Lorraine stretched. "She's not any raving beauty."

* * *

Byron got out of bed while Lorraine and Bobby were still asleep. He opened a large brown envelope, took out the typewritten pages, and started to read as he lit a cigarette. He still was not sure he liked the title: *Tom Cane*. And he had never been satisfied with the way the book started. It was too vague. He knew what he wanted to say, and he knew enough about writing to know he had not even come close to saying it. He had never been able to write about anything close to him, anything involving much of his own emotions. He had never been able to stand back where this story was concerned. It was just too much a part of him.

What he had tried to do was explain how he, the writer, had met and become acquainted with this "Tom Cane." How they had met while moonlighting at a business school back in Eanes, Alabama. This Tom Cane had been an English instructor at the community college. The writer taught English and creative writing in a high school. Byron had been trying to capture the first encounter between them. Thumbing through the unfinished manuscript, pages faded round the edges, he came to the part he wanted, and he began to read...

"...Contrary to Tom's viewpoint, I am certain it was I who was sitting at the desk that evening, reading from an anthology of short stories, when he walked in, late, to replace me at the business school where we, having state government accepted college degrees, were supposed to teach English and writing. The place was a farce, posing as a school, deceitfully awarding to veterans benefits for signing in and hanging out, gambling on the farthest city stamped on bottoms of Coke bottles. 'Winter Dreams,' I told him when he wanted to know what I was reading.

"Tom has always sworn the story was 'Three Players of a Summer Game,' Tennessee Williams, and it was he who was reading when I arrived late…"

Byron turned several more pages, skipped over several paragraphs, coughed several times, lit another cigarette, then read some more:

"…when he opened one of the desk drawers where he had left a bottle of vodka…"

After reading the next two paragraphs, Byron reached for a pencil and Xed over them.

Lorraine rolled her big self over in bed and grunted. Byron looked at her for a moment, turned another page as Bobby, naked, got out of bed, and stepped over for a cigarette off the desk. "How is it going?" he asked hoarsely, tapping his cigarette on the desk.

"Not well," said Byron

"You'll get it. Take your time. Don't be so hard on yourself," Bobby said, turning toward the bed. "Woman, get your fat ass up. And clean up this place. Since you've been here it looks like a pigsty. Byron's trying to write, and don't you disturb him. He's writing about me." Bobby took a drink out of Byron's plastic glass, then sat in the armchair, crossing his chalky dark legs, and staring down them at his yellow toenails. "I grow old, I grow old," he said.

As Byron continued to read, Bobby said, "Lorraine, Byron is writing a novel about me. I'm the main character. Byron, read Lorraine the beginning."

"I don't want to."

"Lorraine, it's good. Let me see it, Byron, I'll read it."

"No."

"Please."

Reluctantly Byron passed the pages to Bobby, who jerked it playfully from him.

"Lorraine, he is so sensitive."

Laughing, Bobby read to himself for a few moments before he began to read aloud. "*Tom Cane*," he said. "Woman, that is me. And it has nothing to do with Cane and Abel, does it, Byron?"

Byron frowned as he reached for a cigarette.

"Oh! Oh!" Bobby shouted after glancing through several pages. "You've got to hear this, Woman." After moving the paper farther away from his eyes, then back some, he hesitated. "Listen, Lorraine. Woman, are you going to listen?"

"I'm listening," said Lorraine.

"Then listen." Bobby held the pages forward once more and started to read.

"...For certain we were there longer than the others..." He stopped reading to explain to Lorraine that "there" meant this night school where he and Byron had once taught.

"Just read," said Byron.

Once more Bobby adjusted his eyes to the page. "…We drank all the vodka; we closed the doors to the school, sat out on the steps that early spring night, in the haze brought on by the liquor, and never missed the mark with one another…" Bobby stopped reading and said, "It's true, Lorraine. This whole thing is true."

"It is not," said Byron. "It's a novel."

"Novel, my ass. Lorraine, it's about me," Bobby said and he continued to read: "…like two children who had, for the first time, discovered someone who shared their thoughts…"

"I like that," said Lorraine.

"Hush, Woman. '…Then Tom would wave his arm as if doing tricks with an imaginary lasso…'"

"Byron, I think you should use 'lariat' here. I like 'lariat' better," Bobby offered.

"I like 'lasso'," said Byron.

"Suit yourself," said Bobby as he went back to reading, '…things that remain out of sight…'

"Lorraine, that's my line."

"Just read," said Byron.

Bobby read to himself for a moment. "He's just talking about my crooked mouth," he told Lorraine as he glanced down the page. "Here's what he says about my eyes. 'There was nothing unusually interesting about his eyes, except to say he used them to look—TO SEE—and he made no apologies for using them without reservation. I suppose I could say they were useful eyes. Useful to him, and useful to me that first night. Useful in my seeing so much clearer what he wanted me to see. They were kind, dark brown eyes—ferocious, probing eyes. Mischievous eyes. Playful and daring eyes. They did not shine necessarily, and they did not turn in hue, or dance by themselves. Oh, his face danced…' I like this. Listen, Woman, '…and his eyes could have been the shoulders of his face. But by themselves those eyes did little in the way of promenading, or curtsying for him…'"

"It's a novel," said Byron.

"Like hell it is. It's ME—and YOU!" Bobby pointed his finger straight at Byron. "Lorraine, he eventually tells about some of our escapades together. He tells some awful things, too. But that's okay, I gave him my permission. I told him to tell anything he wanted to about me. I have nothing to hide. He tells everything about my divorce. Everything."

Byron stood up and put his open hand over the top of his head, then turned to Lorraine. "It's a novel. Not everything in it is true."

"But it is, Lorraine," said Bobby. "The story may not be absolutely the way it happened, but it's certainly not just a novel."

"It's about…"

"Something that remains out of sight," said Byron.

Bobby let his arms fall to his sides as his shoulders

drooped. "Yes!"

"And he can't get it right," added Bobby. "Lorraine, one of the things he's trying to explain is how I left my family for a younger, more beautiful woman, and how she broke my heart and took my boys."

"Oh, hell, Bobby, that's not it," said Byron.

"Lorraine, he is lying."

FIVE

Bobby and Byron left Lorraine in the room Saturday morning and went downstairs to Tiny's, not returning until the middle of the afternoon. They wanted to meet the Indian woman Lorraine had told them about. When they entered the room they did not immediately realize that she had been crying.

"Woman, get up off that bed and let's go wash some clothes," said Bobby. Lorraine only turned to her side the best she could. "Look at that sorry woman."

It was then that Lorraine started to cry out loud. "Oh me," she moaned. "Oh me."

"Oh you, hell," said Bobby, "Get your lazy rump up and let's go meet your Georgianna friend."

Lorraine began to bellow. "Bobby, I'm hurtin'. Can somebody help me?" The two men went to the bed, and even in their drunken stupors realized something was surely wrong. Bobby began to talk softly and gently. "Woman, are you alright?"

"No," she moaned. "I'm hurtin'. Oh, Lord, I'm hurtin'. Help me!" she screamed.

Bobby put his hand on her huge shoulder. "We will. Don't you worry. Where are you hurting?"

"Oh Lord," was all Lorraine would say. She kept saying that over and over while the men moved about the room trying to decide what to do.

"You think a drink of whiskey would help? Byron, pour her some whiskey."

"Oh Lord!" moaned Lorraine.

"Bobby, I think it's bad. You think we ought to take her to the hospital?"

"Lorraine, do you want to go to the hospital?"

"Oh Lord, I'm hurtin'" was all she could say.

"Can you walk?" asked Bobby.

"Oh Lord!" screamed Lorraine.

"Get her arm, Byron."

They tried to encourage her to get out of the bed. They pushed and pulled her, but she only screamed louder.

"Let's carry her," said Byron. And they began to tug on her until she was at the side of the bed. Then Byron took her huge legs and Bobby grabbed beneath her arms and they heaved. But when they did, Lorraine fell to the floor and the men fell with her.

"Ya'll hurtin' me!" she cried. They tried once more to pick her up, but it was no use. They were drunk, too old and too weak. And she was just too large and help-less. Byron went to the phone and shortly an ambu-lance arrived with a stretcher. It took the two paramedics and Byron and Bobby to carry her down the stairs. On the way down, Bobby slipped, the stretcher with its overwhelming contents tilted to one side so that Lorraine was saved from a fall all the way down the stairs by the strength of one of the younger men.

Climbing into the back of the ambulance with Lorraine, Bobby told Byron to bring the car and not to forget the vodka.

At the emergency room things got worse. Lorraine was bellowing, the nurses were complacent, there was no doctor immediately available and the paramedics, having determined that Lorraine had no insurance, wanted payment for their services. Worse, there was a runaround about not being able to provide Lorraine treatment without some assurance that the hospital would be paid. Cursing and ranting, Bobby demanded better treatment, which did accomplish Lorraine being put behind a curtain onto a bed.

Two nurses calmly went about their business as Bobby continued to complain while Byron tried to console Lorraine. Bobby was saying to the two nurses, "Do you think we can't pay to have this woman looked at? Is that it?"

The nurses had begun to ignore him completely, it being obvious these were indigents, reeking of alcohol, belligerent winos.

Half an hour later, Lorraine was feeling better, Bobby had calmed down, no doctor came, so Byron suggested leaving, going to another hospital.

As they helped her off the bed, noticing her sneakers, one of the nurses did not hesitate providing a wheelchair. "I'm terribly sorry," she said.

"I hope you aren't a Christian," said Bobby as Byron rolled Lorraine toward the emergency exit.

When they got to the car, Lorraine, starting to complain again, badly needed to lie down. As weak as she was, they had to help her out of the wheelchair, but after several attempts to squeeze themselves and her through the opened door, her screaming when they applied too much force, let her back into the chair while they thought of possible solutions. They stepped to the back of the Pontiac, deciding to have a drink of vodka, and Lorraine heard Byron say, "We have no choice."

Reaching for the handles of the wheelchair, Bobby said, "Lorraine, we're going to have to put you in the trunk."

"Oh, Lord," said Lorraine before they wheeled her to the back of the car. "Just take me back to the hotel."

From the ramp outside the emergency room, two nurses watched the spectacle until the old Pontiac left the parking lot.

When Byron stopped for a traffic light, from behind the backseat they heard a cackle.

***

The next day Bobby and Byron got unusually drunk and laughed all morning recounting the most minute details of the ordeal with Lorraine. Lorraine's appetite got back to normal and she went through a family pack of coconut macaroons. In the afternoon, the men passed out and slept until after dark. Byron was the first up. Lorraine was sitting at the window munching on a piece of cheese. Byron coughed away the debris lodged in his throat, lit a cigarette and poured himself some vodka.

"I've got to quit drinking," he said. "I've got to get out in the sun before I die."

"Me too," growled Bobby from the bed. "But pour me a drink first."

"We're out of juice."

"What's that in that glass?" Bobby asked as he sat up.

"Byron reached across the desk, smelled the contents of a glass. "No smell."

"Then pour me some vodka in it."

Lorraine had been watching Byron. "What were ya'll…" she cackled.

Byron and Bobby looked at one another and laughed.

"I mean, before ya'll got all messed up, what were ya'll like?"

"Byron," said Bobby, "she said we were messed up."

"I agree," said Byron.

"Byron, how long were you married?" Lorraine wanted to know.

"Long time," said Byron.

"Listen to him," said Bobby. "Lorraine, he was married for ten years to a pretty woman, wise woman. She left him. I didn't blame her. Byron mistreated her. Byron got down, depressed, and it was his fault."

"I've never been down in my life," said Byron.

"Oh ho! No, he's never been down. Not old stone heart. That's always been his defense, Lorraine. He can't admit it, but he's been pining over that woman half his life."

Bobby slid off the bed onto the floor so he could reach the ashtray. He stubbed out his cigarette and leaned back against the bed. "Lorraine, he met her in high school. She came from New York, and his folks never approved of her. They lived together about ten years and she left him. Why? Because he was just as stubborn then as he is now. He had to prove he could fuck every woman in sight, because he had an inferiority complex, see." Bobby threw up his hand, "And she left him. Then, instead of getting down on his knees and swallowing his pride, he let her go. He had the idea that she would come back to him. Well, you see what happened. Pride goeth before the fall."

"Why didn't his folks like her?" Lorraine wanted to know.

"Because she was low class. But, Lorraine, she was more than that. Oh my, she was something else. She was pretty, I mean, pretty. She had this look about her that..."

"She was a fucking nymphomaniac, Bobby. If you're going to talk for me, tell the truth."

"You don't mind?"

"Go ahead," said Byron. "Lorraine, the woman is dead."

For a moment no one spoke.

"It's a hell of a story, Lorraine," said Bobby.

Byron left the desk and went to the opened window, sat in it, gazing toward the street.

"Lorraine, when Byron was a high school…"

"I know, ya'll were football players."

Bobby laughed. "Heroes! Byron, she remembers everything."

"How could I forget?"

"Close that damn window, boy!"

"I'm not gonna do it."

"Lorraine, do you hear that?" asked Bobby. "He can be so stubborn. He's always defying me."

"What was she doing in Alabama?" Lorraine asked.

"That's not important, woman." Bobby stepped to the window, taking a drag from Byron's cigarette before handing it back to him. "Her name was Katherine Flowers…"

Bobby told a story about a girl who moved to Eanes with her mother and sister, who lived in a rundown housing project that happened to be owned, ironically, by Byron's father. It was not known round Eanes why they moved there from New York City. However, the girl soon developed a reputation as an easy lay. Rumor got

out she had actually entertained a considerable group
of the football team on more than one occasion. This
supposedly took place during the summer before
school started back. Byron had spent the summer
working in the wheat fields in Kansas. When he got
back home, even the grown-ups had heard about the
girl from New York.

The first day of school, curiosity was at a peak
about this Katherine Flowers who would be entering
the eleventh grade at the same high school Byron was
beginning his senior year. The halls of the school were
filled with students and teachers waiting her arrival.
Even several leading citizens and some others had
parked near the school to catch a glimpse of the town's
new celebrity, tainted celebrity. That morning the
behavior of those who already knew what she looked
like prompted those who did not to shuffle and peek
over shoulders as she, along with her mother, arrived. It
was the first time Byron had seen her. He watched
along with the others as they walked up the walk to the
entrance. Byron was struck by her looks from then on.
She was a slender girl, bordering on skinny, long legs,
long straight hair, and Byron was close enough to look
into her dark brown eyes.

Weeks passed, Byron was busy with school, football
and the popular girls he was expected to be with. Byron
was at least one of the most popular boys in school. He
had dated one of the majorettes regularly since the

middle of his junior year. But throughout that first senior semester he could not get Katherine Flowers out of his mind. He watched her from a distance until that spring, fearful of the ridicule he knew he would receive if he showed any blatant interest. However, he spoke to her in passing and often met her eyes. Then, in late spring he asked her out. Byron had told Bobby that he had intercourse with her that night, after only an hour parked behind one of his father's unrented buildings. Soon afterward, he took her out again. It was that night she had touched Byron so, accusing him of being ashamed to be seen in public with her. It was also that night Byron took her to the most popular hangout in town, where his clique gathered. When he entered the place with Katherine Flowers, no one could believe it. His reputation with the good girls took a nosedive, but the boys' admiration for him intensified.

Late that night, the only light coming from St. Charles Avenue, Lorraine lay on her back, her huge legs narrowly cocked while Bobby grunted, sweated and engaged her, as rolls of fat ebbed and flowed. She turned her face away from the stench of old whiskey and tobacco, conscious of only the now, interrupted with images of this man as a little boy, barefoot, in blue jeans, grinning, as she rubbed the oily thin hair of a temporary beau.

* * *

The day Lorraine took the men to meet the Indian woman was warmer, inspiring Bobby to go without his shoes. He wore white bell-bottom pants, polyester with a flawed fly exposing the zipper.

Lorraine led the men up a stairway outside a run-down house converted to apartments, a block from Magazine Street. Vines, overgrown shrubbery, and several boarded windows characterized the neighborhood.

"How do I look?" Bobby asked Byron.

"You look okay. How do I look?" asked Byron.

"Your hair's sticking up," said Bobby, licking his finger and brushing the back of Byron's head, just before a tall dark woman opened the door at the top of the stairs. "Come in, come in," said the woman with long black hair in a dark green ankle-length dress. "Ya'll this is Georgianna," Lorraine said. "And this is Bobby and Byron."

"You are tall," Bobby said. "What, six feet?"

"Six one," the woman said with a faint smile. She had dark eyes, high cheekbones, a long narrow face with a prominent chin, enhancing her odd appearance.

"Cherokee?" Byron asked.

"Apache," Georgianna told them.

"Then that must be Geronimo," said Bobby who had just noticed a large painting of an Indian warrior on the wall.

"That is my great grandfather," said Georgianna.

"My mother was a Creek," said Bobby, Georgianna invited them to sit down. Byron had begun to take in the room, cluttered with Indian artifacts, cacti and a strong scent of incense. Music from a radio on a shelf featured a flute. "Christ, what happened to your foot?" asked Georgianna as she was opening a bottle of red wine.

Soon talk dispelled some of the unfamiliarity among them. Bobby asking the Indian woman about several relics displayed round the room. After she explained her acquisitions of a painting and several artifacts, Bobby told a story about an Indian who had lived in Eanes when he was a boy. "Georgianna, as far as we knew, nobody had any idea where he came from. He just appeared, started doing odd jobs for this boot-legger for room and board." Bobby elaborated a story of a huge red Indian who had been such a mystery to the kids of his hometown. "I never heard him say a word. Then one day he just disappeared. No one ever knew what happened to him."

With no response from the others, Bobby jumped to another subject. "Did Lorraine tell you she was a mental patient, Georgianna?" Georgianna could not decide if she should laugh or not. "Well, she is," said Bobby. "We take care of her, though. We see that she doesn't run out in front of a car and things like that. She's bad about going off into her own little world sometimes."

"She's nice," said Georgianna.

"Oh, we think so too. But we have to watch her. We don't know when she is going to embarrass us." Seeing

Georgianna not catch his humor, with a chuckle, he said, "I'm only joking. Lorraine doesn't mind. She's one of my favorite people."

Suddenly recognizing the tune of a song coming from the radio, Bobby said, "Oh, Byron, do you recognize that? Georgianna, would you like to dance?"

"I'm not a good dancer," she told him.

"What, an Apache?" said Bobby while Byron unconsciously leaned his head to look beneath a little Indian girl doll's dress while Lorraine brushed its hair with a tiny brush she discovered on the table beside her.

Not sure how to respond, Georgianna laughed.

"Byron, doesn't she have nice breasts?" Bobby then asked. "Georgianna, are those your original breasts?"

Not amused, she said, "The last time I looked."

"Well, they're nice," Bobby said, leaning back on the sofa where he and Byron sat.

When Bobby asked the Indian woman what her religion was, Lorraine got up and disappeared down a narrow hall.

"Pentecostal," the woman said.

"That surprises me. I would have guessed an American Indian faith, Hopi perhaps. Byron's Catholic."

"Georgianna, he means I was once married to a woman who was Catholic," Byron explained.

Lorraine returned. "I like your bathroom," she told Georgianna. "Bobby, she has this real big cactus in her bathroom. You ought to go look at it."

"Lorraine, have you been plundering again? Woman, you don't go in people's houses and sneak around everywhere."

"I've just been to the bathroom."

"Well don't announce it. Now sit down. I was telling Georgianna about the time I saved Byron. Georgianna, Byron studied theology. That was before he got a master's in literature. But I'm going to heaven and he isn't. Byron's a heathen."

Later, when Byron was shown the bathroom, Bobby followed him. "Of course I would," said Bobby as the two men stood over the commode.

"Watch where you pee," said Byron.

"Would you?"

"I might need a little more wine."

"Byron, when we get back in there, ask her to dance."

* * *

After Georgianna insisted on not dancing and the men had drank most of her wine—Bobby getting louder, Byron high stepping more frequently to the bathroom, as though he were wading through unsure knee-high swamp water—Bobby, grinning crookedly, made a proposal. "Georgianna, would you mind showing Byron and me your breasts?"

"Pardon?" said Georgianna as Lorraine cackled.

"Byron and me will show you ours."

"Is he serious?" Georgianna asked Lorraine.

"Uh huh," said Lorraine with another cackle.

"Better yet, why don't we all go back to your bedroom and explore one another?" said Bobby.

"Child, where did you find this man?" Georgianna asked Lorraine.

"Lorraine will, won't you, Lorraine?" said Bobby.

Lorraine leaned back in her chair and stretched her arms above her head, locking her hands together. "I'm not saying anything," she giggled.

"But you would if Georgianna would."

"I'm not saying I will, and I'm not saying I won't."

"It wouldn't be anything but fun," said Byron.

"He's right," said Bobby as he told a story about when he was five years old, crawling under a blanket with a neighborhood playmate, both taking off their clothes to investigate one another, and how her mother discovered them, sending Bobby home before spanking her little daughter. "Did you ever do anything like that, Georgianna?"

Lorraine's laughter was beginning to assure Georgianna of the harmless babbling of an eccentric egomaniac, who she had to admit was amusing her.

"We're still just children. We may have lost some of our innocence, but we're really nothing but little boys and girls. The only difference is now there is no one to spank our butts, and mine is starting to droop. Jesus understands. I'm lonely. Byron is lonely. That woman over there is lonely. You're probably lonely sometimes, too."

"And it's not like we are bad or anything," added Byron.

"Not Byron and me," said Bobby.

"All we would do is rub one another," said Byron. "We could go in there and rub one another, and if somebody didn't like it, we could stop. I'm a good rubber."

"I'm sure you are, Byron," said Georgianna while Lorraine cackled her loudest of the afternoon.

SIX

One day in February, a warmer day, the first hint of spring not being far away, Georgianna joined the excursion in Byron's Pontiac. After being turned away from the Admiral's Table restaurant because of the likelihood that Bobby's big toe could be contagious, they stopped by a streetside hut for po' boys to eat as they rode out of town into the country-side toward Thibodaux. Bobby, driving, insisted Byron read a short story from one of the literary anthologies scattered about the car. When Byron selected "Bernice Bobbed Her Hair," Bobby said, "No, boy, read, uh, read…Sherwood Anderson, or…'Girls in Their Summer Dresses.'"

"I'm going to read 'Bernice Bobbed Her Hair.'"

Throwing up his hand, Bobby said, "Read 'Bernice Bobbed Her Hair' then. Georgianna, he always does this to me. That boy can be so contrary sometimes. Read then!"

As Byron started to read, Bobby took the cigarette from his hand, returning it after a draw, as he turned off a four-lane onto a narrow paved road, interrupting the story now and then to elaborate or explain something. As he turned south toward Thibodaux, the woods and foliage became thicker, darker, encroaching Louisiana swampland.

In the backseat, Lorraine ate one of her favorite snacks, a package of Oreos dumped into a family-sized bag of potato chips as Byron continued to read while mixing new screwdrivers for himself and Bobby, who had to interrupt again to point out to Lorraine a sugarcane field of scattered dead stalks. After turning again, alongside a narrow canal running adjacent to the road as Byron was approaching the end of the story, Bobby pulled the car off the road and stopped. "Look, let's walk down there and sit by the water and Byron can finish the story."

They took the book, vodka and potato chip bag down to the edge of the canal for fishermens' boats to enter the Gulf of Mexico. The women, Georgianna, sitting side-legged accommodating her long dress, and Lorraine, legs spread forward, sat on the slope of the bank while Byron finished the story. "I liked that," said Lorraine as the men poured fresh vodka in Styrofoam cups and Bobby, inspired by the familiar story, recited a poem with flailing arms and dramatic stances:

"'The Red Rose is a Falcon

The White Rose is a Dove...'" he began, finishing with acceptance of applause from the women.

As the afternoon went on with talk of mostly sex

and other recitation, Byron, at Bobby's insistence, sang "Lord Randall" while he stepped about seemingly oblivious with his head held high. It was afterwards, Lorraine heaved herself up, went to the car and brought back a large brown paper bag, handing it to Byron before she worked her way back to the ground. Inside the bag was a baritone ukulele. "For us?" Bobby asked as Byron plucked the strings of the little instrument. "Lorraine, where did you get it?" asked Bobby.

"From that Salvation Army place," Lorraine told them. I kept it in that trunk ya'll put me in."

The men laughed and Bobby had to tell Georgianna about the night Lorraine went to the hospital.

"I got tired of listening to ya'll sing without music," Lorraine said. Soon the men stood side by side, Byron plucking the ukulele, harmonizing with Bobby to:

"Blue Mooooooon,

You saw me standing alone,

Without a dream in my heart,

Without a love of my own..."

Bobby added a smooth, slower version of the Alabama Shuffle before finishing and darting into:

"...With rue my heart is laden..."

(he paused to grin)

"...For golden friends I had,

For many a rose-lipped maiden,

And many a lightfoot lad."

As the sun was going down, they walked back to

the car. The men mumbled awhile in the backseat, Lorraine having insisted that she drive, before they passed all the way out.

*　*　*

A rainy day kept them in the room, except Lorraine did walk to the convenience store. Bobby and Byron spent most of the morning playing gin rummy. In the afternoon Bobby took a nap and Byron sat at the desk and tried to write. But the liquor he drank kept him from it. He did pick up a pencil, and he did write, several pages of notes concerning a scene he had considered adding to his novel. But even in the haze he knew it was too melodramatic, so, throwing it in the trash can, he reread several chapters to see if something had improved with time.

Late that night, after a visit from Georgianna, the men having slept off the afternoon's liquor, Lorraine went with them downstairs to Tiny's. They sat next to the opened front door so Bobby could listen to the rain patter on the sidewalk. "I love that sound," he told them. "It reminds me of something. What is it, Byron?" They spoke to Nick, the barkeep, who stood behind the bar talking to old men at the far end of the place. Lorraine complained about her stomach hurting while she munched potato chips. "Nick," said Bobby, "Would you mind bringing Lorraine an Alka-Seltzer. She has the indigestion again. And, a couple of shots of tequila, and two Miller High Lifes."

When Lorraine did not feel like talking, she knew all she had to do was ask a question and the men would take over, allowing her to relax. "What did ya'll do that was so bad?"

"What, Woman?" asked Bobby. "Byron, she's drifting again."

"No, I was just wondering why ya'll think the people in your hometown thought you were bad? Was it the whiskey, do you think?" Lorraine asked.

"Woman, you look awful, do you want another Alka-Seltzer?"

"I'm alright."

"Well, don't just sit there and die on us. No, it wasn't the whiskey. It was life, Woman! Experience. With Byron it was too much knowledge, too fast. Not only was he a football star, he was a bookworm. And he loved women, too much. I did too. We have always had too much lust for life, and never understood people who did not. We've always been livers of life. Spectators, we never were."

At the back of the bar, a young man was setting up sound equipment, preparing to play a guitar and sing.

"I think I have always put too much stock in the written word," said Byron. "Sometimes I think I lost touch with something."

"Lorraine, what that boy means is he lost interest in

most of the mundane people he met."

"That don't make a lot of sense," said Lorraine.

"He's just complicated, Woman. He's always been that way."

Soon, the young guitar player started to sing. Bobby strolled to the back of the bar to sit at a table near the music, stomping his foot until the song ended, saying, "Play something Cajun."

Soon, Byron and Lorraine joined Bobby, who had begun to dance a Cajun waltz alone.

It continued to rain as several more patrons came in, Bobby asking one of two women with two men to dance, showing her the Alabama Shuffle to the party's amusement. Byron tried to talk Lorraine into a dance, but she was still not feeling well enough.

In a while, Bobby sang a duet with the young guitar player, who sang several more songs while a couple of couples danced, then took a break, leaving a microphone, too much of a temptation for Bobby after several more vodka and tonics. Nick the bartender seemed not to mind as Bobby introduced himself then did his "Little Elf Man" poem that prompted a round of applause, only to feed his inebriated ego. By then, Byron was ready when Bobby had him come up to the microphone to help him sing "My Gal," a song perhaps written by someone who would not have approved of the changes in lyrics they had, while on one of their excursions together, concocted, adding their own lewd stanzas. When they finished the song, an old man at the bar yelled, "Now, that'll get a man some pussy." When several in the audience laughed, Bobby felt, since Nick was one of them, he had license to share his, in some circles, infamous "Pussy Story." Bobby's timing and patience lasted just long enough to grab everyone's undivided attention before he started: "If I don't offend anyone, I have a story to tell, about the first time I ever saw a piece of pussy…"

"Whoa, shit!" someone said.

"James, I want you to hear this," Bobby said continuing. "Ladies, I assure you this story will not offend you. So, please, give me your undivided attention." Bobby swallowed long and deeply, "It's an innocent story, true, too. This happened to me. I was seven, eight years old at the time. Seven, maybe. I lived in this neighborhood where most of the boys were older than I was—not a lot older, a couple of years in most cases." Bobby had to preface the story with talk of the small Alabama town where he grew up. "Now understand, we did lots of things, played ball, went swimming, sneaked peeks at the breasts in the *Playboy* magazines at the bus station when the cashier and waitresses weren't looking, masturbated like all normal seven year old—James, how old were you?"

"Whoa, shit," said the old fellow sitting alone in a corner.

"Bobby," said Nick, "we Louisiana boys didn't do that."

"And I don't have hair on my palms," someone else said.

"Hush now," said Bobby. "Anyway, among other things that went on in those days of my innocence was talk about something called pussy. Pussy. And I never was sure what it was. Oh, I knew it had something to do with a girl, and I just about knew it had something to do with her bottom—I just wasn't sure. And I didn't want to ask anybody. Even I, had sense enough not to go ask my mother. Pussy. Isn't that an amazing word? Pussy. Ladies, we men would all like to shake the hand of the coiner of that word."

"I'm here to tell you."

"Now, don't interrupt me, James."

"I used to go around saying it to myself. And even though I didn't know for sure what it was, I knew it was something very very special—because of the way it was always spoken about. I loved girls—even then. And I knew that somewhere between each one's legs was something I wasn't allowed to see—not to speak of touching. I really don't know how I knew that. I think we were all just born knowing that." A couple of the old drinkers smiled and tipped their beers. "Pussy. That word was the most important word in my life at seven, eight. I loved pussy and I didn't even know what it was." Building his drama, Bobby stepped from the microphone, reached and took a cigarette from Byron's pack before returning to his story. "Anyway, one day we were all out in this broom sage field playing baseball—most of the boys in the neighborhood—and up rode Leon Tuberville on his bicycle. Leon was a delinquent, twelve, thirteen years old. He may be incarcerated by now, or dead. Leon liked to hang cats by their tails and steal—and talk about fucking, which was something else I didn't know about. Leon told me one time what fucking was—which was my second favorite word—but I didn't believe him. 'My daddy and mama don't do that,' I told him. Anyway, we were playing ball and Leon came up and was standing over with a couple of other boys and I walked over to where they were. I had just struck out, I think, and Leon had this ball of something, tossing it up and catching it." Bobby illustrated a toss and catch as he went on. "'What's that?' I asked him. And he looked at me with this nasty little grin of his and said, 'What? This? It's a piece of pussy, Long.' And he went right on grinning. That's all he said, 'It's a piece of pussy, Long.'" Bobby swallowed and spoke softer. "Ohhhhh-hhh, people, at that moment I could feel something churning in my stomach that started going down on me. My face got hot, and I felt like I was out of breath." Bobby took on the expression of a mystified little boy. "Ohhhhh, my. My hands got clammy and I started to sweat. And every time Leon threw that ball in the air I would follow it with my eyes until it dropped back in his dirty little fingers. Leon had cigarette stains on his fingers even then." Bobby took a drag off his cigarette and stepped to the table for a sip from his vodka and tonic, returning to the microphone to continue. Byron had been studying the reactions from the faces of the enthralled audience.

"That ball," Bobby continued, "that piece of pussy looked like this dirty piece of wax—paraffin, or a melted-down candle that had been rolled around in the dirt and grass. Or something, slick looking, moist. I'm telling the truth, I was mesmerized, kept looking at it and wishing. And the more I watched it, the more frustrated I got. I had seen it, men. I had seen a piece of pussy, finally, and I was still just seven years old. Lust was what I was feeling. I didn't even know what lust was, but I was lusting after that...piece of... pussy... I still wasn't sure what it was—but I damn sure wanted some of my own. I knew it had something to do with a girl, I just didn't know what. I imagined that Leon had gone off somewhere and stooped down between some little girl's legs and let it pour in his hands, or had reached up there somewhere and pulled it out and balled it up and taken it." The men all burst out laughing, and Bobby waited.

"And then it turned hard and you were supposed to eat it or lick it or something that would surely send you straight to hell, but Leon Tuberville was still standing there, rolling that stuff in his grimy hands."

Both men and women were laughing, slapping each other's backs, shuffling in their chairs and stools.

One old man coughed so much that Nick had to give him a glass of water.

"I just had to have that piece of pussy," Bobby went on. "At least smell it, touch it. I was starting to believe that there really was such a thing as fucking. Then old Leon finally took that piece of pussy, jumped on his bicycle and left. And there I was, knowing—knowing, my life would never be the same again." Speaking meticulously, Bobby, slowly, allowing more distance between his words, said, "I would have given every marble I owned, every ball, comic book, cap pistol…hell, I would have given my little baby sister for that piece of pussy." Bobby stopped and took a drink of vodka while the men laughed and sneezed and coughed. Then he wound up his tale with, "I quit playing ball. I went off by myself and all I could think about was I had finally seen a piece of pussy, and some way or another I was going to have to get some…some of my very own. Just one little piece, just one little piece that I could carry with me all the rest of my life."

Several people started to clap, as others needed to reflect momentarily before responding.

"Bobby," one of the old men shouted, "You the craziest son-of-a-bitch I ever met. You alright, Mister… Mister Alabama."

Unnoticed, Lorraine had left the bar during the story.

It was long past that February midnight when Bobby and Byron finally left their good company, staggered out into the drizzling rain, the quiet stillness of St. Charles Avenue, and up the stairs.

When they got to the room, Lorraine was lying in the bed with potato chip crumbs all over her breasts. Beside her lay the empty bag. Her eyes were closed, but the two men had needs, so they tried to wake her. Byron called her name. Bobby sang and started taking off his clothes. But Lorraine did not wake up.

***

Byron sat at the desk with his hands in his pockets, legs stretched out front of him, staring blankly at an empty beer bottle that stood beside his incomplete manuscript.

Lying on the bed, Bobby glanced over, "You look nice." They had just returned from the cemetery. "You should wear that suit more often."

Byron smiled. "Does that mean you want to go to bed with me?"

"Not yet," said Bobby, grinning.

Neither of them spoke for a while, as Byron stared at his shoes and Bobby took his off. "Bobby," Byron finally said.

"What?"

"You wonder how much longer we're going to live?"

His hand clasped at the back of his head, Bobby said, "Boy, don't talk like that."

"Which one of us do you think will go first?"

"I hope to hell it'll be you."

"We came from good stock, don't you think? Your folks lived a long time. My folks, most of them, have."

"Yes, but they didn't abuse themselves."

"I need to quit drinking."

"Me too."

"I need to get out in the sun. It's been so long since I felt the sun on my back."

"Me, too."

"We aren't that old."

"No."

"Do you think they have been right about us?"

"Who."

"Our people."

"Probably."

"Goddamnit, I've tried."

"Me too."

"I want a woman, Bobby."

"Me too."

"You have to have something to offer them. I have nothing to offer them."

Bobby went to the window, raised it, sat on the side of the bed and lit a cigarette. "Byron, why do you think Carolyn left me?" Byron laughed as Bobby chuckled with him. "Why do you always laugh when I'm trying to be serious? I asked a serious question, and you laugh. You always do that to me." Bobby reached across the table for the bottle of vodka. "I bought her a house, Byron. She wanted a house, and I bought her one. I sure as hell didn't want a house."

"She bought the house, Bobby."

"She did not," he said defensively. "We bought it together."

"She paid the payments."

"I helped." He knew Byron would laugh. "To start with."

After reflecting Bobby said, "I should have been willing to mow the lawn."

"Fuck, Bobby, that wasn't it."

"Women appreciate a lawnmower. I should have taken her more places. I should have shown that flaxen-haired thing to the world. She was pretty. Didn't you think she was?"

"Very."

Bobby looked at Byron. "What do you mean, 'very'? Byron, did you ever—"

"Nope."

"Try, I mean?"

"I tried."

"But she wouldn't let you?"

Byron's eyes brightened as he looked out the window.

"Look at me, Byron."

Grinning, Byron turned to face Bobby. "I'm looking. Now what?"

"She wouldn't let you?"

Byron barely chuckled.

"You son-of-a-bitch," shouted Bobby. "You fucked my fucking wife."

"I did not fuck your wife. I was just trying to piss you off. I did, too."

"Byron, I'll ask you one—"

"No."

"Swear?"

Byron stood up. "Bobby, you know something?"

"What?"

"All we ever talk about anymore is women."

"So?"

"So we ought to go fishing sometimes."

"You don't fish."

"Well. Maybe we should start."

"Byron, did you fuck my wife?"

"No!"

"Just asking," said Bobby. "I don't want to talk about it anymore."

Within the hour the two men were sitting across from each other on the floor playing rummy and drinking. The sun was about to go down. Byron had shed his coat. A streetcar rumbled by and somewhere outside a bird whistled.

THE OCCURRENCE

T he young girl climbed the stairs carrying a considerable sized brown vinyl bag strapped to her shoulder. When she reached the top, taking a piece of paper from her shirt pocket, she began to compare a number written on it to the numbers on the doors. Eventually, matching the number, she set her bag on the floor and knocked. Byron came to the door wearing khakis and an unbuttoned shirt, while Bobby, seeing the girl, stood from the bed as she said, "Are you Bobby Long?" Byron stepped back acknowledging Bobby. "I'm Lorraine's daughter," the girl said.

"Then you must be Hanna," Bobby said. "Come in, girl."

The teenager wore a dark green beret with her sandy blond hair, a light orange shirt beneath her Navy peacoat, a knee-length gray skirt and black, thick-soled shoes. She was fair skinned with a light scattering of freckles across her nose. Her slenderness gave her an appearance of being taller than she actually was. "Is this where she stayed?" the girl asked as she glanced into the room.

"It certainly is," said Bobby, "come on in." The girl did not move.

"She stayed in this little room with ya'll?" she said, her eyes darting about the place.

"Sure did," said Bobby, "don't you want to come in?"

"I'm Byron," Byron told her as he reached for the desk chair. "Come in, have a seat."

Still the girl did not move, except to brush back her hair with her hand as she looked away. "I'm not staying. I just come to see. I hadn't seen her in a long time. I come just to make sure everything was taken care of. She didn't have anybody else is all. I didn't hardly know her and all." Hanna glanced at Bobby, "Did ya'll bury her?"

"We did," said Bobby. "We gave her a nice funeral. You may feel assured of that. I wish you would come in."

Hanna stepped inside the room. Byron, noticing her bag, took it from the hall to set beside her. She glanced at him suspiciously. "Did all of ya'll sleep in that bed?"

"Not really," said Bobby, "mostly we slept either on the floor or the bed, or that chair there."

"Much of the time we slept at different times," Byron contributed.

"If you are asking if we slept with your mother, yes, we did, with her approval," said Bobby.

"I'm not surprised," said Hanna glancing round the room.

"You're welcome to sit down," Byron said, offering the armchair.

Hanna, pushing strands of hair from her forehead, then sighing, said, "The truth is, I came to see if Lorraine left anything that was worth keeping. Just to make sure if everything was taken care of. She was my mother but I didn't hardly know her."

"Just some clothes, a purse, several paperback books," Bobby told her.

"That figures," said Hanna. "I didn't expect she had much. She probably didn't have no money either, did she? Or would ya'll tell me if she did?"

As Byron was about to speak, Bobby said, "Your mother received a disability check every month. After the funeral expenses and all…"

"I guess that means no money, huh?"

"We all three pitched in equally," said Byron. "We had expenses, this room, food…"

"Now, won't you have a seat and tell us about yourself," said Bobby.

"No, I guess I'll just go. I thought it was a bad idea for me to come. I sorta expected this is what was gonna happen." Hanna reached for the strap of her bag.

"How did you get here?" Byron asked.

"Bus."

"Do you have a bus ticket back?"

"No."

"Do you have enough money?"

"About five dollars."

"Well that won't buy you very far," said Bobby.

As she lifted the bag, blowing a strand of hair from her face, she said, "I don't suppose she left enough money for a bus ticket."

"Come on, girl, sit down," said Byron. "You're probably tired. Just rest awhile before you go."

"No, I'm going."

"Just have a seat first," said Byron, nudging her toward the chair.

Hanna reluctantly backed into the desk chair, crossed her legs but did not sit back.

"So, tell us about yourself. I understand you've been living somewhere in Florida," said Bobby.

"Nothing to tell," said Hanna, glancing at a pack of cigarettes on the desk. "Could I have one of your cigarettes?"

Grinning, Bobby said, "Help yourself." Byron passed her a book of matches. Hanna glanced round the room as she raised her head to blow smoke. "So, this was where she stayed, huh?"

"She did," said Bobby. "Your mother was a very good friend of mine. I've known her for a long time."

"Um huh," said Hanna, continuing to study the room.

"What does that mean, 'um huh'?" asked Bobby.

When Byron reached to close the door, Hanna said, "Please don't close that door."

"What's the matter, girl, you don't trust us?" Bobby asked.

"I don't know ya'll," she said, her eyes catching a glimpse of the vodka bottle on the top of the chest of drawers. "Ya'll drink all the time?"

"All the time," Bobby said, grinning.

"Ya'll alcoholics?"

"He is," said Bobby nodding toward Byron.

"And I guess you're not."

"I am too," Bobby confessed, "Look, Hanna...what's your last name?"

"Is there a bathroom in this place?" she wanted to know.

"Down the hall, take a right," Byron offered.

As she stepped to the door reaching for her bag, Byron said, "You're coming back, aren't you?"

"I don't know," Hanna said as she started down the hall.

Byron looking at Bobby, both with raised brows, was about to speak before Bobby whispered, "Don't let her leave."

When Hanna came out of the bathroom, Byron was standing outside the door.

"What are you doing?" she wanted to know.

"I was afraid you would leave. Bobby and I are concerned about you."

With cocked head, her foot turned, she said, "Well, if ya'll are so concerned about me, why don't you give me some money for a bus ticket?"

"We'll talk about it. Just come back to the room and stay for a while. We want to talk to you."

"About what?"

"About you. Your mother. Where you are going. What your plans are."

"Why the fuck should that matter to ya'll?"

"Because I know you don't have any family, and you're…How old are you?"

"Look, I'm not going to hang around here with the two of you. Just tell me now, are you going to give me the money or not?"

"Come back to the room, just for a while."

Reluctantly, with a sigh, Hanna started down the hall. On the way back to the room, Byron, behind her, could not help admiring her walk.

Bobby was sitting in the window with a glass in his hand, smoking a cigarette. "Do ya'll mind if I have another cigarette?" Hanna asked after she sat stiltedly in the desk chair and crossed her leg and twitched her foot. After lighting her cigarette, she said, "Well, are ya'll going to give me the money or not? Byron, do you have to discuss it with him?"

"Girl," said Bobby, "where are you planning to go? I know you have no family. Lorraine told me your grandmother died last year. Do you have any relatives?"

"Nobody I would have anything to do with. I'm just gonna go back to where I came from. I don't know. Anyway, what's it to you?" she said, glancing toward Bobby.

"Where will you stay? Do you have any friends, a boyfriend? Where have you been staying?"

"With this guy, if you must know."

"Is he your boyfriend?"

Hanna leaned her forehead against the hand that held her cigarette. "'Boy enemy' is more like it."

"He's not good to you? How old is this boy?"

"Twenty something."

"Does he work?"

"He's a mechanic," Hanna mumbled.

Byron spoke. "How old are you, Hanna?"

"Seventeen. Look, are ya'll going to help me or not. I got to go," she said, uncrossing her legs, bringing her knees together.

"It doesn't sound like this guy, man, is all that special to you. Why do you want to go back and stay with him?"

"Well, what else do you expect me to do?"

Bobby glanced round at Byron, "Would you like to stay with us for a while, long enough to get your head together?"

Leaning forward, glancing toward Bobby, she said, "Are you serious? I will walk back to Florida first."

"Look," said Byron. "I know this room is not much, it's small, but it sure beats the hell out of you traipsing off to nowhere without knowing what you want to do. Hanna, this is a big point in your life. It sounds like it's been pretty fucked up so far. Girl, you need to make some serious decisions right now. This is no time for you to be floundering. You have your whole life ahead of you...what grade are you in?"

"Look, forget it, I'm not about to stay in this room with ya'll. Shit! I can't even believe ya'll, especially ya'll would think I would..."

"What grade are you in?"

Growing more frustrated, running her hand through her hair, said, "No grade. I don't go to school. I quit school halfway through the ninth grade for the second time."

"How long have you been living on your own?"

"A while," Hanna said, then suddenly, with a change of expression turned to Bobby and said, "Wait. What about Lorraine's welfare check? Has she gotten one since she died, since she cashed the last one?"

"What difference would that make?" asked Byron.

"Maybe I could cash it."

"Girl, are you more stupid than you look?" said Bobby.

"What?" Hanna asked.

"First of all," Bobby began, "No, she hasn't received one since she died. It always comes the first or second day of the month. Second, even if we did have one, if you tried to cash it, do you know what would happen?"

"What? I'm her daughter."

Byron spoke. "What he means is you could be arrested for forgery. And if that happened, you would probably not go to jail, since you're under-age, but more than likely you would be put in some institution for minors. If that didn't happen, something would. Since you have no family, most likely you would be placed in a foster home or an orphanage until you were eighteen, at least."

"What if I didn't get caught?"

"Do you want to chance that?"

As Hanna's enthusiasm faded, dropping back in the chair, folding her arms, she said, "Fuck. Motherfucking son of a bitch!"

"Listen," said Byron. "Just listen for a second. If you would consider just this, Bobby and I could get another bed..."

"Don't start that shit again," said Hanna. "If ya'll don't plan to give me bus fare, I guess that's it. I'm going."

"Just hear me out," Byron continued, "We could get a rollaway bed and some blankets from the hotel to make a curtain, a partition, between us and you. You could have some privacy, at least some—"

"What day is this?" interrupted Hanna.

"What?"

"When is the first of the month?"

"Today is the...twenty-seventh, twenty-sixth of February," Bobby offered. "Something like that?"

"Why?" Byron asked. "You're not still—"

"If ya'll loaned me the money to get back to Florida,

and mailed me her check when it comes, I could pay you back from it."

"Damn, Bobby, we've got a nutcase here."

"Better yet," Bobby suggesting as he stepped from the window for a cigarette, "you could stay with us until the check comes and solve all your problems. It would only be for a few days, the first of the week. What is today?"

"Friday," offered Hanna.

"Well, then, if today is the twenty-eighth, then Monday will be, what? Hell, the check will be here Monday. You can stay here that long, can't you, girl? Fuck, I'll forge the check for you." Bobby winked at Byron who until then had not bought the plan.

"Where am I going to stay?" Hanna asked.

"Here," said Bobby.

"I ain't staying in this room with ya'll."

"Well then, hit the road."

Hanna said nothing for a moment, leaned forward, elbow on her knee to prop her fist, glanced around, then finally said, "And ya'll would get me a bed and put a wall up between?"

"I'll check on it, but I'm pretty sure we can find you a rollaway, and I know we can find something to make a partition," Byron offered.

Hanna said nothing before Bobby said, "Look, girl, we're not going to molest you, if that's what you think. Byron is a schoolteacher and a writer. I am a college professor."

"Uh huh, and I'm a ballerina?"

"It's true."

"Ya'll do talk like ya'll might have been something, maybe before ya'll got to be alcoholics."

"Byron was an English teacher. Girl, we're not just some unprincipled sons-of-bitches. We're honorable people."

Hanna glanced about the room, bowed her head, scratched her leg, then took a deep breath and exhaled before finally looking at Byron, accepting defeat and saying, "Will ya'll buy me some cigarettes?"

"Hell yes. As long as you will smoke our generic brand."

"Is he really, like a professor, like college?" Hanna asked Byron.

"He was."

"Girl, are you hungry?" Bobby asked.

In the afternoon, after a trip to the grocery store for a loaf of bread, mayonnaise, packaged ham, a tomato, potato chips, and three packs of cigarettes, they made sandwiches in the hotel room.

"What do you write?" Hanna asked Byron while Bobby was making a screwdriver with a dab of orange juice.

"Pardon me?" said Byron.

"He said you was a writer, what do you write?"

"He writes novels. He's writing one about me,"

Bobby told her. "Byron is going to be famous one day and he's going to make me famous."

"I can only imagine," said Hanna.

"It's true," said Bobby. "Girl, I will bet you've never read a book in your life."

"I read sometimes."

"What do you read, *People Magazine*, the *TV Guide*, romance novels?"

"Well, what do you read, Mister College Professor."

"Being a ninth-grade dropout, you wouldn't understand," said Bobby handing Byron a drink in a plastic cup.

"Is all ya'll do is drink vodka?"

"Well, Miss One and a Half Years in the Ninth Grade, what do you do?"

"I don't know. Ya'll don't even have a television or a radio."

"No," said Bobby. "We have no television and we don't want one. What a terrible waste of an invention. The propaganda, opiate of the slaves."

"What?" said Hanna.

"We have cards," said Byron. "Would you like to play gin rummy, Hanna?"

"No. I don't know how anyway."

"We'll teach you. Byron where did you put the cards?"

"I don't want to play cards, ya'll can."

"Oh, hell, girl, let's play. What do you know how to play?"

"About all I know is poker, five-card draw or five-card stud."

"Well, let's play five-card stud. Do you feel like losing some of your five dollars? Nickel at a time, I mean. Nickel limit."

It occurred to Hanna that the little money she had was of little use to her, and that if she happened to win more, who knew.

They spent the afternoon playing poker, the men showing no remorse when Hanna said she would play with her own money rather than let them loan her some of their pocket change. The men drank, showing no signs of intoxication, except for Bobby's loudness and overexuberance after winning a hand. After finishing off half a fifth of vodka, Hanna having lost most of her five dollars that the men wanted her to take back, Bobby suggested they go downstairs to Tiny's for a drink. When Byron said something about Hanna's age, Bobby said, "Oh, fuck, Nick won't check her ID if she's with us."

Hanna thought it was a good idea.

They sat at a table at the back of the bar where it was darker. Bobby went to the bar, ordered two gin and tonics, a Sprite and an empty cup.

He poured half his and Byron's drinks into the cup and set it before Hanna as she stared at it for a moment.

"Don't tell me you don't drink," said Bobby.

"I do, but mostly beer."

"Well, drink that. It's free."

The bar was nearly empty, except for one old man sitting at a table by himself and an emaciated woman at the bar near the front. "Where is she buried?" Hanna asked, taking a cigarette from her pack.

"Across town," said Byron. "Would you like to see?"

"Fuck no. I don't like cemeteries."

"Me either," said Bobby. "Don't ask me where my father lived, but did he live. Hanna, I have a story to tell you."

Later, they bought several rounds of gin and tonics. The bartender never questioned Hanna's age. The sun was going down, the bar getting darker, Hanna was feeling the alcohol and occasionally slurred a word when she spoke, mostly about Monday and the promise Bobby had made to her.

Hanna wanted another drink when, after dark, they got back to the room. She lit a cigarette, took off her coat and flopped down in the armchair. The alcohol allowed her to tell the men more about herself, that she had not known all that much about her mother, had started sneaking out of her grandmother's house before she was a teenager, the old woman being nearly senile and going to bed early. She said she began to lose interest in school after the sixth grade because of boredom mostly.

"Girl, what were you doing sneaking out of the house when you were such a young kid?"

"I don't know. Just things."

"What things? How old were you when you lost your virginity?" Bobby asked.

Hanna had an inebriated grin when she said, "Twelve."

"Goddamn, girl!" said Byron.

"Mother fucking son of a bitch," said Bobby. "How old was the boy?"

"I don't know, sixteen."

Byron felt it was time to change the subject. "Let's play some cards. Fuck this."

"I'm not doing shit till ya'll get that bed and a wall between ya'll and me."

The men's good fortune was the two blankets, a rollaway bed, sheets and an extra pillow, compliments of the hotel. They opened the rollaway next to the window facing St. Charles Avenue, then fumbled with the blankets while Hanna, between nods, watched their mechanical awkwardness. "Ya'll don't have a fucking idea what ya'll are doing," she said as one design after another failed until near midnight they managed with the heel of Bobby's cowboy boot and a nail from the wall, meant for a picture sometime in the past, to attach the corner of one blanket, then tie the second at the top and bottom before pinching the other end in the top drawer of the chest. Hanna, believing they had done the best they could, accepted the very temporary wall for one night, if they would do something about the opening where the two blankets met. It was Byron's idea to conceal it with several of his and Bobby's shirts tied and draped. "I'm so tired, I don't give a shit," said Hanna. "But tomorrow, ya'll are gonna have to fix it better. God, I don't know what I'm doing here."

TWO

F inally crawling on their bed, sometime past midnight, Byron could not sleep, but he was not aware that neither could Bobby. Late-night light from St. Charles dispelled complete darkness while the men, separated by inches and their separate images of the young girl, so close by, plotted sinister strategies. Byron knew she had fallen asleep with her clothes on, however, he wanted to believe she may, sometime in the night, undress, at least possibly take off her shirt, bra, since it was warm enough in the room, by some absurd miracle, maybe.

While Byron was dreaming, Bobby had slid off the bed like a thief and, on his hands and knees, began to crawl toward the corner of the blanket partition, sneaking, careful not to disturb anybody, with images of doubtful grand possibilities. The floor was completely dark; light from the window penetrated only the upper half of the room on his side of the partition. Creeping along, Bobby touched something, a beer bottle and quietly moved it from his path, afterwards fanning his way for possibly another obstacle. When he reached the wall, lifting back the blanket, peeking behind it where the light brightened the rollaway, there was nothing to see but disappointment. Hanna, lying on her side, knees bent and fully clothed, was sleeping soundly. Suddenly, from outside the window, the blue light of a police car and the shriek of a siren broke through the late-night silence, startling Bobby enough to drop the corner of the blanket to back away. However, as he started back toward the bed, he crashed heads with Byron, who was in the act of committing the same foolish indiscretion, their good fortune continuing since their curses did not wake Hanna.

*　*　*

Byron opened his eyes the next morning; the partition was down at one end. Hanna sat on the cot cross-legged, eating a candy bar from a vending machine in the hotel lobby. Her hair was stringy and damp. She ate with her mouth open, until it occurred to her that she was being watched. Byron smiled. "What?" said Hanna.

"I see you found some nourishment."

Bobby rolled over to his side. "Not me."

"Which one of you snores?" Hanna asked.

"Not me," said Bobby.

"I don't snore," said Byron.

"I saw something on television where you could have something cut out of your throat to stop it," said Hanna.

"Bobby doesn't have anything in his throat," said Byron.

"Girl," said Bobby, "I'm getting out of bed. And I don't have anything on. You can turn your head or watch, it doesn't matter to me." Hanna quickly turned to face the window before Bobby got out of bed wearing nothing but sheer black panties—a skimpy garment stolen from his young ex-wife before she abandoned him.

"I don't mind you looking, girl."

"Just put some clothes on or I'm out of here."

Bobby lit a cigarette and Hanna wanted to take a bath. The hotel bathrooms had showers, so she took her bag down the hall, returning with damp hair combed straight down beneath her shoulders as the men were prepared to take her to breakfast down at the Hummingbird. The men slipped a little vodka in their coffee while Hanna ate a large stack of pancakes. "Girl, do you fool with drugs?" Bobby asked.

"No. A few times."

"You're not hooked on anything, are you?"

"No."

"Byron and I aren't either."

With her fork stuck in a pancake, Hanna looked at them, "Umm huh."

"We learned our lessons about drugs. Hanna, one time Byron and I had gone to visit this lady we knew and she gave us something she said was marijuana. You know, we grew up when bootleg and beer were all we ever experienced. This was when drugs were starting to become popular in the South. This woman rolled these two cigarettes for us before we left. So, we're riding down the road this morning and we decided to see what all the hoopla was about. So, we lit up and started sucking on this cigarette and behold, oh hell. It wasn't long before we felt it. Hanna, we started giggling, ridiculously. We couldn't stop. Could we Byron?"

"Tell her about the road," said Byron.

"Oh, the road. Girl, the road started to disappear. Byron would say, 'Did you see that?' And I'd say, 'What?' 'The road just disappeared, no wait, there it is' then he would giggle and say, 'There it goes again.'"

"We would be riding along, puffing on that…whatever it was. And all of a sudden…all of a sudden the road would go away. I started seeing it, too. We got scared, all the time giggling uncontrollably.

"Then there came this bridge…it appeared and then it was gone, at the same time we were going over it. That's when we decided we'd better get off the highway. Byron kept saying, 'Bobby, stop the car.' No, I would say. I was afraid if we stopped and a patrolman came by, well, hell, there was no way on earth we could have explained ourselves without exposing ourselves. But by then, we started really getting scared. We started crying, then giggling again. One minute Byron would be giggling while I would be crying.

"But finally we did stop. Out front of this old country church. There was nobody there. It was a Saturday morning, I remember. And there we sat, giggling and crying. Paranoid. Scared."

"What did y'all do then?" Hanna wanted to know.

"I went to the toilet," said Byron.

"He did," said Bobby. "There was this outdoor toilet, an outhouse, out behind that church, and Byron left me alone." Bobby's chuckle had a moan in it. "I was scared to death—and started crying again. I thought he had gone off and left me. I stayed in the car and cried, and kept thinking something was going to get me. I was scared to get out of the car. Finally though, I did it anyway. It got so scary inside, I thought the outside couldn't be any worse."

"And so I wandered about and cried—until I came to this outhouse. I knew what it was, and at the same time, I didn't know what it was. I thought it might be a mineshaft, or a place where some strange creature lived. But the crazy thing was, I opened the door anyway. As scared as I was, I opened that door. And when I did, there was Byron, sitting on the stool. All he did was look up at me like it didn't matter if I was there or not.

"Now you have to understand, Hanna, he had been there for no telling how long. It could have been several hours. I mean, this thing went on all that day. So I said, 'Byron, are you all right?' And he just looked up at me and said, 'What?' Then he said, 'Hey Bobby, have you been watching this?'

"'I'm scared,' I told him. I said, 'Byron, come on, let's go.'

"And Byron said something like, 'Bobby, this is the most beautiful place in the world.' And I kept saying, 'Come on, Byron. Please, I'm scared. Something is going to get us out here.' But Byron just sat there." There was a whine in Bobby's voice as he went on. "Byron kept telling me about how beautiful the inside of that outhouse was. He started pointing to these knotholes in the walls, and these spider webs, and telling me all the things he had seen. And I kept saying, 'Byron, come on. We have to go.'"

"How'd y'all ever get out of that place?" Hanna wanted to know.

"We finally left. It was late that afternoon. It got to where the stuff started wearing off. It would come and go, enough for us to realize these periods of reality. Short periods at first. And then it would start all over again—the laughing, the crying. We even thought about getting out on the road and trying to flag somebody—a patrol car or something. By then we were ready to go to jail—anything, as long as we could get somebody to help us. What was that stuff, Hanna?"

"I don't know. I think y'all were just crazy."

"Oh, Hanna," said Bobby, leaning back and stretching out his legs. He propped himself up with one arm and pointed at Byron with the other. "This man and I have done so many things in our lives. We know so many things that remain out of sight. You aren't just looking at two old men here. We've been through so much. We've lived!" he shouted. "And girl, we've had our time in the sun, too. We've had pretty women. Beautiful women. And some that were not so beautiful. And we were good to every last one of them."

"What happened?" asked Hanna.

Bobby grinned at her for a moment, then dropped his head and chuckled. "What happened, she wants to know."

Byron laughed, too.

"I mean, what happened that day?" said Hanna.

Bobby looked at her with his head tilted to one side and grinned crooked-mouthed. "Hanna."

"What?"

"Have you ever had sex with two men at once?"

Hanna stabbed a pancake and slid to the edge of the booth. "I'm outa here," she said, about to stand up.

Bobby put his hands together. "I'm sorry, girl. I swear I didn't mean that. I don't know where that came from. Please don't go."

"I want to go," said Hanna. "This whole thing is crazy. Just forget everything, I just want to go."

"Go where?" Byron asked.

Standing, Hanna brushed back her hair with both hands and sighed. "I don't know. I just want to go. I just want to go upstairs and get my things and go, somewhere. Y'all scare me."

"We don't mean to, Hanna," said Bobby empathetically. "We just talk too much sometimes, darling. Please sit back down, finish your breakfast."

Hanna sat on the edge of the seat. "Could y'all please loan me enough money to get a bus ticket? I'll pay y'all back, I promise."

"Now, girl, you agreed to stay until the first of the week. Now relax. Bobby did not mean to suggest anything. You just have to know him better. He might say things like that, but he's harmless. Finish your breakfast. We'll go do something, show you the French Quarter or something."

* * *

It was still light outside when Byron passed out across the bed. But no matter how much Bobby drank, it did no good; he could not go to sleep. He sat on the rollaway and leaned against the wall with the ukulele. He lit one cigarette off another as he strummed the little instrument aimlessly. He felt so terribly lonely. Was this the way he was going to end up, in a city where no one knew or cared that he had been worth something at so many different times in his life? Nobody cared that he had been a grand running back in his day. No one cared that he knew the poems he did. No one cared that women had loved him, that he had been quite a debonair young man, that he once dove from the highest bank of the creek back home. It was documented. For years afterwards the townspeople had talked of that feat, something, as far as he knew, that still had never been repeated. And he was an educated man, had advanced degrees from a fine school, had been a fine English teacher. Had been a fine Marine officer until he had been passed over for a promotion one time too many.

Bobby let his hazy mind drift back to thoughts of the swimming hole, and the dive from the highest cliff. People were there, people that had mattered. He relived the event several times, until his mind began to drift to connections of the day: his father, who never missed one of his football games; a girl named Sally Coffner, whose virginity he took behind the curtain of the auditorium. It had been such an innocent occurrence, the scent of Tabu and leather from her white jacket, so clean, his girlfriend the last two years of high school, a good girl who got pregnant, her parents, to keep her reputation pure, set up the abortion out of town.

The sun had left St. Charles Avenue, the room was almost dark, and Byron's breathing and occasional shifting on the bed were Bobby's only reminder that he was not absolutely all alone. Maybe if he had one more stiff drink it would take the edge off his melancholy.

Hanna came back from a walk up St. Charles, flopped down in the armed chair, took her cigarettes out of her coat pocket and said, "I'm bored to death."

"Well, hell, let's do something," said Byron. You want to play some stud poker?"

"No. Shit, that sounds boring-er."

Bobby stepped from behind the partition he and Byron had managed to improve. "'Boring-er.' What a word. Girl, you had better go back to school."

Hanna turned her eyes up at him, sighed heavily, then a moment later said, "I guess I had just as soon play cards as listen to another one of y'all's stories."

"I'm going down to Tiny's," said Bobby.

"No, now," said Byron, "sit down here. We're going to play poker with our houseguest. Fix us all a drink." Sitting on the floor, Byron started shuffling cards.

"Well, hell," said Bobby as he stepped to the desk where used plastics cups were stacked. "Girl, do you mind drinking out of a used cup?"

"Go wash the cups, Bobby," said Byron.

"I'll go," said Hanna. "Hand them to me. I don't trust ya'll washing."

When she left the room, Bobby said, "Let's see if we can get her drunk."

"How old is this orange juice?" Hanna asked when she returned.

"It's fine," Bobby told her, as Hanna watched him pour the drinks.

"I would like for mine to look like orange juice," she said.

"Alright," said Byron after everyone was seated.

"Five-card stud, nickel ante, nickel limit."

They all took change from their pockets before Byron began shuffling the deck and dealing each of them a single card. Hanna, after several swallows from the vodka and orange juice Bobby made for her, won the first hand, seventy-five cents. A while later, Bobby, while fixing them all drinks, added slightly more alcohol to Hanna's.

As the evening went on, breaking for the bathroom, drinks, and intermittent talk, Hanna began to feel the effects of the alcohol, and was opening up, telling the men more about herself, that after her grandmother died she had stayed with a girl for a while who got arrested right after Hanna left to go to Colorado with two other girls older than her. That ended with her returning to South Florida where she got with a guy who was in his thirties, even though he told Hanna he was twenty-five, who slapped her around before she took up with the guy she left to come to New Orleans.

"Did you fuck them?" Bobby asked.

"Who?" Hanna said.

"Who?" said Bobby. "Girl, how many are we talking about?"

"I cunzider that none a you bidness," she said light-headedly. "You're fucking with me again."

"Deal," said Byron.

"It's my dee-ul," said Hanna.

Little money changed hands as the smoke-filled

room began to swirl for Hanna who had fumble-hand-edly dealt her next turns.

It was near midnight, Hanna nodding and mumbling, said she had to lie down. They played a couple more hands before she finally fell to her side, asleep. Bobby nudged her several times before he and Byron put her in their bed. "I'm fine," she said, then was out for the night. Bobby and Byron looked at her for several moments before Byron started unbuttoning her shirt, soon exposing her off-white bra, containing considerable heaving fair flesh. Bobby carefully unzipped her jeans, exposing her slender white transparent panties, below curls of dark brown. After feasting their eyes awhile, Byron meticulously undid the hook between the cups of her bra, opened them to gaze upon the loveliness of her restful young breasts. At that moment, the young girl shifted slightly in her sleep. Leaving Hanna, they got off the bed, sat in the chairs, not saying a word as they finished their drinks and continued to gratify themselves with the loveliness upon their bed. After a while Byron stepped over the bed to zip back up her jeans and re-attach her bra, neglecting to re-button her shirt before turning out the light and stepping behind the partition to sleep on the rollaway. Bobby closed his eyes sitting in the armchair.

***

It was daylight when Hanna woke up. She felt terrible, head hurting, face feverish, while her mouth felt thick and tasted rank. An odor of men's old sweat and musk rose from her pillow. Hanna raised her head at the moment it occurred to her where she was, and, at that moment, caught sight of Bobby asleep in the chair. A second glance verified what she thought she had seen, Bobby's limp penis lopped outside the opened fly of his trousers. With overwhelming disgust, Hanna sat up in bed, frowned from her aching head, and realized her shirt was unbuttoned. She did not remember unbuttoning it. She did not think she had. Anger began to replace her disgust as she ran her fingers through her hair. She got off the bed, picked up her shoes and vinyl bag and quietly left the room.

It was mid-morning when Byron stepped from behind the partition, lit a cigarette, then turned to immediately realize the bed was empty. He glanced about seeing that Hanna's bag was gone. That was when he turned to Bobby, whose limp penis caught his eye. "Motherfuck!" he said, stepping into the hall, walking down to the bathroom and returning to where Bobby had not moved. "You son of a bitch!"

"What?" Bobby shouted.

"Look at yourself, you vulgar, grimy, lewd bastard. Somebody ought to shoot your filthy ass."

"What?" Bobby repeated just as he recognized the situation.

"Bobby, who on this entire earth is capable of fucking up even close to more than your ugly excuse as a human being?"

Zipping his pants, Bobby said, "Maybe she just went out for something."

"I'm going to see if I can find her," said Byron, putting on his shoes.

"Well, I'm going, too."

"Do you really expect her to want to see your stupid fucking ass?"

"I'm going," said Bobby.

They had been parking the Pontiac wedged between a Dumpster and the back wall of the Hummingbird Café. Driving out, entering St. Charles, Byron took a wrong-way street toward Lee Circle. Looking for a teenaged girl with a brown shoulder bag, they went up and down side streets, barely considering stop signs and one-ways. After half an hour, the gas gauge reading empty, they drove back to the hotel and made themselves drinks, sat for a while before Bobby said, "The bus station."

They stopped for two dollars' worth of gasoline and asked the attendant for directions to the Greyhound bus station. They eventually found the station; Byron went inside, but found no sign of Hanna. Despondent once more, they started back toward the hotel when Bobby said, "What about the Trailways station?"

They stopped at the entrance to a hotel parking lot

on Canal Street to ask an attendant for directions. When they found the station, they parked, both went round to where the buses were lined up, then went into the lobby. There on a bench sat Hanna, legs crossed, staring at a travel brochure. "When she saw Bobby and Byron walking toward her, she put down the brochure and crossed her arms. "Girl, what do you think you're doing?" Bobby asked.

"I fucking don't know," she said.

"Why did you run off?" Byron wanted to know.

"Now, why in the shit do you think I ran off," Hanna asked.

"You saw Bobby's dick."

"Look, just go away and leave me alone!"

"Damn, girl, haven't you ever seen a peter before?" Bobby asked. "I apologize. I was drunk and I fell asleep."

As her leg started to bounce, she said, "What ever."

"Girl, you're not going to let a little thing like that come between us, are you?"

"Watch what you say, Byron," said Bobby.

"We thought you were starting to like us."

"No more," said Hanna. "Now will ya'll please get away from me?"

Byron sat beside her. "Look Hanna, you still don't have any money, and your mother's check won't be here until the first of the week, tomorrow. Now, come on back to the hotel and at least wait till the mail comes."

"No way," said Hanna angrily looking into Bobby's face. "My shirt was unbuttoned this morning when I woke up. And…" glancing toward Byron, "I sure as shit don't think it was me that did it."

Byron and Bobby glanced at one another. "Well, I certainly didn't unbutton it. Byron, did you unbutton her shirt?"

"No. I damn well did not."

Hanna looked away from them.

"Hanna," said Bobby, "you were pretty drunk, remember? You passed out and we put you on the bed, that was all. Are you certain you could not have unbuttoned your shirt yourself?"

"Now, why would I just unbutton my shirt for no reason? I was drunk, remember, I passed out. And why'd ya'll put me in your bed instead of on the rollaway." Tears welled up in Hanna's eyes. "Ya'll I'm just a girl."

"It was closer," said Byron. "Look, girl, we did nothing to you last night. You passed out, we put you to bed, I slept on the rollaway, and you saw where Bobby slept."

"Oh, yes," said Hanna.

"Darling, I am so sorry about my exposing myself like that. I do not remember pulling my…dick, penis, peter, out at any time. I must have, well, done something…to myself. I don't think I did, though. I feel so ashamed. Please forgive me."

Hanna's crossed leg continued to bounce as she

blew a strand of hair from her face. "Alright, now will ya'll please go."

"Girl, you haven't heard a word we've said," Byron said.

"What do you plan to do?" asked Bobby. "No money, no place to go."

"No family," Byron added.

"I'm gonna call Ray and ask him to send me the money for a bus ticket."

"Yes, now that's a fucking good idea," said Bobby. "You go back and stay with that boy and just fuck off for the rest of your life. Get yourself pregnant, live in a house trailer and watch *Let's Make a Fucking Deal*...and teach another child how to screw up her life."

"That's my business," Hanna said.

Bobby turned away. "To hell with her, Byron. She's not going to stay. Let's get out of here. She is as stupid as I thought."

"Look, Hanna," said Byron putting his hand on her knee as she shifted to rid herself of it and gave him a smirk. "I know you don't think much of us right now. But just think. If you were to stay...for...say, a few days, see us in a better light. And give all of us time to help you make a good decision or two, maybe help you find a better situation than you have in Florida. Hanna, I want to ask you something, and don't jump to conclusions."

Hanna jumped up, "Look, goddamn you both. I just wish ya'll would leave me the fuck alone." She knelt to rummage through her bag. "I just want ya'll to go. I'm gonna call Ray."

"What are you doing?" asked Bobby

"If you must know, I'm looking for some fucking change."

Bobby held out two quarters for her. "Thank you," she said standing and looking for a phone booth. Byron grabbed her wrist. "Let go of my hand," she said. "I'll fucking scream my head off."

"Then scream," said Byron, "scream or sit back down." Hanna stared him in the face for several moments before sitting back on the bench.

"Listen. What if we were to help you do something like get your GED?" Byron glanced up at Bobby. "Isn't that what you call it, the test you take to get an equivalent of a high school diploma?"

"I don't want no fucking GED," said Hanna.

"Let's go, Byron," said Bobby.

"Sit down, Bobby."

"Look, ya'll…" said Hanna.

"No, you look," said Byron. "You seem like a pretty bright girl. At your age, what kind of job do you think you could get, burning hamburgers, maybe a cashier at a convenience store, pulling off your clothes for a bunch of assholes? Or, like Bobby said, go back to Florida and make your living on your back?"

Hanna turned her head away.

"If you were to get your GED, at least you would

have a better chance of taking care of yourself, not having to depend on some loser to keep you up. With a GED you could get into a trade school or something."

"Or something," said Bobby.

"Bobby, shut the fuck up," said Byron. "Look, girl, whether you choose to believe it or not, Bobby and I have formal educations and we have taught school. I've even taught kids your age. We could help you with the GED test in no time. We could be your tutors."

"You two teach me? That'd be the day."

Bobby, seeing where Byron was going, said, "He's right you know. We aren't just some kind of derelicts. We both have rather impressive formal educations. I have a Ph.D. Byron has a master's degree in English literature…"

"That was before ya'll got degrees in alcohol, I guess."

Bobby chuckled. "Girl, you are something."

"Just listen to ya'll. Ya'll stay drunk all the time." Hanna looked at Byron. "And you can't even write your book. How in the world…besides, why in the world would ya'll want to help me, just supposing you did?"

"Well for one thing, you happen to be the daughter of a woman we loved," said Bobby.

"Look, Hanna," said Byron, "Bobby and I have nothing to do. We've pretty much done all we planned to do. You are seemingly a nice kid and we could help you. Stay a week, see. And if after that you decide to go, we will help you do that. You have no business out here on your own. And you know as well as we do, you do not want to go back to that Ray character."

"Ya'll really expect me to stay in that room with ya'll for a week, Bobby showing hisself all the time?"

"Hear me out. If you did—and I'm not suggesting you do—decide to stay longer..." Byron glanced at Bobby. "We...look, we are not without income. I have some money from selling a business, not much, but some. Bobby gets a check, and he's applied for food stamps. We've already talked about it. We have been thinking about renting a little house somewhere down near the river. If, by any stretch of your imagination, you decided, or needed to stay longer, we could get a place where you could have your own bedroom."

Hanna ran her hand through her hair. "Look, if I decided to stay at all it would only be till Monday or whenever Lorraine's check comes. Shit, why am I sitting here talking to ya'll."

Bobby and Byron knew they had turned a corner.

"Let me ask ya'll this," said Hanna after reflecting. "What if I just stayed a day or two till I could find a job? Then I could get my own place."

"Hanna, darling, nobody is going to give you a job worth anything without at least a GED. Somebody will take advantage of you. You don't want that."

Bobby was fidgety, he needed a drink. Byron did, too.

"I'll go back with ya'll if ya'll will give me the money for a bus ticket. That's all."

"No, that's out," said Byron, knowing Hanna was indecisive gave them something to bargain with. "Two more days, no more, no less, if you decide not to."

"Byron, let's go," said Bobby.

Byron looked at Hanna, who swung her crossed leg, folded her arms, and stared toward the floor.

"Shit!" she finally said, glancing at both men. "Do y'all swear that one of y'all didn't unbutton my shirt?"

"Swear," both men said simultaneously.

"And will y'all promise to keep your stupid things to yourselves?"

THREE

New Orleans felt strange to Hanna, the little she had seen of it, certainly nothing like the photographs in magazines and travel brochures. People she knew had talked about the Big Easy, Sin City, Mardi Gras, and the jazz festival. She had images of lots of wrought iron, jazz and blues. But the places in real life were somehow different. The colors were not like the pictures, much too glossy, not the sepias, shadows, and earth colors she saw with her own eyes. The buildings, walls painted over so many times, still unable to hide the oldness, filth, and decay, captivated Hanna. The badly worn streets, smells coming from the restaurants, bars, and under-building parking lots were bizarre.

Hanna woke up Monday morning back in the hotel room; she sat on the rollaway painting her fingernails with light green polish. Despite what people might think of her, she felt she was different. She was a keen observer, aware of not belonging, not to a group, not to a family, gang, church or social group. She knew what it would be like to pretend to be other than what she was.

She had tried before, tried to behave as if she had come from a family, had as much going for her as the people she had mingled with, realizing however the foolishness of being a phony. If she could see through others, she was aware of how she could be seen through. And she was beginning to be aware of the differences in Bobby Long and Byron Burns, in spite of their sloth and drinking. She had observed the little ways their mannerisms betrayed their facades, the way they moved, handled eating utensils, courtesies they took for granted, their speech, their clothes, how they seemed so unaware, even in their unkemptness, of belonging to a world Hanna knew nothing about. She knew the clothes Byron wore were not bought in a discount store, and even though Bobby wore cheaper clothes, he did so knowingly. It had already become obvious to her that they had come from the opposite side of the tracks. And as much as she tried to deny it, there was some resentment when they behaved as if she was a charity case.

When Byron and Bobby, having slept in their clothes, got up, Byron went out and came back with donuts and coffee. "Where is Bobby," he asked Hanna. She only shrugged her shoulders and went on painting her fingernails. In a moment Bobby returned. "Here," he told Byron as he handed him a broom.

"What?" said Byron.

"It's your turn."

"For what?"

"For convincing the little lady we're not slobs."

Byron began to sweep while Bobby sat down, lit a cigarette, then poured vodka in his coffee. Hanna ate two donuts and drank most of her coffee while she smoked one of Byron's cigarettes, saving the few she had left of her own.

"Where would someone go to find out more about the GED test?" Byron said as he pushed the broom here and there.

"Wait," Hanna said from behind the hung blankets, "Y'all said two days."

Byron drew back a corner of the curtain. "All it would take for a smart girl like you is a little help from us and you would be out of here with a high school diploma in no time."

"Not me," said Hanna, "I ain't going back to school."

"Aren't," shouted Bobby.

"I'm leaving here tomorrow," said Hanna.

Bobby flung back the blanket, "And this is the thanks we get for all we've done for you," he said.

"What the shit have ya'll done?"

"Well, for one thing, those are my donuts you're eating."

"Mine," said Byron as he swept dust into the hall.

"And that cigarette you're smoking…"

"Whoooo hoo!" said Hanna. "Big spenders."

Bobby could not help but laugh. "Girl, I ought to whip your rear end."

Byron threw down the broom, clapped his hands, saying, "What can we do today?"

* * *

Walking along Royal Street, Hanna stopped to look at an object hanging in a display window of an art gallery. "Look," she said to the men. "This is weird. Somebody just took a bunch of trash and hung it."

"One man's trash…" said Bobby. They walked on, Bobby wearing a collarless navy blazer and jeans, and one saddle oxford, Byron in a gray sweatshirt over a dress shirt and wrinkled khakis. Purposefully, they drifted several steps behind to watch Hanna as she walked along in jeans and a worn brown sweater.

Inside a vintage clothes shop Bobby tried on a motorcycle jacket to Hanna's grimace, while Byron studied another girl in a tight skirt. After urging Hanna to try on a wide-brimmed, forties movie star hat, they walked down toward Jackson Square, where Bobby stepped into a bar, returning with a cup of orange juice. They sat on a wrought-iron bench while the men had shots from a pint bottle of vodka and Hanna became intrigued with the mime down the way. Later they shared a large muffuleta, Hanna with a root beer, before drifting over to Bourbon Street, overtly ignoring the sex paraphernalia shops.

"This is one weird place," said Hanna while they sat

at a table near a window inside a bar.

"How would you like to live here?" asked Byron after a swallow of Dixie beer.

"I don't know," said Hanna. "It's not Florida."

"Girl, let's talk some," said Bobby, propping his elbows on the table. "You have been terribly deprived. And yet, you seem curious and you seem to have a pretty good mind. Why are you so reluctant to make something of yourself?"

"Like what?"

"Like, first of all getting an education."

"I'm not going back to the ninth grade just so I can fail again, if that's what you mean."

"But you wouldn't fail if you were to try. Hell, you have more sense than a lot of students I've had. Something innate."

"What's that?" said Hanna, wishing she did not have to ask.

"Something you just naturally have," said Byron.

"Look," continued Bobby. "You said something about becoming a beautician."

"I never said nothing about a beautician," said Hanna.

"Whatever. Child, that kind of thing is nothing. Even if that was the best you could do, you would still have to have a high school equivalency education. And to tell you the truth, even with a GED you won't have a real high school diploma." Bobby lit a cigarette, leaned more toward Hanna. "You're only seventeen. You could zip through the ninth grade; at eighteen you—"

"Would be in the fucking tenth grade," said Hanna.

"Well, hell," said Bobby. "But...What if we could do something about that. Byron knows a lot about this stuff. What if we could find a way for you to start in the tenth grade? Could that be done, Byron?"

"Possibly," said Byron.

"And hell, with our help, who knows, we might be able to maybe accelerate you some way."

* * *

They took a streetcar back to the hotel. Along the way, Hanna could not help admitting, at least to herself, she might like New Orleans. It was interesting. Maybe she could find a guy, at least not go back to Florida, find work, any kind of work, possibly even get her own place, on her own. There was a lot to do in Sin City.

Hanna took a shower. When she returned to the room, Byron was plucking on the ukulele. Bobby sat on the bed, back against the headboard, smoking and drinking. "I'm not staying, but ya'll still ought to get a house. I don't see how ya'll can stand this place," said Hanna as she brushed her hair.

"Byron, let's sing Hanna a song. Let's sing 'Barbara Allen.'"

Byron sat on the bed, picked an introduction, then

Bobby started to sing as Byron filled in harmony. "In Scarlet Town, where I was born…"

Hanna had not expected what she listened to. They really could sing. The old English ballad about a tragic love affair intrigued her as she sat in the armchair continuing to brush her damp hair.

"church house wall, grew a lovers knot."

"That was nice," said Hanna when they looked at her for approval. "Ya'll know anything else?"

"Child, you should never ask troubadours that question," said Bobby. "Byron, let's sing 'If You Were Mine, Hanna.'" They had charmed women of different names with the song. "If you were mine, Hanna, know what I'd do? I'd take the world, Hanna, and give it to youooouoouooou. If you were mine, Hanna, know what I'd do? I'd say that I love Hanna, all through the dayaayaay'…"

When they finished, Hanna had to admit she felt somewhat charmed before she said, "Ya'll, I bet the real words are about whatever woman ya'll are singing to. I bet ya'll have sung that song to…I wouldn't trust either one of you for one second."

"But we're cute," said Byron.

"I reckon, for old men."

"Old, girl I'll bet you Byron and I could both outrun you."

"Yeh, but how far?"

"Byron, that little chick is a bitch."

Hanna laughed.

"What else do ya'll do?" Hanna asked.

"Do you mean, besides sing?"

"Yeh."

Bobby got off the bed, posed, then began his best rendition of the little elf man poem.

Later Byron stood to sing "Lord Randall" while Bobby strummed the ukulele. Hanna was fascinated at his carefree stance, lost in the words of the song, wandering about the room, as if he were all by himself, singing to the walls and furnishings, not in the least conscious or concerned with anyone listening. Hanna was not sure she liked what seemed to be happening to her.

Sunday afternoon, after they gave Hanna enough money to have a hamburger supper at the Hummingbird, the men went to Tiny's. They were still out when she crawled onto the rollaway with her clothes on for the night. She could not sleep, though, too many thoughts, especially about the short story Byron had read late that afternoon, about these ignorant prejudiced people who could not see how this intelligent black man forgave them for their abuse of him. So much had happened to her since she arrived to see if Lorraine might have left her something of value. There was turmoil in the young girl's mind. Who were these men, these strange men who had slept with her mother, who were something other than what they appeared to be. Were they trying to take advantage of her, trying to fuck her, manipulate her. They frightened her at the same time she was starting to be drawn to them. Some things about them reminded her of things about herself she had never acknowledged, or perhaps, recognized.

* * *

"I want to ask ya'll something," said Hanna, Monday afternoon when the mail did not deliver a disability check for Lorraine. Irritated and angry at first, she decided to live up to the agreement to stay one more-day and that afternoon had a bowl of gumbo from the Hummingbird. Byron was redlining aspects of his manuscript while Bobby was reading *Our Town*, a play he once directed during his university days. "What if...I mean, just what if..." she was sitting in the armchair rubbing the nails of her hands together. "...I did decide to stay for a while, at least till I could decide what I'm going to do, until maybe I could find a job, get my own place..." She sighed and lifted her head. "...And think about the GED thing. Are ya'll really thinking about getting a bigger place?"

"Absolutely," said the men simultaneously, both wishing they could step over and give the young girl a hug.

Later that afternoon, Byron took his drink, went down the stairs, sat on the curb of St. Charles Avenue in his bare feet. He had the shakes bad, and when he thought about all the promises they had made to the young girl who had bounced into their lives, he became depressed. What had they done? It had all sounded so exciting, so worthwhile an endeavor. But there, sitting alone, watching a streetcar rumble by, it all seemed so overwhelming and ridiculous. To think they could actually make a difference in that poor child's life. All he ever wanted was a young "piece of ass"—to drink his liquor and sleep and maybe one day finish his novel. What good would it do to try to help her? What would he get out of the deal? The more he thought about the whole thing, the more absurd it all seemed. And Bobby, how could he have let Byron make all those goddamn promises? They were drunk, that was all there was to it. A potentially fine piece of ass had done this to them in a moment of drunken weakness.

Well, there was only one thing to do—go back and tell her to hit the road. Get on back to Florida and finish fucking up her life all by herself. What was going to happen if she stayed much longer was that some welfare people were going to start coming around and the next thing anyone knew they were going to end up in jail for child molestation. That was all Byron needed, to spend the rest of his days in some jail wondering how it all happened.

Nothing about the morning offered itself inspiration for teaching a young girl school subjects. They could send her away, see Georgianna whenever they felt like it, drink and get on with their lives, the lives they had decided to live, without much responsibility, certainly not mixing them up with a ne'er-do-well young girl. Who knew, something good still might come their way. At least they were their lives. Byron remained there on the dirty concrete trying to conjure up images of better times; they would not come. Everything had been settled some time ago, but now something just didn't set right. What was it? Yield, he kept telling himself; but to what? What a ridiculous thing this life was.

Byron picked himself up from the curb and went back upstairs. He would talk about it with Bobby first, then they would give Hanna the money to go back on. That would be the end of it, and he and Bobby could get on with what it was they were doing before she came. What were they doing before then?

But when he opened the door Bobby was standing at the far end of the partition and he heard Hanna say, "I don't mind learning. Fuck, I'm pretty curious, you know."

FOUR

Bobby stepped into a 7-Eleven to buy a quart bottle of beer inside a paper bag. It was a fine, almost springlike day and people moved about briskly. As they walked, the men, passing the bottle back and forth, talked about the wonders of libraries as they were approaching the Garden District where the rows of old and antebellum mansions began to appear. Hanna had ears for the men's talk as her eyes were astounded by the grand display of wealth. "Ya'll," she said as they passed one of the homes. "That fence cost more than most people's cars and houses together."

Later she said, "Where is that fucking library? I'm tired of walking."

"Walk on," said Bobby. "Byron, who said that?"

"Lao Tse, I would guess."

"Hanna, Byron is a Taoist."

"A what?"

"Byron, explain it to her."

"Walk on," said Byron.

As a young woman, perhaps a college student, walked by, Byron asked her how far up was the library.

She suggested they catch a streetcar.

"Now, why didn't ya'll think of that," said Hanna.

"Walk on, girl," said Bobby.

As they were passing a grand old church, Byron said, "Bobby, if you were to design an education for someone, say, someone Hanna's age, how would you go about it. What kind of curriculum would you develop?"

Bobby needed to rest his flip-flop and rotting toe. As he sat on a low stone wall in front of a granite mansion, he said, "I would start with having her read *Moby-Dick*."

"Not I," said Byron. "I would start with an overview of the major disciplines. Try to show her the big picture first, so she could see what a well-rounded education would involve."

"But, Byron, that would be overwhelming."

Hoping Hanna was listening, Byron said, "There are only six subjects people of all societies throughout the world have in common: economics, politics, religion, society, aesthetics, and education. An adequate education would include a basic command of all six."

"I don't disagree," said Bobby.

"Isn't that what they call a double negative?" asked Hanna.

Bobby and Byron looked at each other. "Girl," said Bobby.

After Bobby's rest, they decided the streetcar might be worthwhile for the rest of the way, boarding one after Bobby caught sight of a young woman driving by in a Navigator. "Byron, did you see that?"

"No."

"I would marry her, not even knowing what she looked like beneath the window."

"I would too," said Byron.

"You didn't even see her."

"I'll take your word, though."

They reached the public library, a stately stone structure set beyond a spacious lawn. Crossing the street, Bobby stepped out of his flip-flop and had to wait for a car to stop to retrieve it.

While Byron and Hanna browsed the fiction shelves, Bobby drifted into another room. Byron took a copy of Thomas Wolfe's LOOK HOMEWARD, ANGEL from a row, telling Hanna the influence it had been in his early years. He then pointed to a shelf devoted to the works of Tennessee Williams, sharing briefly information about the famous playwright who did much of his work in New Orleans. "I bet you've read half the stuff in here," said Hanna.

"Lots of it," said Byron. "Often, though, I've weeded out so much by reading the backs of the covers and thumbing through things."

"God, I can't believe all the books in this place. The words. I wonder how many words there must be in this place."

"So much redundancy, though," said Byron as

Bobby joined them with an opened 1970 edition of a *Sewanee Review*. "Hanna, look. Do you recognize this name?" he said pointing below the title of a short story, "Breeze Land."

"Byron…Burns," Hanna read. "No."

"Do you remember Byron's last name?"

Hanna turned to Byron. "Burns? That's you?"

"He wrote this right after finishing his master's."

"Are you shittin' me?" said Hanna. "Byron, you're in the library?"

They left after checking out Carson McCullers' *A Member of the Wedding*, *The Diary of Anne Frank* and John Steinbeck's *Cannery Row*, taking the street-car as far as the K&B where they bought a bottle of Popov.

* * *

Her name was Hanna Marie James and she knew so little about so much. James was the name on her birth certificate, but Hanna had never been sure what that meant. To the best of her understanding James could have been one of several men who might have been her father. Lorraine had never married, but Hanna's grand-mother had told her about several men who could have been her father, one an offshore oil rigger, another who was supposed to have been pretty smart, and a preacher. The old woman knew no more about it than that. Hanna had lived with her mother off and on for the first eight years of her life, and otherwise stayed with the grandmother, who, being sickly, had never been capable of much in the way of childrearing. Hanna's memory of Lorraine was mostly limited to a nearly two-year period in which they had lived together in a boarding house in Birmingham, Alabama, when the girl was about six or seven. Those days Hanna often relived in her memory as the best ones of her life. She could recall vague memories of sitting on a linoleum floor while her mother read *True Romance* magazines upon the double bed they slept together on. Hanna could not remember any men in Lorraine's life during those days nor could she remember much more about that time. She embellished though. She often envisioned her and her mother laughing, going for walks and her mother loving her.

Then suddenly that was all over and she was back with her grandmother in Florida, and the years ran together in her mind.

She did well in school for the first six years or so, then she began to stay out more. Her grandmother would complain, but not so much that Hanna changed her ways. She watched a lot of television and day-dreamed, her body started to mature and boys started hanging around her.

Hanna did not know why she decided to take Bobby and Byron up on their offer. It certainly was not something she considered permanent. She had no money, and no place she really wanted to go. She did, however, less frequently, think about returning to Florida, and more than once thought about sneaking the money out of one or the other drunk man's wallets, and slipping away while they were too inebriated to stop her. In the meantime, why not stay. She could leave anytime she seriously had the notion. However, they fed her, had other ways spent money on her—and they left her alone enough. They flirted with her, but not nastily. Occasionally one or the other would comment on something she wore with insinuations. Once, Bobby said, "Now, girl, don't tell me you aren't aware of that pretty little ass of yours." She behaved as if she resented him, but secretly, she had valued the remark. Nothing consistent, but she noticed their attempts to clean up their language. Still, Hanna did not trust them, not hardly.

Even though they most often appeared like the bums they most likely were, there was no doubt they knew some things about books and education. At times they used too many big words, and in such confusing ways that she could not help but wonder about the things that might be going on in their heads that might be interesting to know about. She had read enough of *A Member of the Wedding* to establish interest in it, then could not put it down. Occasionally she caught Byron looking over his manuscript and once writing, but whenever he was aware of anyone noticing, he would stop.

They continued to check the classifieds for places to rent, along with hanging out down at Tiny's, going out for the cheapest vodka they could find, usually Popov, and cigarettes along with marathon gin rummy games.

One day they put a book before her, turned the pages to a story called "The Lottery," then left her while they went out. When they returned, Hanna had finished and was taking a nap. Asking her about it later, she told them it was a dumb story about this girl who won this lottery and her prize was that all these people threw rocks at her. "Why in the world did ya'll want me to read that stupid thing?"

But they were terribly drunk and said some things that had not made any sense, then went to bed.

One afternoon, Byron came in while Bobby was still out, hair mussed more than usual, flopped down in the armchair, pulled off his shoes and said, "Hanna, what's the difference between knowledge and education?"

When he drew back the blanket she saw that his eyes were redder than usual.

"You're drunk, aren't you?"

"Just answer the fucking question."

"I reckon education is stuff you learn so you can get a job."

"Wrong. Not even close. What is knowledge?"

"I don't know. Information, I guess."

"Right. Throw me one of your cigarettes." Byron picked a cigarette up from the floor and put the wrong end in his mouth and lit the filter. Hanna laughed and threw him another. "Education, Hanna, what is it?"

"I don't know."

"Then let me tell you what education is. It's what it takes to have a happy life. Knowledge is just information and education is what it takes to be happy. Any knowledge that does not contribute to your happiness is not part of your education."

"You don't seem so fucking happy."

"Not now, goddamnit," said Byron, scratching his head. "You're mixing me up. I had it all clear in my head when I came up here. You aren't listening. Listen! What I'm trying to tell you is that…is that…" Byron leaned back and took a deep breath. "Goddamn. Girl, you don't hear a thing."

"Well what then?"

Byron crossed his arms and looked away. "I don't want to talk about it anymore. You're confusing me."

"You're just drunk is all."

Byron sat forward again. "Understanding. That's the word I'm trying to think of. See, if you don't have understanding, you don't have anything. Now, think about it. Why did Bobby want you to read *Moby-Dick*?"

"Cause he don't like me."

"Wrong." Byron sat back in the chair pleased with himself for the moment. "You see," he said a moment later. "If you ever read, say, *Huckleberry Finn*, it will be helpful to know that Huck lives in Missouri. And if you know where Missouri is on the map, it will give you a picture in your mind..." Byron stopped himself. "Goddamn. That's not what I mean. Language. That's it. That's the word I've been trying to think of. Language is tricky, girl."

Hanna looked at him with confusion.

"Language isn't what it appears to be sometimes. Do you know what language is?"

"Of course."

"Of course. Of course. What does that mean?"

"It means I know what language is."

Byron put his hands on his hips but one slid off. "Then what is language?"

Hanna pursed her lips. "Shoo," she said. "I'm not even going to answer that."

"You may be wrong."

Hanna sighed and rolled her eyes. "It's what we use to talk."

"Yes! But...did you know that language is fucked up? It doesn't always work."

"You're drunk," said Hanna. "I don't want to talk anymore." She got off the window ledge and went to her cot.

"What I'm trying to tell you is that until you understand what language is, and how it works, you aren't going to understand a hell of a lot of anything. Take the word 'love' for a minute."

"You take it. I don't want to talk anymore."

"Well don't talk, just listen. 'Love' is a lousy word. It doesn't have any meaning. Watch this." Byron was leaning way forward now. "I love my dog. I love God. I made love last night. I would love a piece of pie. See there, I used the same word four different ways. Now tell me, what does the word 'love' mean?"

"It just means a strong feeling you have."

"Goddamn," said Byron. "Now I don't want to talk anymore. You don't understand. See what I mean. It's all got to do with understanding. You just use the hell out of words, but you don't understand. And that's what I meant by trying to explain the difference in education and knowledge. You're going to end up with a little bit of information and no goddamn understanding."

"So?"

"So you still don't understand that words don't always explain things. And until you do, you won't ever begin to get an education. The word 'love' is a fucked up word that's been used and abused so much it no longer means shit. The same thing is true about 'beauty.' 'Beauty' doesn't mean anything anymore. Idiots use the word, and look at what they use it for. Nothing! Anything!" Byron leaned back once more. "If you ever become educated, and I doubt if that will ever happen, you will have to understand that most of what you will learn is going to be just a lot of shit." Byron stood up at this point. "I think I'll take my nap."

Love, Hanna thought, it never meant much to her either. She attributed Byron's unusual state of inebriation to his frustration about not being satisfied with his writing.

The next morning, Byron threw a bottle of vodka in the trashcan and announced that he was going to stop drinking and get his mind straight. Bobby, retrieving the bottle, argued in favor of a less drastic approach; that they should instead taper off gradually. Later that day, Hanna went with them to the French Quarter where they spent the afternoon in pursuit of some illusionary joy that did not come. Hanna caught a streetcar back to the hotel.

* * *

It was late one afternoon when Byron returned from a visit with Georgianna that he told Bobby about the house.

"You fucked her, didn't you?" Bobby wanted to know. "You went and fucked her without telling me anything about it. Byron, there's nothing I hate worse than a goddamn sneak."

"Never mind about that. Where is Hanna?"

Bobby was still pouting. "Gone to the store. Why didn't you tell me? I would've gone with you."

"Bobby, I saw this house, a small shotgun house—"

"And I thought we were friends," said Bobby.

"—Off Magazine Street. Down near that Warehouse District. There was a For Rent sign out front. It's in a rundown neighborhood. The rent is probably nothing. I wrote down the number."

Putting on his shirt, Bobby said. "I'm going over to Georgianna's."

"She's not there."

"What?"

"I left her going out. Will you forget about that and listen to me?"

"When is she coming back?"

"I don't know. What do you think of my idea?"

Bobby sat on the side of the bed. "Did you fuck her?"

"Yes."

"Sonabitch, that makes the third time, Byron."

"Fourth."

Bobby put his fist to his waist. "And, shit ass, when was the other time?"

Byron laughed. "One day when you were gone to the library with Hanna."

"And you didn't even tell me. What, are we starting to keep secrets from each other?"

"I didn't think about it."

"Didn't think about it? Well, that means I get two more turns before you can do it anymore."

"Okay. That'll be all right. But what do you think about a house? Let's go look at it at least."

"Do you think we can afford it?"

"My guess is it's a hell of a lot cheaper than this room."

With persuasion, Bobby went with Byron to see the house while Hanna was out. It was one of a row of shotgun houses, not far from the river. The one Byron spoke of, a narrow-front, faded pink clapboard structure with two missing boards on the outside close to the ground. It was on a narrow street where, absent of driveways, tenants parked alongside the road, allowing only one-way traffic, even though it was a two-way street.

Byron and Bobby walked around the place and stared in several of the windows, including one that exposed the kitchen. "Hey," said Byron, "it has a stove and a refrigerator. More or less."

They sat on the front steps, had shots of vodka to think. "I'm not in this for my fucking health, you know," said Bobby.

"Bobby, did you see the hair on Hanna's pussy?"

"Did you see those tits?"

"God, I would love to feast on that thing."

"Have you noticed those little hairlets above where she shaves her legs?"

"I would eat everything outside and inside of that…"

"But you know, Byron, fucking isn't everything."

"I know."

After a laugh, they had another drink before glancing back at the house and driving off.

FIVE

One Saturday morning in late April, they moved out of the hotel. Hanna complained about the house at first, but Byron painted such a picture of how the place could look with some fixing up that by the time they actually moved in, she was starting to change her mind. At least she would now have a room of her own, and a bathroom. Actually, the little house had two bedrooms, a living room with a large window facing the front and another facing the side with a rusted old fence grown over with scrub trees and vines. However, besides that, the new address was aesthetically barren. The floors were covered with worn and nasty linoleum rugs, especially the one in the kitchen. And the appliances were corroded with rust, old grease and grime.

When they were all inside, Bobby stood by the light switch and said, "Hanna, look! Lights!" as he turned the switch. Hanna was not terribly impressed. "What are we gonna do about furniture?" she said before entering the kitchen, saying "Ug," and opening the door to the bedroom that would be hers. "There's not even a bed."

"One step at a time, Sweet Jesus," Byron sang.

"How much did ya'll have to pay for this place?" Hanna wanted to know.

"The rent here is a hell of a lot better than that hotel room," said Bobby.

"Oh Lord," said Hanna.

Bobby was serious. He made himself a drink and helped carry some things into the house, then toward noon, he went next door and knocked. An emaciated man in his undershirt appeared behind the rusty, torn screen door.

"Yeh?" he said. "You ain't selling nothing, are you?"

Bobby laughed. "No, I'm your new neighbor. We're having a party and you're invited. You want to come to a party?"

"Party?" The man stepped out to what was left of a porch. He was barefoot and had several days' growth of gray whiskers. "You ain't having no party around here, I hope."

"Hell yes," said Bobby. "And we want you to come. Bring anybody living with you."

"You have a party around here you gone attract every wino in a square mile. You shore you got the right street?"

"Right next door," Bobby pointed.

The man scratched at his stomach and coughed hoarsely. Then he spat off the porch. "You gone have something to drink?"

"Oh, yes," said Bobby, "We want you to come."

The man looked down at his feet and studied the matter for a moment. "You ain't some kinda weirdo, are you? I mean, they's all kinda weirdos round here."

"No. As a matter of fact, I'm a poet. And my partner is a writer. And we have this girl we're raising. We're decent people. We just want to meet some of the neighbors."

"Yeah, I'll be there. When?"

"Whenever you get ready."

"And you got some wine?"

Bobby promised the man he would have plenty of liquor and left the porch. He was feeling good. They were going to be doing something, and they had a house. He went to the next house and discovered it abandoned. Then, as he was about to cross the street, he noticed a clutter of people in a vacant lot just beyond. The overgrown corner lot, trashed, with beer cans, wine bottles and faded fast-food boxes, was a gathering place for winos, derelicts and other low-lifes. Toward the middle was an oak tree where a small group of men of different colors dressed for the occasion, talked, stared at the ground and slept. The weeds and grass of the gathering place had been stomped down by much use, exposing the dark delta dirt beneath. Scattered about the clearing were the furnishings—a large rusted oil drum for fires and two weatherworn old sofas, one with popped-up springs, the other with upholstery rotted away over the arms. Four chrome and vinyl kitchen chairs stood randomly about the living area. Stuffing tumbled from rips in the red plastic seats.

On the rump-sprung sofa a man lay napping, his long-toed, bony feet propped on the arm. The other sofa was occupied by two men, one with bloodshot eyes half-closed under a Minnesota Vikings cap, his toenails thick, yellow, and rimmed with dirt. A man slouched at the other end, scratching at a grimy undershirt.

A thin, sallow man hunched forward in a kitchen chair, a brown bottle of Taylor's wine resting on the damp earth beside him. Several others stood about, contributing to the conversation. Popeye's chicken bags, burger wrappers and beer bottles attracted a buzz of flies and a steady stream of ants. As Bobby approached, the conversation stopped abruptly. "Morning, gentlemen."

The gathering studied the intruder suspiciously. One man, wearing a shirt with "Toys 'R' Us" printed on the pocket, slid his Jim Beam bottle out of sight.

"My name is Bobby Long." None of the gathering spoke. "I just moved in down the street…"

* * *

By mid-afternoon their new house was buzzing with laughter and drunkenness. Byron had gone out and bought a whole case of cheap wine, a couple of bottles of bourbon, and a case of beer that they iced down in the bathtub. It was no doubt the best time the neighborhood had had all year. It was no exaggeration to say the man next door was right—they had gathered all the winos and derelicts for at least a square mile. Byron played the ukulele, and he and Bobby sang all the songs they knew and started several over again. Bobby told stories, and the neighborhood drank its fill. It was certainly not a black-tie affair. There was lots of polyester, though, gaudy and colorful. It could have been a modeling show for the Salvation Army thrift store.

Bobby was the host and he made everyone feel at home. He had something good to say about even the least of their guests. He made sure no one was left out—no one but Hanna who disappeared inside her new room early on. She made a pallet with some of her clothes and turned on the radio and tried to drown out the commotion that grew worse as the afternoon went on. She was miserably scared and thought about trying to sneak out of the house. But she finally decided that would be even more frightening, so she waited and tried to sleep, but it was no use. And just after dark she opened the door and screamed for Byron. The whole house got silent. "Whoa, Mister!" said one of the derelicts above the quiet.

"Byron, please come here," Hanna cried. When Byron got to her, she pulled him inside her room and shut the door. The noise slowly returned in the rest of the house as Hanna sobbed on Byron's shoulder. "I want to go back to Florida."

"Whatsa matter, girl?"

"I'm scared."

Byron held her at arm's length. "Of those fellows? Shoot, girl, they're not going to hurt you. There's not a bad one in the bunch. They just like to drink is all. Come see for yourself."

Hanna shook her head frantically.

"Hanna. Look at me girl." Byron nudged her gently. "Look at me." Hanna looked into his red eyes and started to cry again. "Come in there with me. I'll prove to you there's nothing for you to be afraid of. You've got me and Bobby to take care of you. Those fellows aren't going to bother you."

"Some protectors."

"Damn right, some protectors. You think Bobby and I aren't going to protect you? Is that what you think?"

"You watn't thinking about me when all this started."

Byron took her by the hand, pulled her toward the door, Hanna resisting, thinking he was going to force her. Instead, he stuck his head out the door and yelled, "Bobby!" Once more the noise dropped as Bobby went to Hanna's room. "Bobby, talk to this girl."

"What?" he asked with a leftover grin.

"She's scared we're going to abandon her. She's scared of our neighbors."

Bobby dropped his head as much with intoxication

as concern for Hanna. "Oh my. We've upset you, haven't we? Well, I'll run them off right now."

"No, wait," said Byron. "That's not it. She needs to see that they are harmless. Girl, please just go out there with us and see. I'll explain it to them."

Hanna shook her head frantically. Byron, still holding her hand, determined, pulled as she reluctantly followed him down the hall and into the living room. As Bobby was to say later, the place looked like a refugee truck wreck. Nearly a dozen derelicts stood round or sat on the floor, all with plastic cups. When Hanna appeared, the sitting men stood, while the others gave the teenaged girl undivided attention.

"Whoa, Mister!" one said, as others moaned or mumbled.

"Folks, this is Hanna," Byron told them.

"Hanna from Texarkana," said one old fellow who had managed to get to his knees.

"Now, Earl, watch yourself," said Byron. "This is our little girl."

"She yo daughtuh?"

"Something like that." Byron with Bobby's help began to tell the derelicts how the girl had come to stay with them and how they planned to make her a home and help her get an education, to which Hanna raised her eyes toward Bobby's. One old fellow who had passed out came to and more or less sat up to hear the story of Hanna.

"But she's scared, Earl," said Byron when they had finished. "She's scared that somebody around here isn't a gentleman, and I'm betting she's wrong. I told her, I said, 'Girl, there's not one bad one in that whole bunch.'"

"Hell yeah, she's wrong," said the man, Earl. "Honey, ain't none of these boys gone hurt you. Shit, man, every last one of us is respekable. Some of us ain't very pretty, like Nip here, and old Fleetwood there. Fleetwood, he's a throwback from the giraffes."

"Who?" a skinny little remainder of a man said from the corner where he sat.

"You sombitch," mumbled Nip.

"Hey!" said Earl, "Watch yo language."

They honestly did seem to be a harmless band of misfits and characters. The place had developed an odor of old sweat and stale liquor, but no one appeared in the least dangerous. Hanna stayed with them, somebody gave her a cold beer, and to the best of their drunken ability, every last one bent over himself to be a gentleman. Earl ran roughshod over anyone who started to get out of line.

"I think it's a mighty nice thing them boys are doing," said a tall, gentle, pink-eyed derelict with an exaggerated belly forcing its way between the buttons of his polyester red shirt. Hanna felt tenderly for the man, who said his name was Cecil, pronounced, "Ceshul," as he shared a few things about himself, particularly about losing one of his testicles to a barbed wire fence years ago.

After several sips of an awfully sweet wine, wandering about talking with the guests, Hanna explained she was getting tired and went to her new room. Sitting against the wall, she surveyed her own personal space while reflecting on the day. It seemed that at every point at which she found a good enough reason to leave, something came along to change her mind. With one of the two blankets stolen from the hotel, she bundled herself on the floor, wondering whether or not one of the reasons she had not left was because of an obligation she was starting to feel toward two strange, fumbling, often disgusting alcoholics.

Rather than ending, the housewarming party did not actually end, it more or less petered out in the early morning. Bobby was the last one up. He had put Earl to sleep with a tale about the time he and Byron went fishing for bream with a lure. "He damn sure did," said Bobby. "I tried to tell him you can't fish for bream with a lure. I said, 'Byron, you got to have a sinker and a cork—and live bait.'" Bobby was still wide awake, but Earl was lying on his side and kept blinking his eyes until they finally closed altogether. "So Byron, hell, he got this top water lure and put this roach we caught on it—with a cork—and slung his line out in the water. And all that lure did was set there, right on top of the water, with a cork about two feet up the line…"

SIX

They lived together the rest of the week with no furnishings, just a stove and refrigerator. They visited yard sales the next Saturday morning and before noon bought a Bambi lamp, two mismatched straight-back chairs, a Bourbon Street souvenir ashtray, a frying pan, two pots, several plates and bowls, assorted kitchen utensils, towels, a few candles, a bundle of forks and two twin-size foam rubber mattresses. The whole lot cost only twenty-seven dollars and fifty cents.

After taking their treasures to the house, they laid the mattresses side by side in the front bedroom. Bobby said, "Okay, girl, I guess you'll have to sleep in the crack. But you're going to have to sleep naked."

In the afternoon, they went to the Waterfront Mission where they bought a not badly pee-stained, full-sized mattress for ten dollars.

* * *

That night Hanna joined them on the front porch, avoiding the warmth not yet diminished from the day. Byron plucked the ukulele and Bobby tried every way he could to strike up a conversation with Hanna about sex.

"What I want to know," said Hanna, her legs tucked under her as she sat on the steps, "is what am I gonna do about the GED?"

"You ever done it in the grass, Hanna?" Bobby wanted to know.

"I've been thinking about that," said Byron, leaning against a porch post. He put the ukulele down.

"You interrupted me," Bobby said.

"Hanna, you did finish the tenth grade, didn't you?"

"I told you I failed the ninth grade and dropped out."

This set Byron's thinking back for a couple of minutes.

"In the pines, in the pines, where the sun never shines," Bobby sang.

"Shut up for a second," Byron said. "Hanna, what do you think about the idea of going back to high school, I mean, as a senior."

"What the shit are you talking about, Byron?" asked Hanna with a grunt.

"Yes, Byron," said Bobby.

"Just wait. Just listen. Suppose, just suppose, now, you could get into a high school, here in New Orleans, next fall. September. And what if you could be a senior?"

"What have you been smoking, Byron?" said Hanna,

lighting a cigarette. "How in the fuck do you—"

"I've been thinking about this."

Bobby interrupted. "Hanna."

"What, Bobby?" she said irritatedly.

"Never mind," said Bobby, feeling dejected.

"I know this high school principal," said Byron. "Back in Georgia."

"Are you talking about Hap?" Bobby asked.

"Bobby and I fixed him up with one of his undergraduates once, while he was an instructor at Auburn. Bobby and I set it up, she agreed to let him sleep with her for a passing grade."

"So what's that got to do with me?" asked Hanna.

"Well, I feel he owes Bobby and me a favor. I was just thinking. I doubt if he would want his community to ever discover what he did. What if we could persuade him to get us a transcript documenting that Hanna not only passed the ninth grade, but she passed the eleventh grade, aced the eleventh grade."

"Son of a fucking bitch of an idea, Byron!" said Bobby. "We could blackmail the hell out of that coot."

"Yeh," said Hanna, "son of...Byron, how in the living shit do you think I could go to the twelfth grade?"

"With fucking honors," said Bobby.

"Um huh whoo hoo," said Hanna.

Bobby, about to go to the kitchen for a new drink, stepped to Hanna's back and bent his knees enough to touch her. "Hanna..."

"What?" she grumbled.

"You could be a high school graduate by this time next year."

"Ha. Ya'll aren't thinking about everything."

"Like what?"

"All kinds of things."

"Like what?" Bobby persisted.

"Like…like…I don't want to talk about it. Just forget it."

"Like what, girl?" asked Byron.

"Like I don't have hardly any clothes for one thing. And another, how am I suppose to pass the twelfth grade if I…if I…"

"Oh," said Byron. "That's where Bobby and I will come in. You see, once you are in regular classes, we can know better what to help you with. The way we're going now we might get you through the GED and all. But Hanna, there's a lot more to an education than passing the GED."

"Like what?" Hanna wanted to know.

"Oh, come on, girl," said Byron, "you know what I'm talking about. Like social things, growing up among people that have some sense for one thing. Like learning a few social graces, and meeting some people who spend their time doing things besides taking dope and polishing their fingernails. You aren't a dummy, girl. I've watched you. Bobby and I have talked about it, you have plenty of sense. Who knows? With a little help you might even think about going to college one day."

"Huh," grunted Hanna. "Me and Mack, maybe."

"Who?" Bobby asked.

"Nothing," said Hanna.

"Who the hell is Mack?"

"Nobody."

"Nobody who?" said Bobby.

"Mack. John Steinbeck's Mack. You know, Cannery Row."

It was almost dark, but not so much so that Bobby and Byron did not look at one another with surprise. Bobby laughed. "Well, goddamn. Byron, she read the book. I'm a son of a bitch."

Nobody spoke for more than a minute. Sounds of automobiles and the New Orleans night were all around. Down the street a screen door slammed. "There's something else," Hanna finally added without stating what it was.

"What?" asked Byron.

"This place."

"What about this place? Bobby and I thought you liked this place."

"I do," said Hanna, turning to face their general direction. "It's just that…"

"What, girl? Spit it out."

"I don't know," she said reluctantly. "It's just not… not the kind of place…"

"For a school girl?" Byron said.

Hanna said nothing, but she knew she had hurt their feelings. She waited for one of them to speak, but neither one did for most of another minute.

"You mean you would be ashamed of us and our house?" said Bobby.

"It's not that."

"Yes it is," said Bobby.

Hanna almost started to cry. "It's just that I haven't ever had nothing."

"Anything," Byron corrected her.

"Anything," Hanna mumbled as she buried her face in her lap.

Later Hanna went to her room and turned on the radio. She had promised them; by the weekend she would start reading one of the new books they had gotten from the library. Opening and thumbing through pages of all the books, she chose one titled *The Heart Is a Lonely Hunter* by Carson McCullers, the lady who had written one of the first books the men had gotten for her, *A Member of the Wedding*.

Bobby and Byron walked over to the outdoor living room, where several lights from cigarettes broke the dark. The derelicts were talking about the old major leagues when Robinson and Ford, Williams and Mays, played. Nip said he once met Willie Mays.

A distinct smell of earth and stale urine rose in the evening while crickets and an occasional frog broke the intermittent silence and lazy conversation.

It was past midnight when Bobby and Byron left and went back to the house, both pleasantly drunk, tired, ready for bed. The light from Hanna's room was still on, the men heard a sneeze from inside, assuring them all was well. Bobby stomped two roaches before turning out the light and lying down. "Byron?" Bobby chuckled.

"Humm?"

"Are you asleep?"

"Ummm."

"I got a story to tell you."

"Umm, not now."

"It's funny. Byron?"

"I'm asleep."

"Please."

Byron shifts in the dark. "Goddamn, Bobby, tell the goddamn thing so I can go to sleep. Damn!"

Bobby chuckles again. "One time I was living in this room where the bed was across the floor from the light switch...are you listening?"

"Ummm."

"I got this idea one night to see if I could switch off the light and jump in the bed before it went out... Byron."

Byron said nothing.

Bobby chuckled once more. "I missed the bed."

SEVEN

The next morning Byron thought he was the first up. But when he got to the kitchen to fix his first drink of the day, Hanna was kneeling in front of the refrigerator with her head stuck inside. She was scrubbing the inside with a rag. She was using a bar of soap and water from the sink.

"You got the wrong appliance," said Byron.

"I don't know what you're talking about," said Hanna.

"If you're going to commit suicide, you're supposed to use the stove."

Hanna got up and wiped her forehead with the back of her hand. "What do you think?" she said proudly.

"About what?" asked Byron as he started to pour vodka in a plastic cup.

"The kitchen. See, I cleaned the stove. And I got all that rust out of the sink."

Byron looked at the stove. He could not believe it. She had stripped every bit of the grease and grime away. It looked like a brand-new old stove. "Well, goddamn. Look at that thing." He went to the sink. "And the sink. How in the world did you get all that rust off, girl?"

Hanna was proud of herself. "I went outside and got some sand, see, and I got this soap, and mixed it with some water, and presto!" She closed the refrigerator door and said, "And look." The refrigerator door was nearly spotless, except for some rusty places around the handle.

"Well, bless my soul." Byron went to get Bobby. "Bobby! Hey, Bobby!"

Bobby moaned from the mattress.

"Bobby, get up. Come in here and see what Hanna has done."

Bobby's head came up off the bed. "What?" he said in a startled way.

"Come see."

Bobby fought off his grogginess. "Is she gone?"

"No, she's not gone. Come see."

Bobby lay back down and mumbled something incoherent. Byron went back to the kitchen. He could not get over Hanna's enterprise. He sat on the floor and looked about the entire kitchen. It actually looked clean. There was nothing in it besides the sink and the stove and the refrigerator, but the place was clean. Even the walls seemed cleaner, and Hanna told him she had washed them too. And as she bent down inside the refrigerator again, Byron noticed something else. She was wearing blue jeans, and all he could concentrate on for the moment was her ass.

Awhile later, he went out and bought some donuts

and orange juice. By the time he returned, Bobby was up and had discovered the kitchen too. So in honor of Hanna, they sat on the floor and had their drinks and bragged on the kitchen while Hanna sat above them at the table eating her breakfast.

Hanna went to the library later that morning. She told them she just wanted to go out for a while. She took *The Heart Is a Lonely Hunter* with her.

"I've got an idea," Byron told Bobby after she had gone. "Why don't we paint the house?"

"You paint the house if you want to, I'm going over to see Georgianna."

"You dumb son of a bitch," said Byron. "Just when we are starting make some headway with our live-in mini-dame."

"Headway, my ass. She's going to sucker us into using the hell out of us is what that bitch is going to do. The only way we're going to ever fuck that girl is to pounce her ass. She's got our number, bud."

"Well, tell me, Mister, what other choice do we have? We aren't fucking running backs anymore. Your big toe is about gone and I might be able to run from here to the back door. As long as she's here, we have a chance."

"You keep believing that if you want to. I'm going to see Georgianna."

"Go ahead. Go ahead and give up. I'm going to paint the house."

"Goddamn, Byron. How much do you think that's going to cost? We can't afford decent vodka as it is. That little bitch is costing us."

"It shouldn't cost more than maybe fifty dollars to paint the whole house. We'll paint just the front and sides."

"I'm not painting a house."

"Neither am I. We can get Earl and them to do it. I would bet, for a couple of bottles of rot gut, those derelicts would paint all day."

Bobby could not help but laugh. He pointed his finger toward Byron, grinned and said, "You're talking about a party."

By the time Byron returned with two gallons of white paint and a case of grocery store wine, he was well on his way to being tipsy. Bobby had gathered up Earl and Cecil and some of the others and they were standing round on the side of the house that had the better shade awaiting their wages in advance. "I got an idee," said Earl, "Let's drink some wine and wait till tomorrow morning to start painting. Hell, it's getting too hot to work."

"I got a better idee," said Bobby. "Let's paint and drink later."

As the derelicts' eyes darted toward one another, Bobby laughed, "Can't you fellows see I was just kidding?"

"I didn't get but one brush," said Byron.

"One brush? How do you expect us to get anything

done with one brush?" asked Bobby.

"I've been thinking about that," said Byron. "We don't want to get too hot. What I thought was, one of us could paint while the rest of us rested, then switch off when we start to get tired."

Earl took the first shift. Since they had no ladder, he painted as high as he could reach without straining himself, while the others stayed in the shade, passed round bottles of wine and watched him.

"Ya'll reckon we oughtern scrape it before we paint it?" old Fleetwood wanted to know. Fleetwood had once been a housepainter.

"It's going to take two coats," somebody said after Earl had more or less spread several feet of paint.

"Maybe we should have scraped it first," said somebody else.

When Hanna got back from the library they had painted almost half of the lower part of the west side. It looked no better than when they started. Earl said he thought it looked worse. There were several shift changes as they went on drinking their refreshments. But soon, however, the sun was interfering with the shade, and shifts were getting shorter, so, with the best of intentions, the laborers all went to the front porch for a break that became the end of a workday. Several of the derelicts were in the process of taking naps when old Fleetwood stepped up from a trip to the bushes and said, "Ya'll gone work anymore? If you ain't, I going to the house." In a while several more had wandered on back to the outdoor living room where naps were more comfortable.

By later that afternoon the remainder of a can of paint stood lidless on the ground near where the men had worked, a brush laid over the top drying in the Southern warmth.

Two neighbors on Annuciation Street were resting peacefully on their front porch, among the gnats and buzzing bugs. Just before dark, Bobby woke up and went inside to make himself a fresh drink. As he passed Hanna's door, on his way to the kitchen, he heard what sounded like soft crying.

"Girl," he said softly. "Hanna." Then he cracked the door and looked inside. She was sitting on the floor with a book open in front of her. When she looked up, tears were in her eyes and one ran down her cheek. But through them she smiled.

"This is the best book I've ever read."

The next morning Hanna decided to clean the living room. She sneaked into the room where Bobby was asleep on the mattress and tiptoed over to where his pants lay on the floor and carefully went through his pockets until she found a five-dollar bill. With it she walked to a store on Magazine Street and bought some liquid cleaner and a package of sponges.

The men were still asleep, so she closed the door to their room, went to the kitchen, filled a pot with water and was soon starting to wash the living room walls. To her surprise the cleaner she had bought did a minor miracle on the place she chose to test it. Beneath the yellow film was white, nearly a stark white, and before long she had washed an entire wall, using one of the straight chairs to reach to the ceiling. She could not remember when she had felt such a joy of accomplishment. And while she worked, she got caught up in a daydream in which she had turned the little shotgun house into a cheerful little cottage on the side of a hill, a place where she lived alone and raised flowers and had a baby and a job where she made enough money to buy the things she wanted. It was not an elaborate dream. She was careful not to be too terribly impractical when she daydreamed. She considered putting a boy in it, but she had had such bad real-life experiences where they were concerned that she did not.

By the time Byron got up, Hanna had washed all of two walls and was starting on a third. She had to rinse out her pail and get new water often. Byron was in a bad mood and for some reason was not sure why he was so irritated by what she had done. "That fucking wall is not contributing one thing to your education. You would do better to be reading something."

"Fuck you," said Hanna. "Alcoholics don't contribute anything either."

Byron mumbled something on his way to the kitchen to fix a drink, then stepped out the back door and sat on the steps. He was not sure why he felt so miserable, something to do with himself he finally decided. Episodes of his life flashed before him. "That Bobby Long and Byron Burns, they're something alright. Both of them, good boys, came from good families. Could have been anything they wanted to be. Smart boys. Damn good football players in their day. Byron should have never married that whore. Alcohol and women. Wine, women and music. Both fair-haired boys, too," he recalled hearing from somebody back home.

Byron would not allow himself to think about all his failures and what might have been his life under other circumstances. He looked inside his plastic cup of vodka, then poured it out at his feet. He had decided he was going to go a whole day without drinking. But as he thought more about it, he could not imagine such an endeavor. Just the thought of it scared him. It scared him so much that he went back inside and poured another drink. And while he was doing this, Hanna came into the kitchen.

"Byron, I finished *The Heart Is a Lonely Hunter* last night."

Byron turned to look at her and he could not hide the tears that he felt welling up inside his eyes. So he quickly turned away from her. "Yeh, well. There's more to an education than a goddamn novel."

Hanna stood there for several moments looking at him, then went back to the living room. Byron felt even worse. He went out the backdoor and was gone for nearly two hours.

When he returned, Bobby was sitting on the living room floor with Hanna. "There's the man to talk to about religion," Bobby said. The walk had taken the edge off Byron's anger. He went to the kitchen and got a beer and returned to the living room. "Byron, explain something to this girl. She wants to know about the Bible," said Bobby.

Byron sat on the floor and crossed his legs.

"What I want to know is what you think about it," said Hanna. "It don't make a lot of sense to me."

"Me either," said Byron.

"Well, explain it to me."

Byron sighed. "Well, it was written way back."

"See," said Bobby, "I told you he was smart."

"I don't know, Hanna. It's suppose to be a history of the Jewish people, thought by many to have been inspired by God," said Byron.

"I know that," said Hanna. "What I'm asking is for you to sorta summarize it for me."

"Summarize it, Byron," said Bobby.

"Oh, shit," said Byron. "Well, go get me some paper and a pencil."

Hanna went to her room and returned with a tablet and a pen.

Byron started to draw a crude map. "Okay, this is Egypt. And this is the Mediterranean Sea...and this is the Holy Land. I'll explain that in a few minutes. Here is what is modern-day Israel. The Red Sea...Byron began to recall some of his theological studies. He talked on for a while about the design of the Old Testament, the dates in history and the story of creation.

"Get to something we don't know about," said Bobby. "Hanna, he gets long-winded sometimes."

"You want to do this?" asked Byron.

"He's so sensitive," Bobby said. "And he's so big on details. Just get to the meat of things, Byron."

"Ya'll are so fucking weird," said Hanna.

Byron talked on for more than an hour, careful to remain chronological. Occasionally, Bobby would insert something that caused Byron's eyes to open wide or turn beady.

"There is also a Book of Thomas that gives a some-what different account of..."

Bobby interrupted. "That's the one about when Jesus was a little boy and when his playmates didn't do what he wanted them to, he would zap them."

They talked all morning about religion. Byron drew a whole stack of diagrams about such things as the differences between a Protestant and a Catholic and a Greek Orthodox. He explained the Gospels, Paul's epistles, the role Paul played in the development of modern Christianity and his conversion on the road to Damascus. He admitted lack of understanding of Revelation.

Hanna was amazed at what both men knew about

religion. Even Bobby knew much more than he wanted to admit. Byron not only had what seemed to Hanna an amazing memory for details about Christianity, but he eventually got into a treatise about all the major religions. He explained the basic ideas of Hinduism and Buddhism and Taoism. He drew diagrams to show the chronological order of the birth of each of the major religions, and Hanna was spellbound.

"It's all pretty simple when you think about it," Hanna said finally. "The big question, I guess, is whether or not somebody believes any of it or not."

"I believe it," said Bobby.

"Believe what?" Byron wanted to know.

"You do not," said Hanna.

"I most certainly do, sometimes," said Bobby.

Hanna laughed.

"How can you believe it just sometimes, Bobby?" Hanna asked. "Ya'll are something," she said after going to the kitchen. "Nobody in this whole city knows that ya'll know all this stuff ya'll tell me. Sometimes I've laid in the bed and thought about ya'll and all the stuff ya'll are probably thinking that nobody knows ya'll think."

"You mean, to look at us?" said Byron.

"Are you saying we don't look like we ought to know anything?" Bobby asked.

"Ya'll know what I mean."

"Oh, Hanna, we sure did used to be something, didn't we, Byron?"

"Yeh," said Byron, "Bobby used to be much of a man."

* * *

Hanna had been with them less than three months, and in the strangest way she was growing. The two men had a way of playing dumb and at the same time sneaking ideas and information in on her without its being apparent. She was starting to realize more that they were not at all the carefree idiots that no doubt a lot of people thought them to be. It was amazing to Hanna how their brains worked so well after so many years of saturating them with alcohol.

"I've noticed something else," Hanna told them one evening when they were behaving themselves. "When ya'll are around Earl and them and anybody else, ya'll act like ya'll don't know nothing."

"Anything," said Bobby.

"Earl and them would die if they knew what went on in ya'lls ugly heads."

"Hanna, can you do the Alabama Shuffle?" Bobby asked her.

"The Alabama Shuffle? No, but I bet you do."

"Go get your radio. I'm going to show you the Alabama Shuffle. I created it, didn't I, Byron?"

"Hanna, I have to admit, it's pretty cool."

Hanna brought the radio to him and Bobby found a

station playing an upbeat song. Hanna thought the dance was hilarious, and it was apparent to her that beneath the aging man's body was a rather graceful spirit; it was the first time it had occurred to her that all his tales about once having been a football hero were probably true. "Come here, girl, I'm going to show you how to do it."

Byron sat on the floor drinking and turning the radio dial to stations that played the right songs, and Bobby taught Hanna to dance. Not only did he teach her the Alabama Shuffle, but he showed her the jitterbug. Hanna was indeed a poor dancer, and Bobby told her it was because she had too much inhibition. Hanna did not know what inhibition was.

"You don't believe in yourself enough," Byron told her.

"Relax, girl. Let yourself go. Do like this."

Hanna tried everything Bobby told her but the stiffness would not leave her.

"Ya'll will laugh at me."

"Laugh at you?" said Bobby. "Who cares? I've been laughed at before. You aren't a goddamn sissy are you? Hell yes, we'll laugh at you. Now dance!"

They had a good evening together. They danced some more, and Hanna was learning the general idea of the jitterbug. They later went out and got Hanna a sandwich while Bobby and Byron drank gin and tonics. Then they drove to the river and sat on the bank and watched barges being towed in and out of the city. Bobby talked about Mark Twain and told Hanna as much as he knew about him. Hanna had read *Tom Sawyer*; it was one of the books they had gotten for her from the library. But she said it was not one of her favorites, that it was more of a boy's book. And she confessed that she did not finish it.

However, she had started reading the books they chose for her only because she had nothing better to do and because she started to have this reluctant urge to please them. She was not sure why, though. But it was after she started reading this short story called "A Field of Blue Children" that she saw for the first time in her life that there were books that really made her think, not like the cheap novels she had been accustomed to reading. And with "A Field of Blue Children" she discovered an emotion she had not experienced before, even though she had no words for it until Byron explained "bittersweet melancholy" to her. She had read nearly a dozen books since she had been around Bobby and Byron. And she had discovered something else; it was fun to be read to. Bobby was by far the better reader, but Byron was fair, and it was he who had most often chosen a book or story that Hanna liked.

As her so-called education was going, she had learned virtually nothing about science or mathematics, but she was certainly learning some things she had not known before. She still occasionally thought about leaving, going back to Florida or someplace new. But those thoughts were becoming less frequent as days and weeks went by. They were opening up a different world for her and she still was not clear about what to make of it.

EIGHT

Summer arrived and the heat had already become almost unbearable. Bobby bought a three-speed fan from a thrift store and Byron and Hanna found two more at yard sales. One was a small window fan with a reverse switch they put in a living room window. The others were small oscillating three-speeds. Bobby was trying to get full disability benefits from the Marine Corps. He told Byron that unless he sold his house trailer in Alabama, they were going to have to do something different. He got a telephone call from the real estate agency telling him they had a buyer, but he would have to go down on his price. Byron decided to hold out for what he originally asked.

They both thought about going to work, but after serious consideration decided it was too hot. They were spending more money than they had expected. Trying to seduce Hanna was costing them, and worse, they were making no apparent headway. Bobby was the one who came up with the idea of making a hole in the wall between the two bedrooms. Some time ago there had been a door between them. However, it had been replaced by panels of sheetrock in both rooms. One morning, while Hanna had gone out, the men began cutting through the sheetrock with a kitchen knife. After finishing a crude hole through their wall, not more than a foot above the floor, they went to Hanna's room and cut another. When they had finished they were able to see from one room to the next, although the holes were not exactly in line with one another. But Hanna came back too soon for them to improve upon their little spying device.

Hanna was becoming even more attractive to the men. It seemed sometimes that her breasts had actually grown somewhat more wonderful, and her coloring was appearing more…more something. Once Bobby caught her coming out of the bathroom and she had not buttoned her shirt. "Byron, I could almost see her nipples. I think I did see a little bit of one. Oh, my! I got a lump in my throat. It's there. It's been there all morning. How do you get rid of a lump like that, Byron? It's no fun, I can tell you that."

One day they had all gone to a store for some things they needed and Byron noticed these aluminum-frame lawn chairs for sale at half price. They bought them, along with a little yellow plastic table and set them up in the living room. On another occasion they found a broken-down wooden table that somebody had thrown out for trash, and put it in the trunk of Byron's car. All it needed was two more legs and for several screws to be tightened. When they got it in the house, against the wall, they stacked books to eliminate one of the legless corners and they found a two-by-four to prop underneath the other. It was almost nearly level.

The little plastic swimming pool was Byron's idea. It had gotten so hot that later in the day there was no way to cool off without taking frequent baths. One afternoon Byron had stopped at a drugstore for some wine when a woman and a young child were putting a little chartreuse wading pool in the trunk of a car. Byron found one just like it for seven dollars and ninety-five cents, with bright little turtles all over it. It was a Mr. Turtle pool. He and Bobby put it in the little backyard and filled it with water and got in. Their social life started to center around their new pool. "Ya'll look like two old walruses lying in that thing," Hanna told them.

"Hanna, don't you have a swimsuit somewhere in there?"

"No."

"Well, put on some panties and a brassiere, same thing."

Hanna laughed.

"Then suffer," Bobby told her.

"If you'll go swimming with us, we'll get you one," Byron said.

"Swimming?" said Hanna.

"But we get to pick it out," said Bobby.

"I wish somebody could see ya'll," said Hanna.

A day or so later the idea had caught on, and old Fleetwood had seen a little pool like it in the backyard of a place on another street. So some child went out one day and discovered not only his Popeye pool missing, but also his dolphin float.

Every day, by noon, the backyard would become a playground for winos and derelicts. The water had to be changed often as the middle of summer came. The sun heated the water to an almost unbearable temperature within a couple of hours and Bobby started charging the derelicts twenty-five cents every time they refilled a pool. And to get the most of their money, they started following the shade cast here and there during the day.

Tempers flared easily as the heatwaves became more intense. And late one afternoon two of the derelicts got into an argument that would have led to a fight if either had had enough energy to bother with it. It did, however, end the festivities for the day when Byron poured out the water of their guests' pool and one of the derelicts dragged their pool back down to the outdoor living room. Earl said it was probably a good idea because he was starting to feel that they might be becoming a bad influence on that precious Hanna. So, for some time afterwards, the derelicts stole water from an outdoor faucet behind a nearby warehouse. Occasionally Byron and Bobby would drag their pool down to join them.

It was August before Hanna agreed to let them buy her a swimsuit. It was a thrift-store find, a solid light brown two-piece that caused the men more misery than joy when Hanna wore it to sit in the pool.

"Ga-od damn!" said Bobby.

They made such a fuss over Hanna in her swimsuit that she would not wear it again in their presence. Still, she would wear it when the men had gone off for a while, always having a towel with her in case they came back too soon or one of the derelicts came to visit. Soon she had developed a fine tan. Unconscious of it, Byron's and Bobby's tempers would flare for no apparent reason, as Hanna grew even more appealing.

* * *

It was one night after Byron and Bobby had been out all day and came back drunker than usual that things turned terribly sour. Byron went straight to bed, and did not know that Bobby had gone into Hanna's room. She was asleep on the mattress, underneath the lamp where she had been reading. She wore only a bra and a pair of panties. Bobby knelt down beside her and whispered "Hanna."

She woke up and when she saw him she jumped and backed herself off the mattress and up next to the wall. "Bobby!" she yelled.

Bobby grinned.

"Get the fuck out of here, Bobby."

"You looked so pretty lying there."

"Bobby, you fuck. Get out of here, I mean it you fucking shit."

"I'm going," he said with his grin. "I just wanted to look at you for a minute. Is there anything wrong with that? Good God, girl, I'm not going to do anything."

"Bobby!" Hanna screamed.

"I'm going. I'm going," Bobby said with a laugh. "You should have locked your door if you didn't want me to come in." He got up and started for the door, but as he did, Byron burst into the room.

"What the hell is going on?" he said.

"Not a thing," said Bobby. "I was just coming in to say good night to our little girl and she got the wrong idea."

"Wrong idea, nothing. Ya'll are gonna start that shit again, aren't ya'll?"

Byron went over to where some of Hanna's clothes were lying and handed them to her. She started putting them on. "I'm getting out of here once and for all!"

Bobby threw up his hands. "No you aren't. Not this time." He was no longer smiling. "This time I'm going. I've had enough of this goddamn game." He looked at Hanna very hard and pointed his finger at her. "You stay here, girl. Stay here with him. I'm the one that's leaving." He was as angry as she had ever seen him. "You keep acting like a goddamn innocent child if you want to, but I've had enough. I'm leaving." Byron spoke to him as he went out the front door. A minute later he and Hanna heard the car as Bobby drove away.

"He scared the shit out of me," Hanna told Byron.

"It'll be alright," Byron said, "He'll be back. Are you okay?"

Hanna had her clothes on and stood up. "Hanna, he wasn't going to do anything."

"I'm not taking that chance another time. I'm going, Byron. Ya'll have been nice to me, but I better leave—right now."

"I don't blame you if you do," said Byron. "But why don't you at least wait until morning. When Bobby gets back—he won't be back tonight—I'll drive you to the bus station. You're probably right."

"Byron, I can't wait till morning. I'm just too upset."

"Not now. I'm not going to let you go walking anywhere tonight. Just go to bed and when he gets back, tomorrow, I'll drive you anywhere you want to go. You don't have to worry about anything tonight. You've been with us this long without anything all that bad—a few more hours won't matter. You'll be all right. Just go to sleep. I'll be in the other room."

Hanna laughed nervously, "Well what makes you think I'm any less scared of you, Byron? I mean, Good Lord!"

Byron reached for the door handle. He spoke with authority. "I'm telling you, Hanna, you are not going anywhere tonight. I don't give a damn what you think about either one of us. Now get some sleep." And with that he closed the door and went back to his and Bobby's room, and turned off the light.

When morning came, Byron was sitting by the front door, drinking and smoking and staring down the hall toward the room Hanna was in. Bobby had not returned.

It was more than an hour later when Hanna came out of the room with her suitcase packed, but Byron had dozed off and did not see her until she stood before him and spoke his name.

He was in his underwear and his hair was terribly mussed and his red eyes blinked open as he sat up. "Is he back?" Byron asked.

Byron got up and looked outside. The car was still gone. He ran his hand through his hair and walked away from the door. "He'll be back. He's just licking his wounds somewhere." Byron looked at Hanna. "Do you still want to go?"

Hanna spoke softly, "Yes, Byron."

Byron walked about for several more moments, then said, "Nothing could change your mind?"

"I don't think so."

Byron walked some more and Hanna stood with the suitcase beside her. "You haven't changed your mind about high school?"

Hanna sighed. "Byron, I can't go back to school. It's too late."

"Yeh, maybe you're right," said Byron, then as an afterthought, "But you could still get your GED."

Hanna smiled at the sadness she felt for Byron's touch of enthusiasm. "I'll get it one day. Ya'll really have helped me—a lot."

"Hanna."

She sighed, "What, Byron?"

"Please stay. He didn't mean anything. You just don't understand him. He gets too excited sometimes."

Hanna walked to one of the windows and looked out front. "Byron, you and him could of probably done anything ya'll ever wanted to."

"I made all-state football."

"I know. Bobby told me," said Hanna, who realized the importance both men placed on their old athletic accomplishments, which made her feel only more sadness.

"Bobby played college football."

"I know that too."

They waited awhile longer and Byron talked Hanna into going out for something to eat before she left. So they walked over to St. Charles and sat at a sidewalk café while Hanna had some orange juice and a pastry. When they got back to the house it was midmorning—still no Bobby. "Let's wait one more hour and if he hasn't shown up by then, I'll get you a taxi."

Hanna went to the kitchen, then to her room where she lay down and turned on the radio. She did not know what to do. A part of her wanted to leave, but another part did not. She stared at the dirty ceiling while in the living room Byron lay on the floor doing the same thing. Then he finally dozed off. Almost an hour went by before he woke up and yelled, "Hanna!" He waited for her to answer, then when she did not, he yelled again.

"I'm right here," she finally said from the bedroom. Several moments later she was in the living room.

"I thought you had gone," said Byron. "Has it been an hour yet?"

Hanna looked tired, like she had been crying. "You think something happened to him?"

"No. He's just feeling sorry for himself somewhere."

Hanna sat in one of the lawn chairs. "We'll wait one more hour."

Noon came and Bobby still had not come back. Byron started putting on his shoes. "I'll go down to the phone booth and call you a taxi." He took his time tying his laces. And when he finished and started to stand up, Hanna said, "Let's just wait till he gets back." She went to get one of the fans and put it where it would oscillate for both of them. Then she got one of her library books and sat down in front of Byron. It was a book of short stories. "Byron."

"Hummm?" He was facing the ceiling with his eyes closed.

"What's a good story to read?"

He raised his head long enough to see the book. "I

don't know. What are you in the mood for?"

"I don't know—not anything boring."

" 'A Rose for Emily,'" Byron told her.

Hanna looked through the table of contents. "Hey," she said. "How'd you know that was in here?"

"It's in all short story anthologies."

"You're lying. How'd you really know?"

"I guessed."

After looking at him for nearly a minute, Hanna started to read the story and soon Byron had dozed off again. The most part of another hour went by before Hanna finished the story and said, "Ooooh!" loud enough to wake him.

Byron jumped. "What is it?"

"Ooooh, God, this story!"

Byron got up and went to the window.

Hanna could not get over the story. "How does somebody make up something like this?" She turned the book to the first page of the story. "William Faulkner. He's weird. What else did he write, Byron?"

Byron did not hear her; he was staring out the front window.

Hanna noticed this, then said, "I'm starting to worry about Bobby. Do you think something happened to him?"

Byron shook his head. "He just wants us to feel sorry for him. He'll get scared after awhile. He'll be back—the son of a bitch."

"Byron, I think I'm gonna stay," Hanna said. Byron turned around and smiled.

They did little else the rest of the day. Hanna read some more, and spent part of the afternoon in the Mr. Turtle pool in a T-shirt and shorts. Byron took a long nap and woke up later in the afternoon, then went down to the outdoor living room. He did not tell Earl and them about Bobby, but he kept looking over his shoulder expecting him to show up at any time. Just after dark he went back to the house and Hanna was in the bathroom. He went straight to bed.

The next day Bobby had still not returned, but Byron told Hanna he was not surprised, that Bobby had done such things before. He would stay away just long enough to feel like he was missed. "He just wants to make sure we feel sorry enough for him that we'll forget what he did. He's sitting in some bar somewhere telling somebody how misunderstood he is. He could walk through that door just any minute." Hanna was not so sure. She was really starting to worry about him. "It would serve him right if we weren't here when he gets back," Byron said after he made a drink. "Hey, Hanna, let's go somewhere. Let's walk over to St. Charles and catch a streetcar and go down to the French Quarter." Hanna was not so sure about this idea. "Oh, hell, the last thing you need to do is start feeling sorry for him. You start that and he will take advantage of you."

Hanna was against the whole idea, and only agreed

to go if they left Bobby a note. Byron put on the trousers to his seersucker suit and a white shirt. Hanna wore some blue jeans and a T-shirt.

They got to Jackson Square just as the vendors and painters and entertainers were setting up for the day. Tourists were already out in full force, taking pictures of all the oldness and the remnants of what they imagined was New Orleans. It was already stifling hot and Hanna sat on one of the heavy wrought-iron benches while Byron went inside one of the bars for a drink. When he got back Hanna was sitting cross-legged. She had pulled her shoes off. "I was just thinking about that first time you and Bobby brought me down here," she said. "Ya'll were so funny, the way ya'll would never agree with one another about anything. I remember Bobby walking up to this lady and telling her he wanted her to know he thought she was pretty. One thing about old Bobby, he's not bashful."

"No, he's just crazy."

"I wish I had some of whatever it is. I'm so bashful I'm scared of my own face."

Byron sat down and leaned back.

"I remember thinking that day how different ya'll were than anybody else I ever knew. The way ya'll thought about everything. Stuff just came out of ya'lls' mouths, like…like the way most people talk about the weather or something. I didn't want ya'll to know it, but ya'll amazed me."

People were all about now, some wandering and others in a hurry. Down the way a mime was entertaining a cluster of children. In the other direction a fiddler was opening up his case and a juggler was setting up his props.

"Byron."

"What?"

"I got something to tell you. Promise you won't be mad?"

"What?"

Hanna tucked her feet tighter toward her middle and looked down. "One day when you and Bobby had gone somewhere I got out that book you've been writing." She waited for Byron to chastise her, but he said nothing. "It's about Bobby, isn't it?"

"More or less."

"It sounds just like ya'll. Is that the one Bobby says ya'll are gonna get published and get famous with?"

"It's just one of his fucked-up dreams."

"It may not be."

"Oh hell, girl. What do you know about it? I guess you're some kind of goddamn critic, huh?"

"I didn't mean…"

"You didn't mean what? Don't start any phony shit with me about your knowing anything about books. You've read a half dozen books in your life and all of a sudden you're this goddamn expert."

"I was just talking."

"Well talk about something you know something about." Before Hanna could say anything more, Byron stood up. "Come on, I want to show you something." He started to walk off but Hanna was hesitant about going with him. He seemed ready to get into some kind of rage. "Come on!" he nearly demanded.

Byron took her down toward a farmers' market, past several trucks unloading fruits and vegetables. They walked briskly until they eventually reached a little wrought-iron fence. Inside stood a lone streetcar on a concrete slab. Byron led Hanna around to its front and pointed up to the word *Desire* encased in glass just above the front windshield. "Do you know anything about this?" he asked.

"No. Should I?"

"Tennessee Williams. That's his *Streetcar Named Desire.*"

As they stood there, Byron told her about the playwright. He told her about how, when he was younger, he read everything Tennessee Williams ever wrote. He tried to explain to her how the playwright had touched a major chord with him. He tried to explain to her about seediness and decadence and how they were just the other side of things people had characterized as good and beautiful. "I tend to think derelicts and whores and drunks are just as significant as anybody else in life. If it weren't for derelicts, who would the fucking do-gooders have to look down to? The fucking good people need the whores and thieves and the losers."

Byron did not know if Hanna would understand what he was trying to say, but it did not matter. He just needed to say it. The best he could hope for was that she could understand enough to want to understand more.

"Tennessee Williams was concerned with the seediness of us all, our secret shames, embarrassments and desperations. Sin and sainthood all in each bundle. I think he wanted to expose, for himself first, the natures we try to deny. It seems to me most people are not capable of grasping the idea of necessary opposites of thought itself. The idea that life itself is made up of opposites. The paradox. Their own fucking paradox. With good arises bad, no way out, as the 'Old Boy' said. We can't not fuck up, unless we deny the existence of fuck-ups. The world speaks as if it can get it right. What the fuck does that mean?"

"Byron," said Hanna.

"What?"

"What the shit are you talking about?"

Hanna had reminded him of his own contradiction, however, he needed to vent something. "People can't help it," Byron continued. We're all victims of being whatever we are, I guess. I certainly don't know. I just wish we would not be so quick to judge one another. Fucking compassion, goddamnit..."

As Byron ranted on, Hanna's ears struggled to receive what he must be saying while her eyes darted toward the unusual sights of New Orleans' French Quarter. She felt something she could not explain, nothing bad, not a good feeling; it was something different, something new to her. Part of it had to do with her wanting to experience a lot more than she had.

They went inside a bar and sat down. Byron ordered himself a gin and tonic and Hanna a Dixie beer. "Girl, let me tell you something."

"What?"

"Listen carefully," he said, staring into the mirrored wall facing him. "There's this secret club, see. And…uh… it doesn't have many members." He gripped his glass in both hands and glanced toward Hanna. "They're quiet, and they lurk in the dark, and right under your nose. And most likely you won't recognize one when you see him. They don't dress any particular way. And they're just as likely to be on a street corner as a brothel or a library or a church or a laboratory. Lots of them are in insane asylums. They come in all sizes and colors and sexes and religions." Byron was leaning closer to Hanna gazing at the side of her face. He spoke near a whisper. "Some of them can dance and some of them can't. Some of them are pretty to look at and some of them aren't so pretty to look at. Most of them are dead, because this club has been around for a long time. There aren't many of them. But do you know what?"

"I'm listening," said Hanna, curiosity mounting along with her need to laugh.

"Even though it's a very secret club, and not many people are even allowed in, it is for anybody who has ears. Remember Jesus Christ—People who have the ability to hear, I mean with their inner being, souls, wisdom, are the only ones who can grasp the…"

"Things that remain out of sight," said Hanna.

Byron smiled. "Exactly. Those are the passwords to this club. If you are capable of hearing, listen."

Hanna noticed the barkeep watching them. "Byron," she said, turning her face toward him, "Does it cost any money to join this club, 'cause if it does, I can't join, and I for sure don't want to die anytime soon."

Byron stared straight into her eyes, "You shithead, welcome to the club."

They left the bar and walked toward Canal Street, passing a small park and an old church set behind a wrought-iron fence. Where the fence ended, Byron turned down a narrow alleyway, explaining to Hanna that he wanted to show her something. They paused before a small store identified only by a wooden sign hanging over the street. As Hanna followed him inside, she lifted her head to better catch the mysterious fragrance of must, mildew and crumbling binder's glue that hung in the air.

Byron navigated first one way then another down a maze of narrow aisles. Books were stacked to the ceiling in a discernible but casual order. Hanna followed Byron from one room to the next, each opening off the last to reveal yet another cache of used books. He pulled one from the shelf, *The Dhammpada*. "Not now, but you want to read this," Byron told her.

"Why?"

"It's a club book."

"Lord God, Byron, I don't even know what it means."

Byron pointed out more than a dozen books he thought Hanna should read sooner or later.

"They're just too fucking many of them," she said. "It would take forever to read all this stuff."

"You aren't going anywhere, are you?"

"Crazy, maybe."

"Okay, let's go," said Byron.

"Byron."

"What?" he said as he started up an aisle.

"Can we buy one? I don't think they cost very much."

"Hell yes. Let's buy one."

"Pick me out one you think I would like."

Byron started to look. He wandered about until he came to an area where all the authors' names started with *P*. Then he moved along until he came to an area of *S*'s. There must have been several hundred *S* volumes in all. Besides the authors all having *S* last names, there was no other order about them. But slowly he combed the books, until some ten minutes later he snatched one from the shelf and handed it to Hanna. It was a book titled *Lilith*, by J.R. Salamanca.

NINE

B obby still had not returned. It had been three days since he had left. Byron had less than twenty dollars left to last the rest of the month of August. He still had money in his savings account back in Eanes, but he had wanted it to last as long as possible. So far they had done all right with Bobby's disability check. Byron's unemployment would soon run out, and he was going to have to make a decision about selling his house trailer. He did not tell Hanna but he was starting to worry about Bobby. He thought about calling the veterans' hospital in Biloxi to find out if Bobby had checked himself back in. But if that was so, he did not want to know about it. Bobby would die if he went back to that place. He would wait. He had to wait.

He and Hanna spent their days quieter since Bobby had been gone. Byron once even got out his manuscript and tried to write, but he actually wrote little that he did not trash. Bobby was just too close to him; there was too much to say; the scenes of their lives together were too complicated. There were too many of them and they kept running together in his mind. He never expected to get the book published, as Bobby had so often dreamed they would. But he still wanted to finish it to give to Bobby as a gift one day—just to give his friend a glimpse of himself as Byron saw him. There was so much more to Bobby than anybody knew. For one thing, he had an amazing mind that he rarely showed to anyone. And he could tell a story like nobody else. His sense of humor…well. And his unorthodox goodwill toward others. Byron knew these things about Bobby Long, even if nobody else did. Byron doubted if he had ever intentionally harmed a single soul. It was just that Bobby got an overdose of some things and an underdose of others. His mind ran too fast. He could not slow it down. He was like a gazelle in a toy store at times, and a moth to a flame at others. He had certainly taught Byron a lot in all their years as friends. They had certainly done some living together.

Hanna read *Lilith* in two days, and had been talking about it ever since. "It's so beautiful," she kept saying. "It was almost like reading a real sad song. Oh, Byron, I'm so glad you gave it to me. I'm going to read it once a year for the rest of my life."

Byron told her about the time Bobby had gotten drunk and drove all the way to Virginia to meet J.R. Salamanca and to tell him how he felt about his book. "Ya'll are crazy," Hanna had said.

They went to the zoo one day, and on another, they took in a movie at the Prytania. It was an offbeat

French movie with lots of sex and nudity, but it did nothing Byron had hoped it would. Hanna showed no sign of any kind of sexual arousal. Byron had enough money left that night to buy a bottle of Popov and Hanna a box of cereal and a quart of milk. He would have to write a check on his savings account sooner than he wanted to.

They went to the living room and sat in the lawn chairs as they smoked and Byron drank vodka and water. They talked some about Hanna's mother, and he told her the truth about her funeral, that it was a pauper's funeral and that the city of New Orleans paid for it. "I honestly don't know how I feel about Lorraine," Hanna said. "I guess she did the best she could under the circumstances. It's just that I never really had nobody to give a fuck for me, is all."

"She was just sick," said Byron. "She was probably sick before you were born. She was generous, though, and could be funny as hell." Byron was about to say something else he thought Hanna might appreciate about Lorraine when they heard footsteps on the front porch and then in burst Bobby with a beet-colored face and a gigantic grin.

"I'm back!"

Neither Hanna nor Byron said anything.

"Well, aren't you people glad to see me?"

"Not especially," said Byron. "You have any money?"

"Have I got any money? Just ask me. Say, Bobby,

do you have any money. Go ahead, ask. I got some whiskey too. Look!" Bobby held up a bottle of Wild Turkey bourbon.

Something suddenly occurred to Byron. He had not heard Bobby drive up. "Bobby, where is the car?"

"What?"

"My car. Where is it?" Byron jumped up and went to the door.

"About that," said Bobby. Byron's car was not out front.

"Where is my goddamn car, Bobby?"

"I'll explain. Just wait. Let's have a drink first." He started for the kitchen. Hanna had the feeling something terrible was about to happen.

"Put on some music," Bobby shouted from the kitchen. "Hanna, go get your radio and find a good blues station."

Byron went to the kitchen. "Bobby!"

Bobby turned to face him, "I sold it." He bowed up like he was waiting for Byron to hit him. "Byron, remember my cheek. You could kill me." He was grinning all the time. Byron could only stand there and stare him in the face.

"We don't need a car, Byron."

Byron's eyes turned their beadiest.

"It was falling apart, Byron. Here, let's have a drink. It's Wild Turkey. When was the last time you had Wild Turkey?"

Byron turned around and started pacing. "How much did you get for it?"

"I made a good deal, believe me. We'll buy another one if you want to."

"How much, Bobby?"

"You haven't said one word about missing me. Did you and Hanna miss me?"

"How much did you get?"

"I missed you."

"Goddamnit, you…"

"Three hundred dollars. He wanted to give me two, but I held out."

"Three hundred fucking dollars for my car. You son of a bitch!"

Hanna had gone to her room and was waiting for the explosion.

Byron bowed his head and took a deep breath. "Let me get this straight. You sold my car for three hundred dollars?"

"Smackers."

"What?"

"Smackers, three hundred smackers."

"I ought to…"

"Now, boy, don't hit me, remember my cheekbone."

"Bobby, have you lost your mind completely?"

"Come on, boy, we don't need a car. The streetcar goes everywhere we need to go. It was costing more to run than it was worth."

"Why?" Byron wanted to know.

"I didn't have any money."

Byron walked to the backdoor and let his head fall against the screen.

"But that's not the important thing," said Bobby. He made two drinks and stepped over to Byron and passed him one. "Now, come on back to the living room. I've got something to show you." As he passed Hanna's room he knocked on her door. "Hey, girl, come out. I've got something to show you. You too, Byron. Come on."

Byron's jaw tightened and his eyes grew narrower, but he finally followed Bobby to the front room. Hanna was already there.

"Sit down right there, Hanna. Byron, you sit here."

"I'll stand," said Byron.

Bobby grinned and said, "Suit yourself."

Hanna sat on the floor.

"Now," said Bobby. "Close your eyes. You too, Byron."

"Bobby," said Byron.

"Just close your eyes."

"I'm not closing my goddamn eyes," said Byron.

"Alright, don't close them. But it won't be as much of a surprise. Hanna, Byron never has liked surprises."

As she closed her eyes, Hanna could not help but find something funny about it all. The two men she had gotten herself so insanely mixed up with were absolutely crazy. There was no other word for it. Byron looked at him as Bobby went right on grinning, as he went about slowly unbuttoning his shirt. When he had unbuttoned it half way down, he jerked an envelope from his chest and held it up. "Now open your eyes." Hanna obeyed as Bobby undid the envelope and pulled out several official looking sheets of paper. He dropped the envelope and started to read the first sheet. He held the paper as far away from his eyes as he could. "This…is to Certify…" he began, "'…that Hanna Marie James…has completed all the requirements for the…Eleventh Grade and is Hereby Promoted…to… the…Twelfth Grade!'"

* * *

The next morning, after Byron had shoved Bobby off their mattress during the night, Hanna woke first and lay in her bed trying to decide what she was going to do next. Although she had thought about it on occasion, she still was not sure she wanted to go back to school in any grade. When she stepped into the kitchen, she noticed Byron's manuscript lying on the table. It was noticeably thicker. She fixed herself a bowl of cereal, sat down and glanced at a few pages. She was about to read a paragraph when Byron walked in.

Later in the morning the three sat in the kitchen while Hanna ate cereal with a cigarette in her hand. Before they had gone to bed the night before, Bobby had explained to Byron and Hanna what had occurred while he was away. He had driven all the way to Columbus, Georgia, where he found and met up with his and Byron's old friend and confidant Hap Woodruff, who, with little persuasion, provided a trumped-up transcript to enter the noble conspiracy.

Byron had not mentioned it before, but he had already been inquiring about local high schools. There was one up St. Charles Avenue, Benjamin Franklin, that he had heard had a fair reputation. Hanna could catch a bus on Magazine.

"I'm not going," said Hanna.

"Now, girl," said Bobby.

"Ya'll, I can't pass the twelfth grade. Shit."

"Oh, yes you can," said Byron. "Hanna, just listen."

"Just listen. Just listen. I'm fucking tired of listening. Motherfuck!" said Hanna.

"Watch your language girl," said Bobby.

"Hanna," Byron insisted, "you are a bright girl. You have a damn good mind. With our help you can do it. Hell, Bobby and I will make you an honor student."

Hanna could not help laughing. "I am an honor student."

"Besides," she said while they continued to talk. "I hadn't got but...I don't have any clothes to wear. I hadn't got but three pairs of panties and they're falling apart."

Bobby and Byron laughed. "Well, girl," said Bobby, just because you let them come between you and Byron and me, doesn't mean you have to let some little old panties keep you out of high school. We'll buy you some panties."

"We can buy you probably two dozen pair at the Salvation Army for no more than a few bucks," Byron added. "If that's all you're worried about."

"It's not just the clothes, ya'll. It's a lot of things...for one thing I'm bashful about meeting new people. And I don't want to be reminded again how fucking low class I am. I hadn't ever been a fucking cheerleader or nothing."

* * *

They found out that school would start back August 22. The week before they took care of the details. The plan was that she would be living with her uncle, but which of them would be the uncle? Byron and Bobby had to argue that out before Byron convinced Bobby that he looked more like one of Hanna's relatives might look than dark-skinned Bobby did. "You racist son of a bitch," Bobby had to at least say to feel better about giving in.

So, Hanna would be living with her Uncle Byron, who had custody of her since her mother died. The good principal in Columbus, Georgia, had already mailed the official transcript to Ben Franklin High School. Uncle Byron would accompany Hanna to school on registration day, and they all three would start shopping for some more clothes for Hanna. "Second-hand Hanna," Hanna had remarked.

The official transcript told the story. The new senior from Columbus, Georgia, had been an outstanding student, all A's and B's, a member of an honor society, was on the debate team and vice president of her junior class. Her religious preference Protestant since that could be faked easier than Catholicism.

The big question had to do with state requirements for graduation: did Louisiana require more than Georgia? They went to the library to find out.

The only difference was that Louisiana required a course in Louisiana history. This meant Hanna would have to take five academic courses. Bobby had made sure that the transcript indicated she had taken the more complicated subjects like chemistry and physics. And it turned out the math requirements and foreign language requirements had been fulfilled in Georgia.

Registration went fine. Uncle Byron wore his seersucker suit and a Windsor knot in his tie.

"Byron," Bobby told him before they left, "Don't put on a show. Just do what you have to do and get the hell out of there. And don't go putting your hands on our girl in front of the principal."

They were gone longer than Bobby had expected because things went so well that Byron thought they should celebrate the start of Hanna's senior year. When they did return, they were acting giddy from Bobby's point of view.

"You're drunk," Bobby told Byron.

"So is she," said Byron.

"I'm a fuggen senior," said Hanna.

"And you both left me out. That's so unfair."

It would be the following Monday before classes started, so they invited Earl, Cecil and the other derelicts who had not wandered off somewhere in search of some mood alteration for a gathering in honor of Hanna.

* * *

Saturday morning, Bobby yelled for Hanna.

"Whut?" she mumbled from her room.

"Come here. You've got a decision to make."

"Ya'll make it."

Bobby and Byron looked at each other, then got up and went to Hanna's room. She was sitting on the mattress painting her toenails.

"What is this?" Bobby asked.

Hanna dropped her head. "Ya'll don't know about all this. Ya'll aren't thinking about everything."

"What do you mean? Goddamn, we've got it all set," said Bobby.

"And do ya'll have it all set how I'm gonna pass all this stuff? Psychology. Lord God, I don't know anything about psychology."

"And what the hell do you think your uncle number two is? Shoot, girl, don't worry. We're going to help you. You're going to be the fucking valedictorian."

"Ya'll don't know everything."

"We know enough to get your pretty ass out of a little old high school," said Bobby.

"And what about clothes? I hadn't got enough clothes to last two days. I'm gonna just be this little old welfare girl that hadn't got no clothes to wear is all. I hadn't even got no panties that don't have holes in them."

"Panties? Girl, you aren't going to be showing your tail to anybody anyhow. What do you need panties for?" Bobby asked.

"I agree with Hanna," said Byron. "She's got to have some clothes."

"Aw pooh," said Hanna. "And where do ya'll expect to get enough money to buy me clothes? Clothes cost money, Byron. Or haven't you heard?"

Byron and Bobby went back to the living room. "How much money do you have left?" Byron asked Bobby.

"A little over a hundred dollars."

Byron walked over to a window and looked out. "Bobby, what in the hell are we doing?"

Bobby put his finger to his lips and frowned, then he went to the kitchen and made himself another drink before going out to the porch. Byron followed him.

One of the derelicts came by trying to conceal the paper sack he had rolled round a bottle. He spoke, but it was apparent that he was not going to stop. Bobby sat on the steps and Byron walked about the yard. "It's not going to work," Byron finally said. "Bobby, let's let her go before we mess everything up."

"Mess what up?" Bobby wanted to know. Then they looked at each other and burst out laughing. Bobby's voice was getting hoarser and he had to cough midway through his laugh. Byron stepped up on the porch and stuck his face to the screen door. "Hanna!"

In a minute, she stepped out on the porch and leaned against one of the posts.

"What would you have to have?"

"Oh, Byron."

"No, now. Just answer my question."

Hanna looked at her newly polished toes. "I can't wear blue jeans all the time."

"Well?"

"Oh, Byron, ya'll can't afford to buy me clothes to go to school in."

"Hanna," said Bobby, "Let me ask you something."

"What?"

"Nothing."

"What, Bobby?"

Bobby grinned and said, "You could at least let us see you naked sometimes."

No one said anything for a couple of moments then all three burst into laughter at the pitifulness of Bobby's remark.

"I swear," said Hanna.

"Well, you could. Goddamnit, it wouldn't kill you."

When that was all over with, Byron got back to the subject of clothes. "I'll tell you what. Down in the French Quarter there are some places that sell used clothes. Why don't we take a trip and go see if we can find something?"

"Byron," said Hanna, "it's nice of you to try, but I can't go to that school looking like hand-me-down city. I know you mean well and all, but I'm sorry. I just can't. I got a little pride, you know."

"A little," said Bobby.

"Well goddamn," said Byron, "we could go look. It won't cost a thing to just look."

"Ya'll keep talking like I'm gonna do this thing. I hadn't said I was going to school no matter what, yet."

"Look, bitch," said Bobby, "You're going to school. It's just a matter of whether you're going in rags or naked. I've heard enough of this talk."

"Oooooow hoo," said Hanna. "Listen to Mr. Mister." She glared at him curling her mouth to one side in contempt.

"Now go get on some shoes. We're going downtown and look at some used clothes. Go! Right now!"

Hanna looked at Byron. "I agree," he told her. So she went inside and soon came back ready to go with them.

When they returned, after stopping off for drinks, the men insisted that Hanna try on her new clothes.

They all went to bed early that night, and nobody said another word about clothes or school or anything else. But when Hanna got up the next morning Byron and Bobby were gone. They were gone all day. It was almost dark when they returned, drunk and acting suspicious. But when Hanna asked them where they had been, they paid her no attention, and finally left again to go down to the outdoor living room.

And the next morning, when Hanna got up, again they were gone. They were certainly up to something, but Hanna could not figure it out. She spent the day lonesome, and it was the first time she realized that she could miss them both. When they got back late in the afternoon, Hanna was mad and told them they were acting stupid and there was no sense in it, that if they had to keep things from her she was going to start keeping things from them. But this did no good. They were drunk, acting terribly silly, before both finally passed out on the living room floor.

Hanna had decided that she was going to get up early the next morning, and if they went anywhere, she was going to follow them. Sure enough, when morning came, they were up early. Hanna stayed in her room and listened, but they said nothing to give themselves away. So when they went out the door she waited a couple of minutes and followed them. She was nearly too late, for when she got out in front of the house they were going around a block headed toward Magazine,

Bobby carrying something inside a large grocery sack. She ran across the street and was careful not to get too close. She stayed about a block back from them as they crossed Magazine Street. Hanna kept nearly a block behind them until they reached St. Charles Avenue where they stood at a streetcar stop. Determined to discover what they were up to, she stood across the street until a streetcar arrived, knowing she had to get on the same car to follow them. So she walked up to the corner and stood behind a tree so that if they boarded from one door she could enter the other. Luck was on her side, several people departed as others arrived from out of nowhere to ride. She was one of the last on, and got lost in a group at the back after Byron and Bobby entered at the front.

The streetcar moved away, nobody signaled to get off; it made no stops until reaching Canal Street. Disembarking, Hanna remained with her clutter until it started to disperse. Catching a glimpse of Bobby and Byron crossing Canal, headed toward the French Quarter, she kept her distance and followed them down Royal Street. There were still enough people moving about for her to feel easy about her concealment.

Soon the two men turned to a side street, and finally, from a block away, she watched them enter the area about Jackson Square. When she reached the corner of a building at the edge of the square, she peeped around and saw them go into a bar. Hanna walked across the way to the wrought-iron fence surrounding the fountain and statues, moved alongside it until she reached the corner, then decided to stand there and wait to see if they emerged from the bar. It was quite a while before they did, with drinks in their hands and Bobby still carrying the paper bag. They sat on a park bench and Hanna stayed where she was and watched them smoke and drink. They talked too, Bobby mostly.

More people were arriving, the scent of horse manure from the buggies for tourists grew strong as Hanna finally moved round the corner, sat on a wrought-iron bench, determined not to leave before discovering the mystery. The craftsmen and artisans were setting up their easels, and the tourists were starting to arrive. Several men went by in tuxedos, on their way to the restaurant to wait tables. Hanna had looked away, and when she looked back, the bench where Bobby and Byron had been was empty. A moment later, she caught sight of them standing against the wrought-iron fence. There was a crowd by then, so she had to mingle and meander round to get a better view from the corner of a restaurant, where most of a hundred feet away the two men stood, Bobby with his hand on Byron's shoulder as he strummed a ukelele and intermittently she heard the broken tune of "Won't You Come Home, Bill Bailey."

With a lump in her throat, Hanna could not help laughing, feeling a mix of shame, absurdity, admiration and embarrassment for them while she noticed Bobby patting his flip-flop to the beat. Sitting at a sidewalk table, she could not decide whether to laugh or cry, so she settled on both, through several more songs as mostly people ignored them, or stood for short stretches to clap along or possibly have a humorous addition to their stories of the Big Easy when they got back to Wisconsin or Minnesota. As she left, boarding a streetcar back, she realized that, at least while she was there, no one had dropped as much as a single coin in the opened grocery sack standing before two of the... well...fairheadedest boys from the state of Alabama.

The day school started Hanna wore a pair of denim pants and a white blouse. It was the best outfit she had. Byron and Bobby walked with her to the bus stop and wanted to ride down to the school, but Hanna talked them out of that. All the arrangements had been made and her transcript had already been sent from Georgia. She was nervous, but the men had gotten her so upset with their instructions and endless chatter that by the time she got on the bus the idea of starting back to school was nearly a pleasant one compared to the ordeal they had put her through all morning.

Byron and Bobby spent the day drinking and waiting until she got back. They talked lots about painting the house and otherwise making the place more livable, but they did nothing toward that end. And when Hanna did finally get back, they were sitting in the swimming pool red-faced and red-eyed and excited. They made her tell them everything, and she did. She made herself a bologna sandwich and they all sat on the back porch while the men overwhelmed her with questions and Hanna answered as many as she could. The day had not been nearly as frightening as she had imagined it would be.

But she had homework, and Byron and Bobby promised not to make any noise. They even moved the kitchen table into her room, put the lamp on it, and made sure she was comfortable before they went to the living room and waited just in case she needed some help. And although they did not tell her, they were very disappointed that she did quite well without them. That is, they were disappointed until they eventually passed out on the front porch.

At school several days later, in her government class, sitting in the front of a row, a classmate, a girl she had another class with, put a little package on Hanna's desk, smiled and said, "This is a little something some of us girls got you as a welcome to Ben Franklin High present," then walked toward the back of the room. After glancing to her back, Hanna opened the package, discovering a pair of white lace panties with a split in the crotch, above which was written starkly in black, SLUT. As the teacher walked into the room. Hanna stuck the package in her purse, determined not to look around.

* * *

They made no money to speak of from singing in Jackson Square. Byron wrote a five hundred dollar check on his bank account back in Eanes. The money arrived

Hanna's second week of school, and when she got in that afternoon they had a super large pizza waiting for her.

And after an early supper with a bottle of cheap champagne, Byron announced that they were going shopping.

"With what, pray tell?" Hanna wanted to know, and Byron pulled out a crisp one hundred dollar bill and flipped it on the floor.

"Where did this come from?" she wanted to know.

"Never mind. Come on."

They went to a discount department store downtown, and by the time they had finished, Hanna had two new pairs of blue jeans, several T-type shirts, a pair of casual shoes and a skirt and blouse that looked downright fairly expensive. And they had only spent just a little over a hundred dollars.

Then, as they were walking down Canal Street, Bobby spotted a huge banner across one of the display windows at Holmes Department Store that read SUMMER REDUCTION. UP TO 70% OFF. So Bobby passed the pint bottle of bourbon he had been carrying in his pocket to Byron, and after they both had a considerable swallow, they crossed the street.

* * *

"Hanna, you got to try on your new clothes," said Bobby as he got out what was left of the champagne.

"Not now," said Hanna, "I got some homework." But the men looked so disappointed that she finally gave in. "Alright. Ya'll turn the chairs around this way, and I'll try on some of them. But then I got to study." Hanna chuckled. "Idn't that something, I got to study. Shit, I never knew I'd be saying that."

Byron and Bobby turned the lawn chairs to where they faced the hallway; Bobby looked at Byron, rubbed his hands together and grinned with a cigarette dangling from his crooked mouth.

* * *

When Bobby got up the next morning, Hanna had already gone and Byron was sitting at the table in her room writing something. After he had finished and stuffed the paper in an envelope, he told Bobby he would be back in a minute and left.

When he returned, Bobby was sitting on the front steps. "What do you want to do today?" he asked as Byron sat down beside him.

"We could go over to Georgianna's."

"You want to?"

"You want to?"

"Not really."

"She would appreciate it."

They bought a bottle of wine and picked a tiny bunch of yellow flowers that were blooming in a patch of weeds next to a vacant house and spent the morning with Georgianna.

And it was while they were walking back to the house that Byron noticed a piece of plywood leaning against a building. "Bobby, look. That would make Hanna a good desk." So they carried it with them and later wandered about the neighborhood rounding up cinderblocks from wherever they found them. They found two at the edge of the vacant lot where the outdoor living room was. And they found six more in a little yard where an old woman lived. She told them they could have them if they would only haul them away, so they went to the outdoor living room for help. Cecil, who knew a kid down the way with a Radio Flyer, loaded the little wagon with blocks. In appreciation for Cecil's enterprising contribution they offered him a screwdriver, which he really appreciated.

It was the excitement of surprising Hanna that kept them working. They moved the kitchen table back to the kitchen, then stacked the cinder blocks upright to make four legs cattycorner in Hanna's room, and put the plywood in place. Then they sat on the floor, refreshing, while they admired their work and eventually took naps to recoup all the energy they had lost working so seriously.

It was the next day that Bobby went to the store for some supplies and brought back a paintbrush. They took turns using the good paint beneath the crust in the can intended for the outside of the house, painting the cinder blocks, and then the plywood. Then they rearranged Hanna's room and talked about trying to round up another piece of wood and some more cinder blocks to make her a bedstead.

* * *

Her name was Nesslie, the girl who gave Hanna the SLUT panties for a present, and soon afterward Hanna made a point of going to the girl's restroom one particular morning after she saw several girls go in, including Nesslie. Among the chatter, as Nesslie came from a stall, Hanna stood before her, lifted her green skirt to expose the boldly printed SLUT panties, took a mischievous stance, one slender tanned leg propped on the knee of the other, and said, "I just wanted you to know, these have been marvelously successful for me, me being so new in ya'll's school and all. I'm starting to feel more popular already. Thank you so much."

"Ooooouu, shit!" someone said as others laughed and another said, "Miss Geoja!"

Among the girls looking on was Dede, a popular member of Nesslie's in-crowd, who had just changed her opinion about Hanna.

It was three days later before Hanna was allowed in her room. She had never seen the men so busy and sober. It was not that they did not drink; they did, but they seemed inspired. Their clothes were splattered with paint and there seemed to be a sense of purpose in everything they did. They were in and out of the house and laughing and secretive. Hanna knew they must be fixing up her room, but school had gotten into full force and she was too busy herself to get too involved in whatever it was that had gotten them so consistently interested in something besides drinking.

However, she was terribly worried and frightful about a speech she had been assigned to make on Friday.

"Oh hell, girl. There's nothing to that." Bobby told her on Thursday. The speech was to be no more than five minutes long and no less than four. And it had to be about an object she owned and prized. She had to take the object with her.

"Take me and Byron," Bobby suggested. "We'll put on our best clothes and stand there and not say a word." They were so involved in the project concerning Hanna's room that they did not pay much attention until they got back from downtown and Hanna was sitting on the living room floor in tears.

"What is it now?" Bobby asked her.

"I can't make a speech in front of all those people. I don't even know what to say. I hadn't even got no stupid object I want to talk about."

"Haven't any," said Byron.

Bobby sat beside her and picked up her limp hand. "Bless this baby's little soul. Byron, we have to write a speech."

"And besides that, I got a test in psychology. Something about this Pavlov man's dogs and how they slobber everywhere."

Bobby reached for her chin and turned her face toward him. He sang, "One day at a time, Sweet Jesus, one day at a time." Hanna's eyes looked so pitiful. "Let's take the speech first. Have you thought of any objects you can talk about?"

"I don't have any objects."

"You have a radio."

"Oh, shoot, Bobby, everybody's got a radio."

Byron said, "It needs to be something you really like."

"Whut?" Hanna pouted.

"I've got it," said Bobby, "your mother's gray sweater."

"Yeh," said Hanna. "I can just see me dragging that old thing in there and telling everybody how it belonged to my big fat mother."

"Hey," said Bobby. "Whoa! You've got a lot more to learn than I realized. What is it? Would you rather Byron and I go out and buy you a silver goblet or something so you can impress a bunch of goddamn high school students? So you can lie?"

"That's not it."

"That sweater and the woman who wore it are both worth a hundred people that wouldn't appreciate them."

It was after Bobby gave Hanna a lecture about honesty and humility that she began to feel even worse.

Byron told them he thought it might be a good idea for Hanna's speech to be less serious and emotional—that she should do something frivolous for her first one. Then after a while they decided a book would be a good object to work with. They decided on the short story anthology that was overdue at the library. The one with "A Rose for Emily."

It took them almost three hours to finally gather up what was about four minutes worth of speech, and it was getting on toward midnight. But Hanna was starting to put the speech together enough to practice it in front of them. She was getting tired, so Bobby suggested she go take a bath and a break while he and Byron looked over the first chapter in her psychology textbook. "But stay out of your room!" he shouted.

It was almost two in the morning before they finally reached a point where Hanna felt she was ready for her psychology test. The speech was another matter. So they set the little clock they borrowed from Georgianna for five-thirty and went to bed. Hanna was given Byron and Bobby's mattress like they had done for the past two nights, and they slept in her room somewhat overjoyed to breathe, besides the fumes of paint, the smells left on the pillows of their main object of affection.

When the clock went off, Hanna rolled over and stopped the alarm, then started to go back to sleep. But Bobby had heard it and was up quickly. He woke Byron then Hanna. He sent her to the bathroom and made her wash her face. Then he filled the tub with water and after making sure she was wide enough awake, left her to take a bath. There were three stale donuts in a week-old package in the refrigerator, so he put two of them in the oven and had them ready when Hanna got out of the bathroom. Byron was not so spry, so Bobby ran him some bathwater, too.

Hanna was not exactly confident when she left for school, but she did promise them she would do her best, and managed a half-smile as she went out the door.

Afterwards, Bobby offered Byron half the remaining donut, but he did not want it, so Bobby ate it, crumbs included. They still had some things to do in Hanna's room, and after talking about the matter over vodka and orange juice, they left the house and were gone half the morning. They spent the other half using the paint they bought and otherwise making the finishing touches. They were so proud of each other, and spent some time just before noon gratifying themselves for what they had done.

And it was Bobby who put into words what both men had been thinking. "This calls for a celebration."

When Hanna opened the door they all jumped out of their hiding places, and yelled, "Surprise!" It was the most absurd sight she had ever seen. The living room was filled with derelicts in party hats, and beneath each hat was a grin—awful rotting and yellowed-teeth grins. And the room was filled with cigarette smoke and the odor of liquor. Earl could hardly stand up. And across the wall was a huge banner that said, "Yea, Hanna!"

Then before she could move, Byron took up the ukulele and Bobby directed the derelicts in a song they had written just for her. They more or less sang it to the tune of "Bicycle Built for Two."

"Hanna, Hanna'
Sweet as a pink bandanna.
She's in scho-ol
Learning just like a fool…"

It was about there that most of the derelicts began to mouth sounds as close as they could remember to the rest of the lyrics, while Byron and Bobby went on with the song.

"…She's got some purty new clothes
And she's got real pretty hair.
She's real sweet
Sitting upon my seat.
And when she's not wearing no clothes.
Hanna, Hanna,
Sweet as a magnolia in Savannah,
Hum Hum Hum Hum
De Dum Da Dee Dee
Come with us and see!"

With that Bobby took her by the hand and led her to her room as Byron flung the door open and switched on the light.

"Oh Lord," said Hanna.

The men had created a relative miracle. First of all, the walls and ceiling were painted a bright clean white, as white as anything imaginable. And in one corner, cattycorner, was a desk. It was not actually a desk but a piece of plywood painted a bright yellow, with cinderblock legs of white. And on the table some books arranged in a row and held together with wine bottle bookends, the mouths of which displayed single yellow flowers. Next to the books was the radio. Next to that was a brand-new paperback dictionary lying beneath the lamp. Before the desk was a straight chair that had been painted bright wine red.

Hanna stepped into the room and then saw her new bed. It had light green cinderblock legs, and the bed itself was covered with a bright yellow nylon blanket. Byron jerked the blanket off the bed to show Hanna what was beneath it, a light green electric blanket, and beneath that was a set of new white sheets. "Mercy!" shouted Earl from the doorway where half a dozen winos had clustered to see what they could see.

"And look, Hanna," said Bobby. "These were my idea." He pointed to the wall behind the bed where two circus posters had been tacked. "Aw," said Hanna. Then Bobby turned her toward another wall where there were more than a dozen cutouts from magazines—young people posing for blue jean and perfume commercials. There was one of a handsome boy and a beautiful girl about to kiss in the rain.

Hanna sat on the side of her new bed and buried her face in her hands. "What are ya'll doing to me?" she moaned.

"That's not everything," said Bobby as he reached under the bed and pulled out a piece of folded cloth. He shook it loose and held a huge beach towel before him. It had a scene of a beach and palm trees in the moonlight. Bobby spread it out at Hanna's feet. "It's a rug for your little cold feet when it gets to be winter. It didn't cost but five dollars. It was on sale."

Hanna's face had a look of both delight and sad frustration.

"Shit, what a rug," said old Fleetwood. "Lord, child don't you step on it. Walk around it. That's too pretty to step on."

"What are ya'll trying to do to me?" Hanna moaned once more.

Bobby laughed. He was so proud of himself and Byron. But Hanna was about to cry. "Hey, girl, you didn't see this." Hanna raised her head and over in another corner were three matching cardboard boxes that had been painted the same wine red as her desk chair. They were arranged like stair steps and inside them were all of Hanna's clothes, folded very neatly. "Look, Hanna. I bet you didn't know these were cardboard boxes. We got them at the grocery store. Tampax came in them." And on the top of one stood a vodka bottle with another yellow flower.

"I wish ya'll hadn't done this," said Hanna. The derelicts had begun to disperse to other parts of the house.

"Oh hell, it wasn't anything," said Bobby in a way that showed that it certainly was.

"Oh, Hanna," said Byron, "how did the speech go?"

"Hanna," said Bobby before she could answer. He cocked his head and grinned his wicked grin. "You can't bring boys in here now. Except me and Byron."

"Bobby," Hanna said.

"Me and Byron will come. But if Byron and I…"

"Bobby," Hanna persisted.

"Do you know what Zorba the Greek said about that, Hanna?"

"Bobby," she said once more.

"If a woman invites you to her bed and you refuse…"

Hanna stomped her foot. "Bobby!" she shouted.

"What?" Bobby shouted back.

"I didn't go to school today, ya'll."

Byron cut his eyes to her and after it occurred to Bobby what she had said he grinned and said, "Girl, have you been out fucking somebody?"

Hanna folded her arms and rolled her eyes, then

pursed her lips and sighed. "I told ya'll not to bother with me. But no, ya'll wouldn't listen. I didn't tell ya'll to fix this fucking room."

"Where have you been?" Bobby wanted to know.

"Nowhere."

"Nowhere, where? Have you been out fucking or what?"

"I've been different places. I mostly just walked around—I don't know. It don't matter."

Nobody said anything for the next several moments, while Hanna stared at the beach towel palm trees. "I got scared, Bobby," she finally said. "I don't belong in that place. Everybody's stuck-up and knows one another. I feel like the janitor, or something, more than I do a student. People have been asking me all kinds of things about myself and I'm tired of lying."

Byron went out of the room.

"Half the students there are rich," Hanna went on. "They all have these nice cars and everything."

"Was it the speech?" asked Bobby.

"That was a lot of it. I just couldn't do it. My legs started to feeling like water or something. And I kept remembering how I'm suppose to be this A student from Georgia that's suppose to know everything." Hanna looked up at Bobby. "I really do like what ya'll done to this room though. It's nice."

The derelicts soon wandered off toward the outdoor living room, and Byron disappeared out the back door.

Bobby sat on the floor and listened to Hanna go on about her problems with the school and said nothing for quite some time. Then later, he went out to look for Byron. Hanna lay on her new bed and stared across the room, wishing she could make everything up to them.

It was almost dark when Byron and Bobby got back. "Hanna, come in here!" Bobby told her from the living room. A minute later she sarcastically pranced in. "Sit," said Bobby. And when she did, he said, "We aren't giving up this easy, girl. Byron and I have decided. Now, whatever it takes, we're going to keep going. Tell her, Byron."

"Hanna," said Byron, "start from the beginning and tell us how you feel."

"I'm not going back," she told them.

"Okay," said Byron. "Okay. It's Friday. You've got two days to think about it."

"I don't give a shit if I have two years, Byron."

"Two whole days," said Bobby.

"Oh, ya'll," said Hanna. "Just forget it."

ELEVEN

They worked all weekend getting Hanna ready for Monday. They told her one story after another about times in their own lives when things had gotten tough. They played the radio and danced and laughed and drank. They practiced a new speech for her, and forced Hanna to stand before them and speak. But no matter what they did, she could not dispel the awful fear she had of standing before her new classmates alone. Then early Sunday afternoon Bobby called Hanna to the living room and told her to lie on the floor.

"Why?" she wanted to know.

"Just do as I say. Lie down."

"Oh, Bobby."

"Goddamnit, lie down."

So Hanna got down on the floor.

"Roll over on your back," he told her.

"Do what?"

"Roll over on your back. Do as I say…Damn it, do it!" Hanna did as she was told. "Now, stick your hands up in the air." Bobby lay on the floor to show her what he meant. "Now stick your legs up the same way." Hanna started to protest, but Bobby persisted and finally she lay on her back with her hands and legs pointed toward the ceiling. "Now, wiggle your arms."

Hanna dropped her hands and legs and sat up. "What?"

"Hanna, I know what I'm doing. Just do as I tell you. Now, lie back down. Lie down!"

So once more Hanna got into the position he showed her. "Now, wiggle your arms."

Very reluctantly Hanna shook her arms about.

"More," said Bobby. "Wiggle them. Wiggle them. Faster!" Hanna started to flail her arms. "That's it. More. More."

"Bobby."

"Wiggle! Now your legs. Wiggle them. Wiggle!"

Again Hanna stopped and rolled over to her side. "Bobby."

"You were starting to get into it, girl."

"Get into what?"

"Just trust me. Please, Hanna. Please. Please."

Hanna started to chuckle for the first time all weekend. And finally she got back into position and continued to wiggle. "I hadn't ever done something so stupid in my life."

"Wiggle. Wiggle!"

Hanna wiggled and flailed and began to giggle.

"That's it. Keep wiggling. Faster. Faster. More.

More. Wiggle."

Hanna started to laugh uncontrollably. "Now," Bobby told her, "say, 'I'm a dying cockroach.'"

Again Hanna stopped and rolled over. "Do what?" she asked.

"You were doing fine, girl. Don't stop. Please don't stop. Quick, get back on your back."

It was his patience with her that finally convinced her to go on with the foolishness.

"That's it. Wiggle. Wiggle. Now, say, 'I'm a dying cockroach.'"

"I can't."

"Yes you can. Say it. Say it."

Hanna started laughing so hard she could not stop. "I'm a dying cockroach," she managed to say.

"I'm a dying cockroach," Bobby repeated. "Say it again. Say it over and over. I'm a dying cockroach, I'm a dying cockroach. Say it."

"I'm a dying cockroach," Hanna began.

"Keep wiggling. Wiggle. Wiggle. I'm a dying cockroach."

"I'm a dying cockroach. I'm a dying fucking cockroach!"

Bobby spent nearly half an hour putting Hanna through an exercise he had experienced in the Marine Corps. He was satisfied when finally she began to scream uncontrollably as she flailed about the floor hysterically in absolute absurdity. Tears were pouring over her face. It was then that Bobby fell over her and began to hug and hold her and kiss her cheeks. "You did it, girl, you did it. See?" After she came back to her senses and calmed down, Bobby explained why he put her through the ordeal. "How do you feel?" he asked her.

Hanna smiled and said, "Weird. I made a fucking fool of myself."

"Great," said Bobby. "That was the point. See, you got outside yourself. You lost your ego."

Hanna was starting to understand. "I did, didn't I? I let go. I honestly let go of everything. I didn't care. I didn't give a shit for nothing. It felt great. Shiiiittttt!" she screamed into her hands. "I'm a fucking dying cockroach. And I don't give a shit about nothing."

"Anything," Byron said from the kitchen.

* * *

Autumn in New Orleans arrives slowly, the grass and leaves are slow to die and the heat of summer does not usually give way to cooler weather until late October or early November. The first cool snap came at the end of October. Bobby and Byron had finished painting the outside of the house, except for the back and about twelve feet of trim on the east side. The derelicts had rolled a new old oil drum to the outdoor living room for nightly fires, and Hanna was doing surprisingly well in school. It was not altogether her work though. Byron and Bobby wrote lots of her papers, and helped out the best they could. This included designing elaborate ways of cheating. Once they wrote vital information concerning a psychology test in the webs between Hanna's fingers. And on another occasion they put some information about the Senate and House of Representatives on the inside of her bra strap. Bobby wanted to write the names of the Supreme Court Justices on one of her breasts, but Hanna said no, and so they put them on the bottom of her shoe, between the heel and sole.

But they all agreed that the cheating was okay only as long as Hanna realized that the end outweighed the means in this particular case, as long as she was growing and grasping the important things, as long as she was moving forward in her education overall. And they would never help her cheat for the sake of taking a cheap way out of something.

And all in all, Hanna was keeping up, often surprising Bobby and Byron with excellence, her superior knack for grasping complex subjects and her uncanny wit. And when she would lose confidence, give up too easily, one or the other would just happen to be sober enough or drunk enough for inspiration or discipline.

It was with the creative writing course and speech that Byron and Bobby had been able to offer the most help. And her teachers in those courses were beginning to take notice of her creative ability. Byron had taught her so much about writing. "The most important thing is honesty, Hanna. If you've got something to say, say it honestly."

It was Hanna's social life that caused the most trouble. She did not have one. Several boys had asked her out, but she had not gone. She was afraid they would find her out. "They think I'm a whore or something," she told the men. "I think it's because of the way I dress." She had met a couple of girls that she hung around with at school, but she had told them little about herself and so far had not felt close enough to either one to confess her secret. She told Bobby and Byron about them, and Bobby wanted to know what they looked like, and if they had big breasts. "They're probably sluts," she told them. "I think that's why I like them."

"Well, stop hanging around with whores, girl," Bobby had said.

The men were so good to her, but Hanna was starting to feel that that was not enough anymore. She was starting to want the companionship of boys, and there was one in particular who drove an old Mercedes Benz who was beginning to cause her some anxiety. She had even gotten to where she would lie awake after she went to bed imagining herself doing things with him.

Hanna daydreamed a lot, and she was starting to believe that it was not altogether impossible that one day she might escape her past. Once or twice she had even fantasized about going to college one day. But she would not let herself carry this idea too far. It was only the kind of stuff Bobby and Byron had put into her head, but in reality she knew the truth. Still, she was starting to actually like school, and her confidence about her ability to learn was even growing.

One morning during early November Byron got out his manuscript and went to Hanna's desk and started writing chapters four and five of his story about Bobby; *Tom Cane*:

There is something strange about agony; the memory of it can be terribly short-lived when the contrast of revival and a pretty spring afternoon have dispelled the regrets. One drink of vodka in a cheerful glass, in the company of good poetry and the scent of blossoms and earth might entice the most well intended to forgo promise of atonement until a worse time. I have at times been just less than amazed how one drink merges with the second, where at some unknown point a mental transformation sets in. I have never been able to ascertain at what point that is—not precisely—and I have been conscious of trying to catch that moment, to try and understand it, to try and prevent it from happening, or at least have a fair chance to decide whether or not to cross over into that other realm. Such an elusive thing, this is.

I was sitting at the back steps of the business school that afternoon, when Tom came from the front. He wore white trousers and sandals and a straw hat, a Key Largo sort of outfit. When he caught sight of me he

stopped in his tracks and grinned with his head bent
nearly to his shoulder. It could have been a grin offered
to a child at play or a woman, or what it was—a grin for
me. He stood with one leg mostly supporting the rest of
him and tipped his glass toward me. "The earth keeps
some vibration going there in your heart, and that is
you..." Now this is the first two lines of an Edgar Lee
Masters poem. It is "Fiddler Jones," from his *Spoon
River Anthology*. Tom recited that poem at the back
steps of that school that afternoon and I would like to
here provide you with the lines for I think it has more
than just a bearing on something I am not altogether
sure of. And as you read it, try to see Tom Cane standing there that spring afternoon with about a twenty
degree slant of his lips and at least several dozen of his
different grins coming and going as he waves, sways,
tips his drink, adjusts his hat, occasionally kicks the
ground and grimaces, and, well...I hope you can see:

> The earth keeps some vibration going
> There in your heart, and that is you.
> And if the people find you can fiddle,
> Why, fiddle you must, for all your life.
> What do you see, a harvest of clover?
> The wind's in the corn; you rub your hands
> For beeves hereafter ready for market;
> Or else you hear the rustle of skirts
> Like the girls when dancing at Little Grove.

To Cooney Potter a pillar of dust
Or whirling leaves meant ruinous drought;
They looked to me like Red-Head Sammy
Stepping it off, to "Toor-a-Loor."
How could I till my forty acres
Not to speak of getting more,
With a medley of horns, bassoons and piccolos
Stirred in my brain by crows and robins
And the creak of a windmill—only these?
And I never started to plow in my life
That some one did not stop in the road
And take me away to a dance or picnic.
I ended up with forty acres;
I ended up with a broken fiddle—
And a broken laugh, and a thousand memories,
And not a single regret.

And when he had finished he laughed loudly and came to sit down beside me, took my cigarette for a single draw, then returned it to my fingers.

"Jess, I'm too old for all this. My chest hurts all the time. When I wake up in the mornings there is a film in my eyes that didn't use to be there. 'I grow old, I shall wear the bottoms of my trousers rolled.'"

"I like your hat," I said.

"I like my hat too. Do you want it?"

"You would give it to me?"

"For ONLY you!"

"Then keep it for now."

He took the hat off his head, "I'll tell you what. It is your hat, anytime you want it. Tell me. And until then..." he carefully adjusted the hat back on his head, "...I'll just wear it. Good enough?" So we shook hands to bond the agreement and he continued to adjust it with the help of an imaginary mirror before him. And I could not help thinking there surely was a mirror there, one that remained before him always.

"Jess, let's close down the school and go someplace."

"We can't do that."

"Sure we can. Watch." He went inside and I could hear him as he moved through the rooms. "Let's go home, men! It's Friday and you should be home with your families or out trying to create one...by the authority I declare I have!" I heard him laugh and then I began to hear the movement of chairs and the shuffling of shoes and soon afterwards the first automobile leaving.

When he returned with a fresh drink, he asked me. "Do you know anything about religion, Jess?"

"Enough to hurt myself I'm afraid."

"The part that bothers me is the adultery part. What does it mean? Does it mean what everybody says it does, or does it mean something else? Does it mean we aren't supposed to take what doesn't belong to us? I can't believe what it says about burning in hell. Do you think that's what it really means?"

"Would it make any difference?"

"Yes! I don't want to hurt. I would do anything to keep from hurting."

"But would you change your ways if you knew for sure?"

I do not think Tom ever had to think long about anything. He already had. He stood up, caressed his chest with his arms, like he was cold. "But I don't want to think about that now. Come, let me take you somewhere."

* * *

Byron sat back, placed his new writing beneath the rest of the incomplete manuscript, yellowed with age, and lit a cigarette. He had written it, rewritten it, and thrown away hundreds of sheets. He never intended the story to be biographical—he only wanted to tell a good story. But somehow, along the way, truth had gotten in his way, and there was something about Bobby Long he always felt needed saying. It had something to do with wanting to explain him to people, wanting them to see what Byron had seen. Bobby Long had certainly abandoned his family for a pretty young woman. No. It was not that way at all. That part was simple. Byron wanted to go beneath all that, to show Bobby as the eternal child he was, who was no more capable of responsibility than a permanent infant. He wanted to tell about Bobby's (Tom Cane's) last terrible encounter with his adolescent son, the night he had so brazenly taken his new young wife to a football game at his high school alma mater. The Eanes spectators, prominent citizens, had seen what they had wanted to see, that Bobby Long had gone way too far this time. The crowd had moved back when the struggle broke out. Bobby had stepped down the bleachers to where his son was sitting to speak to him. They saw a fallen man beating his son for hating him, a disgusting sight, Bobby on top of his son, who struggled to get away from the grip of his too-familiar assailant.

Byron had seen it all, and had tried many times to make it as fictional and dramatic as it surely was, to show the depths of the tragedy, how the boy had struggled to free himself from his father's hold, how they had fallen to the bleachers, Bobby on top, with his arms locked around the boy's neck, trying desperately to whisper what he wanted to say, that he loved him, that it made no difference what else happened, he loved his son, knowing well his son hated him, and not just for leaving home. Bobby was drunk and filled with compassion that night. It was the compassion the crowd could not see. His young wife had tried to discourage him from using that occasion to speak with the child. But Bobby knew nothing about occasions, timing, he only knew what he lived. That was the way he had lived his whole life. To him things were simple. You reached out and took, and if you felt like it, you gave, with intensity you wanted to give with.

Men that night at the stadium had dragged Bobby off his son, and while the crowd was thick enough, hurt him. They beat him badly, broke his jaw that never healed, in the name of justice. Those who did the pounding thought themselves more than justified. And the son managed to get away—forever. Byron wanted to tell of the awfulness of the whole episode, but also the truth. The community never knew how that night had affected Bobby, how he had carried its memory with him ever since. In his writing, Byron had never been able to show what had really happened, what might have been if the whole scene had never taken place. It probably would have made no difference. Sooner or later it certainly would have happened. Those in the community, who had not made up their minds about Bobby, surely did so afterwards.

Then, not two years later, his young wife left him— took their first child by the hand, the other still in her belly, and left in the middle of a night when Bobby was out carousing. They had been living at the university, where the woman eventually got a degree and remarried and forbade Bobby to see his youngest children. Bobby returned to his hometown where he took to drinking and debauching conclusively.

Byron had tried to write about this, too—from tales he was told by those who had watched, along with those things he saw firsthand. By then, Byron was

working on the tugboat, and only returned to the community occasionally—to drink, play poker, occasionally
sleep with an available woman, and to run with Bobby
Long. Bobby had stopped taking baths, most often went
about the town without his shoes, speaking to anyone
who would listen, about anything he wanted to say at
the moment. Often he appeared downright crazy. He
began to gamble with money he did not have, frequent
the worst places in town and, uninvited and unwel-
come, the respectable places. He spent more than one
night in jail, and more than once was beaten up by
shady gamblers. He would beg money unashamedly and
tell his stories too often and too loud. He carried photographs of all his children in his wallet and showed them
to everybody. Byron wished he could have blamed it all
on a war, a broken home during childhood, some terrible handicap, and make the reader of the book he
would probably never finish believe that there was
some good in Bobby. But the truth was more likely that,
his friend, with all his sins and faults, with his unusual
mind—enhanced or diluted with years of alcohol and
too many thoughts—was neither good or bad, just a
conglomeration called Bobby Long. Byron could have
done this, but he had not. And if his society wanted to
believe in some form of justice, Bobby Long got nothing
he did not deserve. Perhaps a considerable segment of
Eanes, Alabama, slept better, their faith in the virtues
of righteousness restored. Perhaps Bobby Long had no

other purpose.

Byron stayed at Hanna's desk all morning, drinking, smoking, and making notes. That he was making little, if any, progress in the story was something he kept to himself.

Byron and Bobby decided one morning just after Hanna got out of school for the Christmas holidays that they were not going to drink for a while—not until at least after Christmas. But it was a cold cloudy day and Hanna had her radio turned on, and the station played "Sleigh Ride." So Bobby got a good tinge of the Christmas spirit. "I got it," he shouted through the house. "Let's all go find a mall and go Christmas shopping! Let's all dress up in our best outfits and go watch the people. Hanna, what did you do with the vodka?"

"You told me to hide it."

"Okay, I did. But where did you hide it?"

"You told me that no matter what, don't let ya'll have it."

"Since when have you paid any attention to what we say?" said Bobby.

Hanna got the vodka.

Bobby wore Byron's navy blue suit without a tie and his cowboy boot and two white socks with a flip-flop. Byron wore wrinkled khakis and a dress shirt with an old herringbone jacket. Hanna put on jeans and a sweatshirt.

"Oh, aren't we pretty," said Bobby as they started to leave.

"Belles of the mall," said Byron.

They walked down to the outdoor living room where Earl and the others were gathered close to a roaring fire that smelled like rubber. "Whoa," said Earl. "You all going to church?"

"Bobby is that a new flip-flop?" old Fleetwood asked.

"We're going to the mall," Bobby said. "Where's the best Sandy Claus mall, Cecil?"

Half a dozen derelicts felt they could lead better than explain.

"Sure," said Byron.

It was Bobby's idea to go by and invite Georgianna to join the party.

They all waited outside Georgianna's apartment while she got dressed. The men passed round a couple of bottles and shivered from the cold. Hanna had a swig of vodka with them.

Georgianna came down her stairway in a long dress the color of her coal-black hair. Hanna only hoped that nobody from her school saw her.

They climbed onto an already full bus. They had to stand in the aisle. Bobby introduced himself to the driver. "I'm Bobby Long, sir. And what's your name?"

"David Poindexter," the driver said.

"Ladies and gentlemen, and little girls and boys. Mr. Poindexter, our bus driver, has given me permission to lead everybody in a Christmas carol. Do all of you know "Deck the Halls"? Why certainly you do."

By the time they reached Carrollton Avenue most of the passengers had joined in. And by the time they reached the mall Bobby had led them in three more songs and was in the process of teaching everybody a song he was making up the words to with the tune of "She'll Be Coming 'Round the Mountain." Even David Poindexter the bus driver sang, but not the little boy who kept looking at Bobby's flip-flop and cowboy boot.

"And I live with him," Hanna told Georgianna as they stepped off the bus.

When the unlikely band entered the mall, Bobby said, "Byron, tell everybody about the time I came to the mall with those crazy people from the hospital."

"You tell it," said Byron once given his cue.

Bobby started to tell his story with little interest from his audience he was losing to the spirit of the mall.

Hanna had already started distancing herself from the party, wandering just far enough away to justify herself. Soon, she and Georgianna were window-shopping while the men looked at the women passing by.

"Happy Christmas," Hanna heard Bobby say to someone, his flip-flop slapping his heel.

They went up an escalator and people continued

to glance in their direction. At the top of the escalator, Bobby stopped the group and pointed to a glass elevator going up to another floor. "Look," he said to them, "you can almost see up that woman's dress."

"Bobby, I swear," Hanna said, having heard him from the distance she kept.

As they walked on, nobody was aware they were leaving old Fleetwood underneath the elevator.

A woman in tight white pants walked by. "Young lady…" Bobby said. The woman never lost her stride.

The seven men still in a pack came to a lingerie shop. "Whoa, shit," said Earl. "Let's buy Hanna some panties," said Byron.

"Don't forget that big woman," one of the derelicts who stayed outside said as Byron, Bobby, Cecil and Earl went inside the store. A middle-aged woman with glasses hung round her neck greeted them. "We want to look at some women's panties," Byron told her. Bobby was wearing his best grin. The woman kept a business expression and led them to a display area. "White," said Byron. "Baby blue," said Bobby as he stepped closer to the woman and whispered loudly, "Do you have any without the crotch. You know, the kind…"

"I know," said the clerk. She very reluctantly led them to a more sleazy section of the store.

"Whoa!" said Earl.

"What size?" the sales lady asked.

"Let's ask this charming lady," said Bobby. He

looked the woman up and down. "What size do you wear?" he asked.

The woman's lip did something strange and ugly before she said, "Maybe if you told me what size dress she wears."

"I don't know," said Bobby taunting the woman with a grin. "One of them is about your size in the hips. Doesn't she have nice hips, Byron?"

"One of them could probably wear yours," Byron told the woman.

"Whoa," said Earl before he and Cecil distanced themselves from their morally inferior companions, and then went to stare at a display of more discreet women's undergarments.

"We don't want to pay too much," Byron said.

The sales lady suggested they try Woolworth's.

After a couple of hours, the unorthodox band got back together, the men red-faced with twinkles in their eyes.

When they got back to Georgianna's apartment it started to rain. "Snow," said Cecil.

All of the derelicts, except for Fleetwood, who took a nap on Georgianna's living room floor, had drifted off toward the outdoor living room to take advantage of the old bright blue tarp one of them had found a while back blown against a fence. Georgianna eventually woke Fleetwood, who thought he was in jail, to send him on his way.

When Bobby, Byron, and Hanna got back to their place, they got blankets and sat on the front porch watching the rain. "I wish it would snow," said Hanna.

"Me, too," said Bobby.

"Me, too," said Byron.

"I wish I had a million dollars," said Hanna.

"Me, too," said Byron.

"Me, too," said Bobby.

Then still later, Hanna said, "I love rain."

"I do too," said Bobby.

"I do too," said Byron.

"I wonder where my children are right now," Bobby said as the rain slowed and it got darker. Nobody said anything in return. "I hope they are warm and dry," he added a minute later.

"Me, too," said Byron.

"Me, too," said Hanna.

*   *   *

Christmas was less than a week away when one morning they drew broom straws to see who was going to wash the clothes. Byron lost and took two grocery sacks over to the washateria. While the clothes washed he sat next to one of the dryers, near the front, and started reading the Gospel according to Luke—the Christmas story—from a Gideon Bible that had been left on one of the chairs. He was just finishing the part about the Wise Men when he looked up and across the street. A well-to-do looking woman was getting out of a station wagon that had a huge Christmas tree stuck out its back. He watched as the woman walked down the street and eventually went inside an antique shop. It took less than a minute for Byron to cross the street, walk past the station wagon, and grab the top of the tree. The next minute he was rounding a corner building headed toward the house.

Hanna happened to glance out a window as Byron came up dragging a tree. "Bobby, I wish you would come look at this."

They opened the front door to help get the tree inside. "Where'd you get this?" Bobby wanted to know.

"We got a Christmas tree," said Hanna.

"It fell off the back of a truck," Byron told them.

"The hell you say," said Bobby.

"Where can we put it?" said Hanna.

"Where did you really get it, Byron?"

"I told you. It fell off a truck."

They spent almost half an hour arguing about where the tree should go. Hanna wanted it in front of a window.

"You put that thing in front of a window, every wino in the neighborhood will be wanting to come have Christmas with us," said Bobby. "Put it here." They finally decided on a place between the front window and door.

"How is it gonna stand up?" Hanna wanted to know. And then she thought of something else. "Byron."

"We need a stand," said Bobby.

"What about a bucket of sand?" said Byron.

"We don't have a bucket, nothing big enough for this thing," said Bobby.

"We could tie a string on the top and hang it from the ceiling," Byron offered

"Byron," said Hanna. When he did not answer, she shouted. "Byron!"

"What?" he finally said.

"Where's our clothes?"

When Hanna got back with their clothes, the men were down on the floor with a stack of some of Byron's old short stories—ones he had intended to throw away anyhow—cutting the sheets into little strips about half an inch wide with a razor blade. "Hanna we've got to use your fingernail polish," said Bobby.

Hanna suddenly noticed the Christmas tree hanging from a string attached to the ceiling, the base some six inches off the floor. "Ya'll," she laughed, "that is the most shit for sense thing I've ever seen."

"Fingernail polish," said Bobby.

Whatcha'll want with my polish?"

"We need some glue," said Bobby.

"What are ya'll doing?"

"Making a paper chain. We need some glue."

"Ya'll aren't gonna use my polish."

"We've got to have something," said Bobby, meticulously slicing the strips of paper.

"Ya'll aren't gonna put it on that tree, are you?"

"And why not? It'll be pretty. We'll lace it all around it."

"The idea," said Byron, "is to not spend any money."

"Yes, and you're gonna have this tree that looks just like you didn't spend any money on it. What about lights?"

"We'll think of something. Right now we have to have some glue."

"A Christmas tree chain," said Hanna.

"Flour," said Bobby. "We could make some paste out of flour and water."

"Except we don't have any flour," said Hanna.

"We could go borrow some from that old lady that gave us the cinder blocks," said Byron.

"We have some Bisquick," said Hanna.

"Hey, yes!" said Bobby. "That'll do."

Hanna made paste with some Bisquick and water, then folded clothes while she watched the men make a chain. Bobby cut the strips and Byron pasted the rings together. Later, Hanna got the radio and found a station that played Christmas music. After she finished the clothes, she helped Byron with the pasting as the chain grew long enough to reach nearly twice around the room.

The next morning Hanna got the men up early. After they had drinks of vodka and orange juice, they were ready to finish decorating the tree. Hanna and Bobby went over to the park between Magazine and St. Charles to pick up pinecones, while Byron went down to Earl's to see if he could get some string. By the time Hanna and Bobby got back, Byron was sitting on the floor with the wine-red paint that had been used to paint Hanna's desk chair, and a spool of thread. It was starting to drizzle outside, and they all agreed it was a fine day for the Christmas spirit. Byron painted pinecones, Bobby tied thread on them, and Hanna hung them on the tree. Then later that afternoon, when they stood back to admire their work, it was Byron who said, "A string of lights wouldn't cost very much." So they went to the drugstore over on Magazine and bought a string of all blue lights. They came back damp from the misty rain and by the time they finished stringing the lights, Byron and Bobby were starting to give out. Neither of them heard Hanna when she said, "I hadn't ever seen a Christmas tree that sways from the bottom." She knew that it would be the next day before they could move it over close enough to the wall to plug in the lights.

Three days before Christmas, Byron got sick. He woke up that morning with a fever and threw up twice before going back to bed. "You alright, boy?" Bobby wanted to know. Byron only nodded his head, closed his eyes, and started to shiver. A half hour later he tried to throw up again, but nothing came. Hanna got the blankets off her bed. Bobby covered him, but still Byron complained about being cold. He shivered and perspired at the same time. "He needs some soup," said Bobby. But Byron was not up to anything, having trouble breathing on top of everything else.

Bobby started to walk all over the house as he rubbed his hands together. "He's really sick," he kept saying. "Do you think we ought to take him to the hospital?"

Then Hanna would say, "I don't know," and they would go back to the bedroom again to see about Byron, who was pale, shivering and trying to swallow. He just kept shivering and trying to swallow. His clothes were wet with sweat.

"Hanna, help me take his clothes off," Bobby told her.

"Bobby," said Hanna.

"Goddamn, girl, get your ass over here and help me. This is no time for you to start that stuff." So they took the covers off, and Hanna did her part to strip Byron of the wet clothes. Afterward, they rolled him over to the floor where once more he tried to vomit and could not. Bobby turned the mattress over and managed to get Byron back on it, then rearranged the covers, putting the wettest on top.

"Bobby, I think I'm dying," Byron told him.

"No you aren't, boy. You'll be alright." But Bobby was not so sure. He started to move about the house again. As the day went on, Byron seemed to get worse. He wouldn't eat or drink anything; his face got hotter, and he would not move for fear of having to go through another attack of nausea. Bobby tried to talk him into going to the hospital, but Byron would only turn his head and blink his eyes. Hanna said she thought his fever was going higher. "Bobby, he needs to be bathed in alcohol or something."

"We don't have any."

"You have vodka. What about that?"

Bobby had to think for a minute. "Will that work?"

"Something to cool him down. I don't know."

"Well, go get it," he told her.

They stripped the covers off Byron once more and Bobby took a drink before Hanna got a towel and soaked it with the liquor. She was no longer concerned with the naked body. And since Bobby was beyond being of much help because of his concern for Byron, Hanna took the towel and washed Byron's entire body. "Keep feeling his head, Bobby. Let me know when it starts getting cooler."

"I need another drink," said Bobby. When he had taken it, he left the room, and Hanna nursed Byron by herself. The vodka rub seemed to be working. His breathing was improving and his entire body was cooler. But Hanna did not stop washing him down. She would wave the towel in the air to cool it, then continue rubbing him. Finally Byron went to sleep. She pulled the covers back over him and fell back to rest herself. Later, she went to see about Bobby who was in the kitchen sitting on the floor beside the stove—crying.

"He's going to die, I know it."

"He's better, Bobby. Honest."

"Nooooo! He's going to die and leave me right by myself. I always knew he would."

Hanna knelt down in front of him. "Bobby, he's gonna be alright." She moved beside him and took his head to lie on her shoulder while she patted the top of it. "He just has the flu or something."

"Noooooo, it's cancer. I know it is. He's going to die and I'll have to go back to the veterans' hospital." Bobby locked his hands around his knees and started to rock himself. "Oh my," he moaned, then started to cry. A bubble of mucus formed at one of his nostrils. Hanna kept his head on her shoulder and lightly patted him on the back. Bobby kept rocking himself as Hanna held him and outside darkness was approaching. In a while Bobby started to whimper. "What is it now?" Hanna asked.

"I just peed on myself."

"Oh, Bobby." Hanna pressed her head closer to his. The kitchen was almost dark. And from the bedroom, the radio played "Santa Claus Is Coming to Town."

* * *

Byron's fever went away sometime during the night, and by morning he was feeling a lot better. He was very weak, but the nausea was gone and he was starting to breathe normally. By afternoon he wanted a cigarette and a drink. Bobby gladly waited on him, while Hanna was gone with the ten-dollar bill she had stolen from Byron's pants pocket.

"See, boy, I told you, you would be alright. You just had the bug or something. Oh hell, I knew you would be alright," Bobby told Byron. "I wasn't worried in the least."

THIRTEEN

Christmas morning Hanna woke up when she heard a knock at the door. It was Byron, with his hair standing on end and his shirttail hanging out beneath his coat. He had a smile on his face and a bottle underneath his arm. "Bobby!" he yelled as he came inside. "Get up. It's Chrissmus! Time to open the presents!"

Bobby rose straight up from the mattress, and in his hoarse voice, started to sing, "Happy Christmas to me, Happy Christmas to me."

When he came into the living room, Byron was crawling around the Christmas tree saying, "I don't believe we have any presents." All three looked at one another. "We forgot Christmas," Bobby said mournfully.

"Well," said Hanna, "I wasn't expecting anything anyway."

"Well, it's a fucking crying shame," said Byron.

Hanna left the room and returned with two brightly wrapped packages. She handed one to Bobby, who gave her his best crooked mouthed grin, the other to Byron. "Aw, you shouldn't have. Bobby, you open yours first," he said.

"No, you."

"No, you."

"Well, shit, one of you!" said Hanna.

"I will," said Bobby. He sat on the floor and tore the package open. Inside a shoebox was a yellow carton of generic brand cigarettes. "Oooooo!" he said, then got up and gave Hanna a big hug. "That's the sweetest thing. And my brand! Look, Byron."

"Now, Byron, it's your turn," said Hanna. He opened his more slowly.

"Hurry up, Byron," said Bobby.

He finally got it open, and inside another shoebox was a fifth of Popov vodka.

"Whoo, damn," said Bobby. It was Byron's turn to give Hanna a hug.

"Ya'll both need a bath," she said.

"Hanna," said Bobby, "if Byron and I go bathe, will you…will you…"

"Nope," said Hanna, "but I'll let ya'll take me out to dinner."

"Oh, child, we can't do that," said Bobby, "we don't have any more money." He looked terribly unhappy.

"I was just joking anyhow," said Hanna. She gave herself a little bounce and went to the kitchen. In spite of herself, she felt hurt that they had not said anything about a present to her. Then while she was running some water in the sink to wash some of the plastic cups that had accumulated, they stepped into the room, and Bobby said, "Hanna, look what Santy Claus brought you." When she turned around they were holding a huge box wrapped very poorly in three different patterns of Christmas paper.

"Well, dog," said Hanna as they sat the box on the floor.

"Open it," said Byron.

"Well, dog," said Hanna again. She knelt on the floor and began to strip the paper away. "Ya'll are the funniest people I know. Who wrapped it?"

"Bobby and I."

"Somebody could use a lesson in wrapping," she said as a knock came at the door. Byron went to see who it was. Earl was standing behind the screen with a grocery sack held in both arms. "Byron, is Hanna here? I brung her something."

"Hanna!" yelled Byron, "it's for you!"

"Just a minute."

"No. Right now. You've got to come right now."

She stopped unwrapping her present, and went to the front door. "Hey, Earl," she said. "You want to come in?"

"No, sugar baby, I just brung you something. I mean, me and some of the boys did." It was not until then Hanna noticed a variety of derelicts standing on the porch and in the yard. She opened the screen and Earl said, "It's heavy," as he passed the sack.

Hanna did not know what to say. Cecil was leaning on a porch post while he looked at his shoes. "Hey, Cecil," said Hanna.

"Mary Christmas," said Cecil.

"Hey, ya'll," she said to the others as she took the package. "Shit, it is heavy. What is it, Earl?" she asked as she stepped out to the porch.

"Turkey," said Fleetwood.

"It's froze," another shouted from the yard.

"Well, goddamn," said Byron.

"Earl, where in the world did you people get a turkey?" Bobby wanted to know.

"This preacher brung it to Cecil," said Earl proudly. "And we giving it to this sweet baby for her Christmas present."

"Well goddamn," said Byron, "we'll just cook that son of a bitch."

Bobby stepped out to the porch grinning. "Okay, now. Everybody go get dressed up, everybody has to wear a tie. Nip, you got a tie anywhere?"

"Albert does," said one of the derelicts. "I got one over at the mission," said another.

"Well," said Bobby. "Byron and I will loan one to anybody that doesn't have one."

"Bobby," said Earl, "Me and Cecil already got on ours best clothes, 'cept'n a tie."

"Well alright then!" said Bobby. "Everybody just come on in. Byron and I will supply the ties."

"I'm gone get mine," said Albert.

Hanna took the turkey to the kitchen.

"Girl, you have to finish opening your present," said Byron. Several of the derelicts were looking round to see if there was any conspicuous liquor anywhere. Earl and Cecil were in the kitchen as Hanna finished unwrapping the box. "Oh Lord!" she said as she took out a heavy white cotton sweater, and held it to her chest before withdrawing a dark brown wool skirt. "Oh, Lord." Then there was the jeans, another sweater, another skirt, shirts, socks, four new pairs of panties, "And Mickey Mouse," she joyfully whined about one.

"Bless his heart," said Bobby before Hanna pulled out a heavy, long herringbone item, prompting old Fleetwood to say, "Somebody got them a blanket," referring to a long overcoat that Hanna had to try on. "There's one more thing," Byron said, so she looked inside the box and took out a dark brown beret. When she tilted it atop her head, Cecil said, "Whoa!"

"Ya'll," said Hanna as she reached to hug Bobby and Byron together.

"Now, can we have some pussy?" said Bobby.

"No, but ya'll can kiss me, if you don't put your tongue in my mouth."

"Then I don't want to," said Bobby before giving her a quick smack on the lips after Byron gave her a quick soft kiss.

After dragging the box into her room and closing

the door, Byron and Bobby made drinks and talked about cooking the turkey. "We have to have some cranberry sauce," Bobby was saying.

"And dressing," said Cecil.

"Do you know how to make dressing, Cecil?"

"Naw. My grammaw did though—'cept she's dead."

By mid-afternoon, in the process of inebriation, having made canned sweet potatoes, rice, and green beans, it was time to carve the turkey, still frozen beneath a golden brown breast.

* * *

The day Hanna went back to school Bobby got depressed and spent all morning talking about his children, the ones from his first marriage mostly.

"I was a good father," he told Byron.

"I know," said Byron.

"I taught them about life."

"I know you did."

"One day I'm going to make it up to them, Byron. When you get your book published and we start getting famous—when you win the Pulitzer Prize—the first thing I'm going to do is see about my children. To hell with their mother. Oh, by the way, did I tell you I called her last week?"

"No. What was it like?"

"She hung up the phone. Milton is staying with her

now. He's going to be just like her. I called back and said, 'Carolyn, why did you hang up on me?' You know what she did? She said, 'Because you are a son-of-a-bitch.' How would she know whether or not I was still a son-of-a-bitch?"

"You still are, Bobby."

"I was a good father, though."

"I know."

"Carolyn ruined my children."

"You ruined them."

"I?"

"Oh, hell, Bobby, let's don't get into this."

"You always say I ruined them."

"I don't mean you ruined them. You just weren't there."

"I was there when he was young."

"They were young."

"I taught them things."

"I'm not blaming you. It was just the circumstances. You just never should have been a father."

"I was a good father." Bobby's lips turned crooked and started to quiver.

"You were a kid, Bobby. You've always been a kid."

"So are you."

"Not as much as you."

"You're an alcoholic, too."

"I didn't abandon my children."

"I don't want to talk about it," said Bobby.

Byron went to the kitchen. When he got back, Bobby was sitting in front of the heater with a blanket over his shoulders. "When are you going to finish your book?"

"When you die."

"What if you die first?"

"I can't finish it while I'm so fucking close to you. It's too much like journalism when I'm with you everyday."

"Do you want me to leave?"

"Would you?" Byron said.

"Fucking A. And you would miss the hell out of me."

"Yeh, you're probably right."

"I'm probably going to die soon anyway. I just wanted to do something to make my children proud of me first."

"You can start by fixing me a drink."

A week after school started back, Hanna came in one afternoon and said her semester exams would start in two weeks. "I'll never learn all that stuff," she complained. The next afternoon, she started talking about quitting and going back to Florida.

"Get out the violin and play something sad for Hanna," said Byron.

"Well, ya'll aren't gonna help me anymore. All ya'll do is hang around that stupid place with Earl and them."

"We'll help when the time comes," said Byron. "All you have to do is get yourself organized. That's one of your biggest problems, Hanna, you are so unorganized."

"I don't know how to organize."

"Well, you need to learn."

"Then teach me."

"You procrastinate, too."

"What's that?"

"Drag your ass."

"High school is so dumb. I wouldn't mind it if it watn't for government and psychology. Who in the world needs to know that mess?"

"That's not the point," said Byron. "You are trying to get from point A to point B. And government and psychology have to be gone through in order to get there."

"But it's stupid."

"That has nothing to do with it. Do you want to graduate or not?"

"I guess."

"Then stop talking about things you can't change. Just get to point B."

The week before the exams, the place took on an air of bedlam. Papers, books and charts were strewn all over the house. Byron had tacked charts to the walls, dividing information into subjects and categories. They made more trips to the library than they did to the liquor stores. By midweek, mostly Byron had turned the house into a well-organized set of textbooks. The living room was set up for government, Hanna's room for psychology, the men's room for speech and creative writing, the kitchen was the dictionary and thesaurus.

Byron bought a different color marker for each subject, underlining and double underlining most significant facts and information. Hanna was learning as much about organizing as she was about the material Byron felt would most likely be on her tests. Bobby would occasionally relieve Byron of drumming information into what Hanna called her busting head. Everything was done on schedule. She had never seen them so difficult, often wishing they would go away and get drunk so she could rest, not that they did not continue to drink while they worked. "Ya'll are plotting against me," Hanna would say, starting to believe that even if she had gotten naked in front of them it would not have mattered. And what was worse, since they were so determined, she could only feel guilty for her resentment. It had been easy to complain when they were negligent. And whenever she talked about cheating, saying that something was too difficult to waste time with, and why didn't they just make up some cheat sheets, they came down on her so ferociously it was better to continue with the drudgery, fluctuating between anger and admiration for their disgusting intelligence. "Ya'll could win the fucking Academy Award for shitheadedness," she once told them.

"You'd just better be glad it's January and there's not a damn thing else for me to do," said Byron. "Otherwise, I'd be doing it. You're the laziest goddamn girl I've ever seen. You should be back in Florida. You're low class and you're always going to be."

"Well, stop bitching and help me!" Hanna screamed.

"I'm going over to Nick's," said Bobby.

"Oh hell no you aren't," said Byron. "If I'm going to help, so are you."

"Ya'll don't have to, you know," said Hanna. "I got along before I got fucked up with ya'll."

"On your back, maybe," said Byron. "You want to go back to fucking your way through life?"

"If I have to," said Hanna.

Byron almost slapped her.

They stayed up past midnight making last-minute cheat sheets. This went on all weekend. Monday morning, with the equivalent of a long short story printed on various parts of her body and clothing, Hanna left for school without eating breakfast. By Friday Hanna looked like she had had the worse of a head-on collision. But the day of reckoning had arrived and she left the house after the men made her eggs, juice, and toast for breakfast, while adding more to her anxiety with last-minute instructions.

On her way to her psychology class her friend Dede appeared. "I'm gonna flunk the living shit out of this thing," she told Hanna.

"You," said Hanna.

When she had finished the day and returned to the house, Bobby and Byron were waiting on the porch. "Byron, look at our little ace," Bobby said as Hanna came up the steps. "'Ace' my fucking ass," said Hanna as if she was returning from a marathon lost.

"Did you get your scores already?" Bobby asked.

"No."

"Well, girl, why so down?"

"That fucking shit was hard, ya'll."

"Great," said Byron. "You did well. I know you did."

Hanna trudged up the steps, stopped, and looked at Byron. "And what the shit makes you so sure?"

Byron put his finger to her sullen lips. "Because you had great teachers, Miss Shit for Sense."

Hanna looked at him cross-eyed. "Give me a fucking beer."

Hanna moped all weekend, stayed in her room mostly, coming out only to eat or several times for a beer. It was her time to make the men miserable for a change. Bobby and Byron drank no less than usual, and left for the outdoor living room when Hanna's wrath forced them out of her way. Hanna hated them for not coming into her room and consoling her. She wanted their arms round her. She needed babying.

She spent most of Sunday afternoon staring at the ceiling from her bed, teary-eyed, imagining the worst, not that she had failed, that she had not done well enough to please the only people in her life were starting to matter to her, more than anybody ever had, and she was going to shatter their opinion of her. She wanted to hate them for what they had done to her, the fucking bastards. No matter how she tried, she could not stop wanting them to be proud of their...their...little pussy. Late in the afternoon she sat up, painted her toenails, still fearful of thinking the best, that she had done well, that if she had, how they would pretend like they knew all along, ignoring her, acting like it meant nothing to them, returning to being the assholes they were. That Sunday was the longest day of Hanna's young life.

When Monday finally came, she tried to delay with no success. Bathing faster than she ever had, barely fixing her face, going without breakfast, she headed for the bus stop. Only one of her teachers had finished his grades—creative writing. She had made an A for the semester. That was fine, but she had felt more confident about that one than all the others. So, she dragged herself back to the house that afternoon still in the dark about her other courses. What was worse, the men were anticipating far too much. Their disappointment showed. That night was awful. They were all cranky with one another, Bobby started talking about going away for a while, and Byron went out for the night.

Then Tuesday came, the men played gin rummy and drank all day. By mid-afternoon, they were so drunk that, had they done what they were about to do—pass out—they would have missed Hanna dragging through the door with the most solemn look they had ever seen her have. Not even the day she ran away from the hotel and they found her in the bus terminal had she looked so awful. Byron was so drunk that when he looked at her he started straight for the mattress. Bobby looked at her with as much pity as he could show under the circumstances. Then, as he was about to get up from the floor, Hanna threw up her hands and screamed, "I made all mother fucking A's, you shit-for-sense cute little assholes! Except for a B in P.E. Now, hit me with one of ya'll fucking excuses for a screwdriver."

FOURTEEN

"O kay, fine," said Byron, "but the little pussy won't give us as much as a goddamn look at her ass." Bobby tried every way he could think of to get her to at least talk about her fantasies, about the boys she met, the one who drove the old Mercedes Benz, about the things she thought about in bed.

Byron used more subtle approaches; he tried to win her over with gentleness and conniving. He would touch her every chance he got, but under the pretense of fatherliness, and brotherly concern.

"The bitch is frigid is all I can see," Bobby told Byron. "I'm ready to kick that tight little ass out of here. If it wasn't out of the goodness of my heart, I would've already said to hell with it. She's getting a goddamn education and we're beginning to act like fucking decent people. It's fucking disgusting. Look at me, Byron; she's got me to cursing worse than her. If it wasn't winter, I would kick her cocky voluptuous ass out the door." Bobby looked at Byron. "What the fuck are you laughing about, you shit-for-sense asshole?"

"Watching you kick her out the door."

"Well, hell," said Bobby as he started to grin. "I wouldn't kick a fucking boy dog out in this freezing fucking weather."

"I have never heard such language from a college professor," said Byron.

"Well, have you ever seen a little wench getting lunch money while a professor has to start drinking grocery store wine and smoking Prince Albert?"

"When have you every smoked Prince Albert?"

"Fuck you, Burns," said Bobby. "And while we're at it, you bought her some new panties, didn't you."

New Orleans was having an unusual cold spell. The house stayed cold. The outdoor living room had been abandoned for the missions; Bobby and Byron spent too much time by the only heater with blankets while Hanna was starting to act too much like a scholar to suit them. The gloomy weather was taking its toll on the men's horniness and moods. Once they did go over to Georgianna's apartment, releasing some of their anxieties. Talking and listening to weather reports, along with gin rummy and optimism that came from the belief that nothing can last forever, kept the men from choking their little pussy. "Fuck the kitchen. Clean it yourself," Bobby would tell Hanna. "Byron and I got along fine without a goddamn kitchen."

Then one night, just before the weather started to improve, something happened that Byron and Bobby would not have expected if heaven and not hell had accepted their unwarranted, inebriated little souls.

It was a very cold night; the temperature had dropped down to eighteen degrees, denying the space heater all but its useless blue light. Bobby and Byron had gone to bed on their mattresses and were bundled trying to swipe the heat from each other's bodies. Then, before midnight, they both seemed to be having the same dream, a dream that often afterwards still seemed a dream. In it, somebody was nudging them apart, Someone, this teenaged girl was crawling into bed with them, beneath their covers, snuggling between them, oozing the fragrances that could only occur in a dream in the lives of two of life's fallen misfits. Later, when they would relive this…dream, one aspect would be different, Byron would recall a magnificent ass tucked close to his middle, while Bobby remembered two voluptuous breasts warming his face. Little did either know that as they dreamed, not daring to believe they could be awake, the little pussy slept the rest of that night like a warm piece of toast.

* * *

The men survived the rest of the winter on the dream of that possible night.

They never mentioned that night to Hanna and she never said anything about it. But for several days afterwards, while she was gone to school, they would bundle themselves next to the heater and attempt to convince each other that dreams may occasionally come true, reliving the most minute details of the night they spent with the object of their affection. By the third day they were embellishing wildly. "I swear, Byron, at one time I had my knee right up against it."

"Did she move it?" Byron wanted it to be a lie, he believed it was, but men never know with one another the truth of such matters.

"Not only did she not move it, at one time I honestly felt her wiggle so that I could get it closer."

"That's nothing, I felt her…"

"Yes, but I wish you could have felt…"

"Bobby, once she…"

New drinks of vodka and juice, along with such talk, would have gotten them through the winter without the news Hanna brought one day from school. "He asked me to the Valentine's dance." The men could feel something like a bubble bursting.

"Who?"

"That boy with the old Mercedes. But I'm not going," she told them on the way to her room.

The bubble had only shrunk, but for the next several nights all Hanna talked about was the boy and the party. She bounced back and forth. "I don't have anything to wear anyway. Besides, I wouldn't know how to act. Miss Hand-me-down escorted by Mercedes Mike."

The men neither encouraged nor discouraged her, both reminded of the inevitable, that sooner or later she would leave them, for some young man who promised things they could not offer her.

"I don't want to hear any more about it," Byron told her. "If you're going, go! But stop this damn moaning. Have you done your democracy report yet?"

"It's not due till next Tuesday."

"Well, do something. Go paint your fucking toenails."

Hanna almost laughed. "Ya'll don't want me to go, do you."

"That's not true," Byron told her.

"Ya'll just want me to stay here, right under ya'lls nose, like ya'll own me. That's it, isn't it? Ever since I first mentioned it, ya'll have been acting funny. I get somebody besides ya'll interested in me and ya'll can't stand it."

Byron got up from where he sat and put his coat on. "Where you going?" Hanna wanted to know, but he said nothing as he went out the door.

"Now look what you've done. You hurt his feelings."

"Oh, Bobby, sometimes I don't know whether to believe ya'll or not."

Bobby went back to reading after she stormed back to her room and shut the door.

Byron was gone for nearly three hours. When he returned, he was damp from the light rain that had just started to fall.

"Where have you been?" Bobby wanted to know.

"Out."

"Have you been over to Georgianna's again, Byron?"

Byron turned his back to the heater. "Bobby, I've got an idea."

"Did you fuck her?"

"I want you to get your coat and come go with me."

"Now you want me to go with you. After you've finished, you call me. Well, it won't work, Mister. I'm not going to take your hand-me-downs. You could have at least invited me along."

Byron went to the kitchen and made himself a drink, then returned to the living room. "Come on, I want to show you something."

"No, it's raining."

"And when has a little rain ever hurt Captain Long? Come on." Byron got Bobby's coat and stood before him with it open. "Come on."

As they walked across Magazine, the misty rain beneath streetlights seemed to float instead of fall. On toward St. Charles, the mist reminded Bobby of something. "Byron, do you remember that time we crawled down that drain ditch to meet this girl, behind that convent?"

"Uh huh," Byron said.

"Remember, we crawled on our bellies past the window where we thought those nuns were sleeping."

"Uh huh."

"Where the hell are we going?" Bobby wanted to know when they reached St. Charles.

"We'll be there soon."

"Soon. Byron, what the fuck does 'soon' mean to you?"

They walked several more blocks before Byron stopped and said, "Look over there."

"Where?"

"Over there. That house across the street."

"What about it?"

"See the way those stairs go up?"

Bobby could barely make out two sets of stairs on a huge front porch. The house was one of the old magnificent St. Charles Avenue mansions, and the stairs Byron meant ascended from both sides of a grand set of front doors, up to a second-story porch that was just as elaborate as the first-story porch. There was only one light on in the house, and it came from a lamp inside one of the great rooms on the lower level. "What about them?" asked Bobby.

Byron lit a cigarette. "When I left the house earlier I was walking around, and I got this idea. I'll bet you some old matriarch lives in that house alone. And I would bet you she doesn't hear very well."

"What do you want to do, Byron, rob her?"

"That may not be the best house, but there's only one way to find out."

"Right," said Bobby, "and there's a bed for you on the third floor of the veterans' hospital, too."

"We're just going to have to watch and see. Do you want to do it together, or in shifts?"

"What the fuck are you talking about? What shifts? Byron do you know it's raining and you dragged me over here to stand in the rain. Did you say shifts or shift?" Bobby chuckled. "Okay, look, here, I'm shifting. Why don't we shift the fuck out of here? I would swear that's water running down my neck."

On the way back to the house, Byron explained the whole thing to Bobby. Bobby's sense of adventure set in and he was starting to like Byron's plot. It would be something to do, and Bobby was the first to admit that things surely had gotten boring lately. "But I'm not going over there by myself."

"We've got to make sure that's the right house," said Byron.

About the same time the next three nights, the men would leave the house, returning a couple of hours later. Hanna could not imagine what was going on, but still indecisive about the Valentine's dance and having homework, she paid them little attention. And they gave her little attention until the third night. After returning, Bobby asked her if she had decided to go to the dance.

"I'm not going."

"I think you should," he told her.

"I do too," said Byron.

"Ya'll don't mean it."

"We're not going to get down on our knees and beg you, if that's what you mean," said Bobby. "If you want to, go."

"That's easy for ya'll to say. I can just see Michael stopping out front of this place. He would probably leave a donation on the doorstep and leave."

"And I would bet you the next thing you're going to say is you have nothing to wear," said Byron.

"Well?"

"Have you ever asked what the others will be wearing?"

"It's a pretty big deal, I know that."

"Formal?" asked Byron.

"I think so."

"Well, goddamn, find out."

"Oh, Lord, Byron, even if it is…"

"This child-rearing shit is costly," said Bobby as he left the room for a new drink.

"I know," said Hanna with a smirk. "We could always go to a junk store and find a nice 1949 evening dress."

"We could damn well try."

"Oh, Byron."

"You get the date, we'll take care of the rest."

"Yeh," said Hanna, then mocking Byron, "Trust me. Just trust me, little girl."

* * *

But the night of the big dance Hanna had a dress, a long slender black dress with thin shoulder straps, and black high heels. "Whoa, shit," said Byron when she came out of her room. Bobby presented her with his best crooked grin, "Hell, no, you aren't going anywhere looking like that. That boy is going to rape the fuck out of you, woman."

"Damn, girl, you look like a princess," said Byron.

Hanna was not so sure. She was scared. "It is a beautiful dress, ya'll. Do you think…"

"Hell yes," said Byron, "if he doesn't, he's got to be blind. And we know that's not true, 'cause he chose the sexiest fucking thing in school to be his date."

"Ya'll sure?"

"Turn around," said Bobby. "Byron was hoping you weren't able to zip it up by yourself."

"It wasn't all that hard."

"Well, you just make sure it stays zipped up, woman," said Bobby.

Hanna presented them as much of a curtsy the dress would allow.

"Now, you'd better finish getting your pretty… black ass ready. Look at that ass, Bobby."

"I wish ya'll would tell me what ya'll got planned. I can't take any more of this. I'm scared to death. Are ya'll sure ya'll—"

"Stop. Just get ready, we'll handle the rest."

"Trust me, trust me," Hanna said as gruffly as she could on her way back into her room.

On the way out the door, Byron said, "Now are you sure you told Mercedes what we told you?"

"Does anybody have change for the telephone?" Hanna wanted to know.

They stopped at a corner phone booth and Hanna stepped inside and made the call to Michael. All she was supposed to tell him was there had been a change in where he was to pick her up, her uncle was supposed to have gone someplace and she was staying with her aunt on St. Charles, and the address.

"All right, now what?" she said after hanging up the phone.

Walking fast made her feet hurt so she stopped to take off the high heels. Along the way Hanna kept asking them to explain things to her, but they would only tell her to walk faster.

It was not until they stood in front of the St. Charles mansion that they began to explain the plan.

"Ya'll are fucking crazy if you think…"

"Shut up and listen," said Bobby.

"I'm going back," said Hanna as she started to leave.

Bobby grabbed her by the arm. "Girl, stop this shit and listen. We don't have much time."

"Ya'll are fucking crazier than I thought," said

Hanna trying to release herself from Bobby's grip, as he pulled her toward the walkway leading up to the house.

"Ya'll."

"Shut your fucking mouth," Bobby whispered loudly.

"Be quiet," whispered Byron.

Hanna wrenched away from Bobby's grip but Byron was there to keep her from getting away. Hanna gave up. "Shit," she whispered.

As on the three nights they had stood across the street, the place was dark except for the one lamplight inside the lower floor. "If I go to jail..." Hanna whispered as they reached the steps leading up to the double beveled-glass doors that sparkled from the lamplight within. "Ya'll," she whispered once more as they let go of her arms.

"Hanna, remember," Byron whispered, "don't come down the stairs until he starts up the steps. Go halfway up the stairs and wait."

They watched her until she reached the stairs, then stepped behind thick shrubbery next to the house and stooped down. Bobby took out a half-pint bottle of vodka and they passed it back and forth to calm their nerves as they waited.

They watched through the shrubbery as cars passed along the avenue. Then one stopped and parked out front of the mansion. "Is it a Mercedes?" Bobby whispered.

"It damn well better be," Byron, holding back a giggle, whispered.

A figure started up the walkway, soon revealing a man dressed in a tuxedo and carrying flowers.

"Goddamn, Hanna, get it right," Byron whispered.

The young man passed within several feet of where Bobby and Byron were crouched as he started up the steps. Suddenly, they heard Hanna say, "Michael?" louder than she should have.

"Hanna?" said the boy.

"Shhhhh," Hanna whispered loudly.

"Is that you?" the boy whispered.

As she came closer, Hanna whispered an explanation for being quiet, that her aunt was sick and had gone to bed early. Bobby squeezed Byron's leg as the couple came down the steps, as the boy whispered. "You look great."

They waited until the second car door slammed before sneaking away. The final stage of the plan was to return at midnight to walk Hanna back.

Back at the house, Byron made a drink and ate a bologna sandwich. On his way back to the living room, he discovered Bobby in Hanna's room sitting on the floor with a pair of her panties in his lap. Bobby grinned, then put the panties to his face. "Byron, do you know where these have been?"

"Yes," said Byron with his mouth full. "In no-man's land."

Bobby held the panties up for Byron to see them. The elastic was stretched and they were coming apart at the waist. "Do you realize that these sad little things have caressed the most beautiful ass in New Orleans, Louisiana? Byron, I had no idea just how gorgeous she really was until tonight. Did you see that ass against that black dress?"

Byron sat on the floor beside him. "Let me hold them."

Bobby took another pair of panties from a shelf, spread them before him, then sniffed. Suddenly he said, "Byron, do you notice something interesting?"

"What?"

"How many pairs of panties does she have?"

The same thing occurred to Byron. "She's not wearing any underwear. No, wait," said Byron. "She had three, we bought her five more. Eight."

But Bobby was ahead of him. "And what do you think this is?" he said as he withdrew six more pair from the box. "Look how clean they are."

"I know. I know. But why do you think she went without any?"

"There could only be two reasons, and I hope one of them doesn't count. Either she's conserving them, or…"

"Or she's going to get fucked."

"Don't say that word, Bobby!"

"And after all we've done for the little bitch."

Bobby left Byron on the floor to study the matter and went to the bathroom. Byron picked up a bra and held it open as he tried to imagine Hanna's breasts inside the thing.

"Byron!" Bobby shouted from the bathroom. Byron jumped up and ran to him. When Bobby turned around he was holding his penis in his hand. He looked scared. "I just pissed blood."

"Oh no," said Byron.

"What does that mean?"

"I don't know."

"Cancer?"

"Oh hell no. It's probably…"

"Probably what? It's cancer."

"Now, don't start imagining the worst, Bobby. It could be anything. You probably have an ulcer."

"An ulcer? Goddamn!"

Byron went over to the toilet to see the water. It was dark red. "God!" he said.

"What?"

"You didn't eat anything red, did you?"

"No. Would that do it?"

"I doubt it," said Byron, "You just peed blood. Do you want me to take you to the hospital?"

"No," said Bobby, zipping his pants. Byron followed him to the living room where they spent the next hour considering all the possible disorders bad living habits might cause. "Let's don't talk about it anymore. Hell, I'm just going to die."

"Why don't you go see if you can pee again?"

"I'm afraid to."

Byron laughed.

"What's so funny?"

"Bobby, you've got to pee—sometime."

"I'll just wait 'til tomorrow."

"Go piss. Right now! Hell, just see."

Byron followed him, stood beside him as he tried to urinate but could not. "What's the matter?"

Bobby whined, with a mournful chuckle. "I can't while you're watching."

"Goddamn, Bobby, I've seen you piss a thousand times."

"Yes, but all of a sudden I'm shy." They both started to laugh, but Bobby did so with tears in his eyes. So Byron left him alone.

Returning to the living room, Bobby tried to grin. "It was white this time."

"Like hell it was. Bobby, don't lie to me."

"It was just a little pink. It was probably something I ate."

"When have you eaten anything?"

It was nearing midnight when the men sat on a bench for streetcar passengers close enough to the mansion to watch for Hanna.

***

"Do you feel alright?" Byron asked.

"I'm fine."

They sat in silence for some time, then Bobby spoke again. "Byron."

"What?"

"She's not going to ever give us any pussy."

"Do you think he knows by now she's not wearing any panties?"

"I don't want to think about it."

FIFTEEN

S aturday morning, Hanna woke to reflections of the party and Michael. The party went well; she had been a hit in her black dress and as far as she knew, she made no unintended revelations about herself. Michael had been nice enough, but she doubted if she would go out with him again, not soon, certainly. She had made so much more of him than was there. Somehow, living with Byron and Bobby had ruined her where adolescent boys were concerned. The ones she had met at school had all seemed too—too something. Even if her classmates thought she was okay, even cool, maybe, she did not feel like one of them, not having had a childhood like she imagined most of them did, not having two parents, even one, with brothers and sisters, a house to be proud of, routine, rules, discipline. Hanna had never had a bathroom of her own.

Byron and Bobby had told her she was calloused. She was not. If anything she was too sensitive, too insightful, too aware. Until those two men came into her life she was aware of so little. Living with Byron and Bobby for one year had seemed like a lifetime. They had exposed her to so much. It wasn't that she was all that innocent or stupid when she came to them—she certainly was not, but the world they had presented her with was more than any seventeen-year-old would have been ready for. She was not sure how much had been, according to her psychology book, negative influence. But Hanna was starting to realize how much she was capable of seeing things that, to quote her reluctant masters, "remain out of sight." And things were not necessarily good or bad, but only different. Like, pretty things and ugly things could be found in the same places. And what lots of people called pretty was not necessarily so, nor were ugly things really ugly if you had the ability to look closely. Right and wrong for Hanna were becoming more and more relative.

If it had not been for Bobby and Byron, she would probably have never read Lilith, or listened to Glenn Miller music, or known who D.H. Lawrence was. She surely would never have heard of Brownie McGee and Blind Willie McTell, not to mention Carson McCullers, Flannery O'Connor, or Edward Hopper. She would have never known the words to "Barbara Allen" and "Streets of Laredo" and the others. Here she was, not eighteen yet, and had already read, or had read to her, practically all of Tennessee Williams's plays. What seventeen-year-old could say that? Oh, some she had not understood very much, some she didn't even like, but they had explained them to her until she was nearly purple in the face. They were crazy all right—no doubt about it—but it was starting to look like some of their insanity was rubbing off on her. That was why Michael had seemed so boring, with his talk about nothing that had feeling about it. Hanna just wasn't used to people who did not show their feelings. That certainly could not be said about Byron Burns and Bobby Long—living with them meant not being dishonest or hiding, certainly not for very long. Those two would find out the truth sooner or later—sooner or later they would. Even with their brains soaked all the way to the bone with alcohol they could see right through anybody. It had been they who explained to her about the woman thing and moods—how honest could anybody get? Hanna could not help laughing to herself when she recalled the time they had sat her down and explained why she got so cranky around period time. She had never even thought of such a thing before. And the time Byron bought her tampons, just before she had started.

Snuggling with her pillow, she tried to think of Michael and the party, but it was Byron and Bobby that kept interfering, their thoughts, words, and God forbid, even their mannerisms were getting mixed up with her own. Her English was improving. She had even considered not saying "ya'll," but she knew they would accuse her of being pretentious, dishonest, attempting to put on airs. The assholes.

Hanna got out of bed and went to the kitchen. "I

got a idee of my own," she mumbled to herself as she put a skillet on the stove. She would make them breakfast in bed—in mattress. Hanna fried some bologna and eggs, then took it to them. Bobby was halfway off the mattress, one naked leg stretched out on the floor. When she woke them, Bobby's other leg came from underneath the cover, exposing his black panties. "Ya'll want some breakfast?"

Byron sat straight up like a corpse that would not stay put.

Hanna handed them plates of food and two barely orange screwdrivers.

"My my," said Byron hoarsely.

"Fried bologna," said Bobby. Hanna sat down on the floor and watched them eat.

"Lord, ya'll should of seen what they had to eat at that party last night," said Hanna.

"You didn't eat with your fingers?" said Bobby.

"No. I ate with a solid silver fork. The thing weighed a pound."

"Well, what we should do is send you out once a week and let you steal us some silver. You didn't steal a fork, did you, girl?"

Hanna laughed. "I thought about it, I swear I did."

The men ate heartily.

"Ya'll, let me ask ya'll something." Hanna said momentarily. "Ya'll both came from rich families, didn't ya'll?"

"No, not rich," said Bobby.

"But well-off, huh?"

Bobby spoke with his mouth full. "I guess you could say that."

"Then, when ya'll were young, ya'll probably learned a lot about manners and how to act, didn't ya'll?"

"Bobby didn't," mumbled Byron. "Look at him eat."

"I've watched ya'll in places. Even when ya'll are so drunk you can hardly stand up, ya'll still eat different from most people I know. It's like it comes natural. I bet when ya'll was young ya'll ate every one of ya'll's meals at a table, with nice plates and all."

Byron stared into space. "Sometimes I think I miss that, too."

"And I'll bet ya'll owned tuxedoes, too."

"Oh, yes," said Bobby.

"And when ya'll went somewhere with a girl, ya'll opened the car door and stuff like that, too."

"Oh, yes," said Bobby. "I noticed Michael opened the door for you last night."

"I know," said Hanna. "It felt good, too. Ya'll, I want to learn how to act."

"Well, the first thing you do," said Bobby, picking up a slice of bologna with his fingers, "is show Byron and me your titties."

"Ya'll could teach me."

"She didn't even hear me, Byron. She's going to be

just like her mother." Suddenly Bobby remembered something. "Oh, oh. Hanna." He looked at her with his wicked, crooked-mouthed grin. "What were you wearing under your dress last night?"

Hanna started to blush. "What do you mean?"

"You know what I mean."

"What?"

"Tell her, Byron."

"You didn't wear anything."

Hanna felt her face warm. "How would ya'll know if I did or didn't?"

"We saw you," said Bobby.

"Ya'll did not."

"We did."

"How?" asked Hanna, embarrassed.

"We have ways. We watched you dressing from outside. We peeked through the window."

"No you didn't."

"Yes we did."

"No you didn't. 'Cause I checked that window. Couldn't anybody see in that window."

"Well," said Bobby, "you're talking like we're right. You didn't wear any underwear, did you?"

Hanna was getting angry. "Well, I might and I might not. What's it to you?"

"You didn't."

"How do ya'll know? There's no way on earth ya'll could know something like that."

"Did you do it for that boy?"

"I didn't do it for nobody." Hanna's defenses were blown.

"Hanna, did you let that boy…"

"No, you fucking shitheads."

"Then, why?"

"Ya'll are really pissing me off," said Hanna.

Realizing they were taking things too far, Byron said, "We're joking. We didn't see your pretty little bottom. Tell her Bobby."

Bobby explained how they had come to their conclusion after going through her things.

"Ya'll are so silly," said Hanna with some relief.

"But it still doesn't explain your not wearing any," said Byron.

Hanna looked away then back at them, "Ya'll want to know? I'll tell you. Lots of times I don't wear panties. Because, I don't want to wear them out."

"Well, I'll be damned," said Bobby, "you poor thing. We can buy you more panties."

"Bobby, why don't you give her yours?" said Byron.

"You want mine?" Bobby asked.

Hanna laughed. "Ewww, gag." Later that morning, she asked them again about their upbringings. "What was it like, really?"

"Hanna," said Byron, "Let me explain something to you. Social class is a strange thing. Like anything, there are some good things about it, and there are some bad things about it. Now, listen to me. Don't ever be ashamed of where you came from. A weed cannot be anything but a weed, a rose a rose, an orchid an orchid. I've seen weeds prettier than orchids. Not that orchids don't have their place in wonder, too."

"One person's weed is another's magnolia," said Bobby.

"A good weed is one of God's grandest creations," said Byron.

"If a daisy tried to be a weed, it would just fuck up," said Bobby. "Now, can we have some pussy?"

SIXTEEN

Their second spring in New Orleans had arrived. The men drank their usual quotas, spent time with Earl and the other derelicts, and occasionally went together, and separately, to see Georgianna.

Often still urinating blood, Bobby one morning agreed to see a doctor. Their checks and food stamps had come, so they could afford one visit without too much of a burden. They found a doctor at random from the yellow pages, one whose office was just off Magazine.

"You have to come with me," said Bobby, "I'll be scared by myself." So Byron called and made the appointment for the following morning, convincing a receptionist there was an emergency. They said nothing to Hanna, and waited until she left for school before getting themselves ready.

"Wash your peter," said Byron.

Byron waited as the doctor saw Bobby. When he came back to the lobby, Byron wanted to know what the doctor said.

"He wants me to go in the hospital to run some tests."

"Did you tell him you had no money?"

"Yes."

"Did he have any suggestions about that?"

"No."

"What do you want to do?"

"I guess I could go back to Biloxi," said Bobby, his flip-flop flapping the sidewalk. They walked out of the hospital.

When they got back to the house, Bobby fixed a drink while Byron took a swallow out of the vodka bottle, then said he was going out for a while. When he had gone, Bobby sat in one of the living room lawn chairs while his mind wandered off in gloom. It was cancer, he knew it was. This was the beginning of the end. He would go back to the veterans' hospital and rot away with the rest of the old soldiers. That was bad enough, but it was pain that scared him most, anything but pain. He imagined himself on a deathbed, nobody there to help him die. And then there was the hereafter to be concerned about. As he drank and smoked, the thoughts became more morbid. Soon he was lying on the floor in a fetal position. He was afraid to close his eyes, afraid they wouldn't open again. He tried to convince himself that his only sickness was in his head, and that if he would get up, go on about life, the urine thing would go away. What in the hell was cancer anyhow? Who knew anything? But nothing he thought helped.

While Bobby continued to suffer, Byron was in a phone booth down the street. He was calling the real estate company back in Alabama, the one that had been trying to sell his house trailer. He was telling the woman agent that he was ready to go down another thousand dollars if she could sell it soon. She told him she knew of at least two potential buyers at thirty-nine hundred dollars. "Sell it," Byron told her.

Bobby was sitting in one of the lawn chairs when Byron came in to tell Bobby he had made arrangements for him to go to a hospital in New Orleans.

"And how did you do that?" Bobby wanted to know.

"I just did it. Don't worry about that part.

"What did you do?"

Byron told him what he had done.

"I can't do that," said Bobby.

"Oh hell yes you can. It probably won't cost more than a few hundred dollars. Now, let's don't talk about it anymore. You need to call that doctor and tell him to go ahead and start making arrangements."

"Nope," said Bobby pulling himself up.

"Yep," said Byron.

"Nope. I'm not going to do that."

Byron went to the kitchen and came back with the vodka bottle choked by its neck. He took one of the lawn chairs just as Bobby took the other. "How much did you get for it?"

"I got a good price."

"How much? Did you get the five thousand?"

"Close. Look, Bobby, do you want the money or not?"

"I'm going to Biloxi."

"Go, then. If you do, though, that'll be the end of you."

Bobby started to cry. "Byron."

"What, boy?"

"If I die, don't just put me in a garbage bag and stick me out front for the trash people."

"I promise."

"Make sure I'm dead, too."

"I will. Now, let's go call that doctor and get going. You'll probably just stay in the hospital overnight or something. They'll run their tests, and you'll be gone."

"Gone?"

Byron could not help laughing. "It's probably nothing," he said as he glanced out the window and saw Hanna crossing the street.

"Why don't ya'll turn on some lights?" she said as she passed Byron and tossed a sheet of paper in his lap. She went to the kitchen and returned shortly with a slice of bread. Bobby was lighting a cigarette. "What's the matter with ya'll?"

"What's this?" Byron asked, holding up the piece of paper.

"It's something the guidance counselor wants me to take."

"What is it?" Bobby wanted to know.

"It's an application for the SAT," said Byron.

"It's got something to do with college," said Hanna.

"I know that," said Byron, "but what are you going to do with it?"

"Throw it in the trash, I guess."

"Well, here," said Byron shoving the paper toward her.

"I don't want it," said Hanna, "what's wrong with ya'll?"

"Tell her, Bobby."

"You tell her."

"You tell her."

"Well what?" said Hanna.

"Bobby's going to the hospital."

"What? What's the matter, Bobby?"

"He's got to take some tests."

"I have cancer," said Bobby.

Byron chuckled "No, he doesn't. He's not sure what it is."

"It's cancer," said Bobby.

"Are you going back to the veterans' hospital?" asked Hanna.

Hanna stayed out of school the morning Bobby went to the hospital. When they were leaving the house, and trying to remember if they had forgotten anything, Hanna said, "Bobby, you aren't wearing your panties, are you?"

"I most certainly am."

"Oh, shit, Bobby."

Grudgingly, Bobby finally put on a pair of Byron's

boxer shorts before they left for the hospital.

A nurse came out to the lobby, loaded Bobby into a wheelchair, and started him down a long hall. Hanna and Byron followed close behind. "I told you I was sick, Byron," said Bobby. "Somebody isn't telling me something."

"Bobby," said Byron, "they put everybody in wheelchairs."

* * *

It was on the bus ride back that Byron brought up the SAT again. "I think you should take it," he said.

"Why?" Hanna wanted to know.

"Because you might want to go to college one day."

"Shoot," said Hanna, "if I get through high school, I don't even want to talk about anything else. Besides, it costs twenty dollars to take it."

"Do you want to take it?"

"I don't have twenty dollars even if I did."

"That's not what I asked."

"It won't mean anything."

Byron thought for a minute, then said, "I think you should take it."

"Why?"

"Because I have twenty dollars, and I don't have anything else to do with it."

"Byron," Hanna said a minute later, "How are ya'll

gonna pay for Bobby's hospital bill?"

"We've already got it straightened out."

"How?"

"What difference does it make? We've done it."

"Where did ya'll get any money?"

When they got off the bus, Hanna waited outside the phone booth, paying little attention to Byron's talk except for the numbers "four, nine, oh," the first three of their address.

"You sold your house trailer," she said when Byron stepped out of the booth. "You sold your house trailer. And you're going to use the money for Bobby. Byron, that's the nicest thing I've ever heard of."

"Yeah, well," said Byron. "The son-of-a-bitch had better not die on me."

"Byron."

* * *

That night, before they went back to the hospital, Byron asked Hanna if she had any studying to do. "Only this test in psychology," she told him.

"Then stay here and study."

"No. I'm going with you."

Arguing with her was futile, so they left the house and stopped at a drugstore on the way, where they bought a twenty-five-cent plastic rose on a wire stem before catching a bus. After sitting down, Byron brought up the SAT matter again.

"What did the guidance counselor say about it?"

"That I should have taken it in the eleventh grade, or last November."

"Hey, boy," said Bobby, without moving, when they walked in. Byron held out the rose and grinned. "Sombitch," said Bobby, then "Girl, come here and put your titties on me. I'm getting out of here tomorrow."

Byron laughed.

"What's so funny about that?"

"I was just thinking about something Lorraine said, about the mental patients always saying they were getting out tomorrow," Byron said.

"No, I'm serious," said Bobby. "I've already talked with the doctor. I told him I couldn't afford to stay any longer. He's a nice man. He said he understood, and he would try to run all the tests he wanted to tomorrow, Hell, all they've done today is clean out my insides. Boy, my insides are so clean a crab wouldn't live there. What have you and the little pussy been up to? She didn't let you have some, did she?"

Hanna unfolded her arms to give him a finger.

Hanna took a bath when they got back to the house. While fixing a drink, Byron listened to water splashing in the bathroom. Lust overtook him and he went to the bedroom where he knelt down and peeked through the hole he and Bobby had cut into Hanna's room, anticipating what might occur when she finished her bath. Hearing her leave the bathroom, he prepared himself. However, when she turned on her light, all Byron could see was light and some kind of obstruction. He guessed it had to do with the hole in one room not being in line with the other. So, after Hanna's light went off, he finished his drink and went to bed.

* * *

The doctor came into Bobby's room, sat down with a clipboard and thumbed several pages. "So tell, me something, George. Do you mind if I call you George?" said Bobby.

The doctor smiled.

"Do you get much pussy in your business?" asked Bobby.

The doctor chuckled and said, "Bobby, you're an alcoholic, aren't you?"

"Byron is, too," Bobby was quick to say.

"Well," said the doctor, "I think you should think about it."

"I'm not going to die, am I, George?"

"No, not yet. The urine problem is just a minor infection. I can treat that with some antibiotics. Otherwise, considering everything, you're not terribly unhealthy."

"I've always thought so," said Bobby. "I've always been athletic."

"But Bobby, you need to stop drinking."

"I've been thinking about that. I plan to. Byron and I both plan to. But it's going to be more difficult for him. He has so little self-discipline."

"And about your foot," the doctor said, writing prescriptions. "I'm going to give you something for it that should do the trick."

The doctor smiled and left the room while Bobby was starting to tell him about Byron's tugboat and fish market work.

"Hell, boy, I told you there was nothing wrong with me," Bobby told Byron when he came to take him home. Before they left the hospital, Byron encountered difficulty convincing an administrator to discharge Bobby before paying his bill. After considerable discussion the woman warned him that not receiving the entire payment within one month would result in legal action. Byron assured her she would have the money within the week.

"I'm sorry," Bobby said on the way out. "I told you I should have gone to Biloxi. But I'm going to pay you back. You can count on that."

"When? When are you going to pay me back?"

"Bobby reached in his pocket and handed a ten dollar bill to Byron. "Here, I now owe you...Wait! What about the gin rummy money you owe me?"

Byron gave Bobby a raised-brow glance.

"Just kidding. Boy, can't you take a joke?" Bobby grinned.

SEVENTEEN

In early May, Hanna was getting ready to take the SAT, spending time in the library going over how to take the test manuals, while the men hung out more at the outdoor living room, emptied the brown water and leaves from the Mr. Turtle pool, cleaned and refilled it and occasionally reminisced about the night Hanna spent in their bed.

One afternoon Hanna came from school in a late-model light green Audi, driven by one of her classmates. Byron and Bobby were sitting on the porch steps in their bare feet, sipping screwdrivers. "Ya'll, this is Dede," Hanna told them as the girl with dark brown hair came round the car.

The men stood up and had a difficult time with their words.

"It's alright," said Hanna, "I told her all about ya'll."

"She really has," the girl said. "I've been dying to meet both of you."

"Alright," said Hanna. "This one is Byron, and that's Bobby. He's the loud one."

"And you, young lady, are very pretty." Bobby

grinned and looked into the girl's eyes.

The girl looked at Hanna, who said, "I told you."

"What did you tell her?" asked Bobby.

"Come on in," said Hanna. "I'll show you where I temporarily live." Hanna looked up at Byron, then Bobby, as Dede followed her up the steps. Byron and Bobby looked at each other and joined in behind them.

"Ooooh, I love it," Dede said when she got inside. "This is like something out of a story." She peeked into the first bedroom. "And there's the mattresses."

The men gawked.

"And the lawn chairs!" the girl exclaimed.

When Hanna led Dede to her room, the girl said, "Ohhhhh!"

"You want a beer or something?" Byron asked.

"Yes!" the girl again almost screamed. "May I? Which one of you writes?"

"He does," said Hanna, pointing to Byron.

"And you are the poet," Dede said to Bobby.

"Would you like to hear a poem?" Bobby said with a flirtatious grin as Hanna closed the door to her room. The men stood in the kitchen, listening to muffled "fantastic," "shit," "cool" and "Oooou" until the radio blasted the girl's talk.

When they came out of the room, Bobby and Byron were sitting in the lawn chairs with beers for the girls. "So, Dede, tell us about yourself."

"Well," said Dede, "Uh, I live on Carrollton. I go to

school with Hanna. I'm a senior, and I plan to attend Tulane—I mean, Sophie Newcomb."

"What is Sophie Newcomb?" Byron asked.

"That's the women's part of Tulane," said Hanna as both girls sat on the floor.

"I've been trying to talk Hanna into going there too," said Dede.

"Damn noble thought," said Bobby. "But Hanna's going to be a beautician. I wouldn't think Sophie Newcomb has a course in cosmetology."

"Hanna's not going to be a beautician," said Dede.

"Bobby," said Hanna, "do that red rose, falcon poem for Dede."

"Yeah," said Dede. "Hanna's told me about how well you recite poems."

***

Hanna was away from the house more, spending time at the library and with Dede who was helping her prepare for the SAT. "You're fucking somebody," Bobby told her one evening when she came in later than usual.

"I've been with Dede. We went to her house after we spent the afternoon in the library. And fuck you anyway."

"Uh huh, and I'm the Sheik of Araby," said Bobby.

"So?"

"So?"

"So I'm going to bed!"

"We're losing our touch," Byron told Bobby.

"Who the hell is touching anything? We ought to just pounce the bitch."

At the outdoor living room the next morning, Earl asked, "Who's the new chick?" when Bobby and Byron arrived to do some serious drinking. "You fellers starting a harem or something?"

"I bet that chicken's got some kinda pussy hair," said Old Fleetwood.

"You bastards don't know the half of it," said Bobby setting a piece of plywood over the springs of a worn-out, legless sofa.

"Great weather," someone said before Byron started badgering women in general. "...conniving bunch of manipulating sons of bitches, all of them, even the fucking young ones who damn well ought to know better."

"Fuck 'em," said one of the derelicts.

They talked on into the afternoon, several of the derelicts frequently wiping their mouths when the wine started running short. Old Fleetwood decided to take his afternoon nap, seeing Bobby and Byron had nothing else to drink either.

When Bobby and Byron got back to the house, Dede's Audi was parked out front. The girls were sitting in the lawn chairs smoking and sipping beer. "Byron, look, teenaged alcoholics."

"Bobby," said Hanna, "I might be a lot of things, but

an alcoholic, I am not. Looking at you two drunk shits has taught me better than that."

Byron sat on the lounge lawn chair beside Dede who moved her legs to accommodate him, just before he grabbed her wrists, drawing her close to his admiring eyes. "You're so pretty," he said.

"Byron," said Hanna.

"Well, thank you," said Dede, with a gleam in her eyes.

"Byron leave her alone," said Hanna.

"I'm going to kiss you," said Byron smiling.

"Ah uh," said Dede staring back with a gleam in her eyes.

Hanna jumped out of her chair, slapped Byron's cheek before he let go Dede's wrist to grab one of Hanna's. "What's the matter, little girl?" Hanna only stared him in the face before jerking away from his grasp and storming out the front door.

"Oh boy," said Bobby as Dede got up to follow after Hanna.

* * *

Hanna returned that evening, making no effort to be quiet after seeing the men had gone to bed, going to her room, turning on the radio, high volume, and finally turning it off to go to sleep.

The next day Hanna came in from school, walking

from the bus stop and going straight to her room without speaking when the men greeted her. They were in the kitchen when she ignored them getting ready for school. That afternoon she did not return. The men waited several hours before growing concerned, before she finally came through the door just before dark. The men were sitting in the living room pretending to be reading. When they said nothing, Hanna said, "Library," then went to her room.

Dede's Audi appeared one morning after Hanna had left for school. Bobby went to the door, invited her in the house. "I just came by to tell you two something." Byron stepped from the kitchen. "First of all, you're either blind or insensitive to Hanna's feelings, or stupid." Dede glanced out the door, then said, "Guys, if you'd get your heads out of your asses, you'd see that that girl wants to go to college."

EIGHTEEN

Bobby and Byron got off the streetcar in front of the administration building, a huge gray stone building facing St. Charles Avenue, and stepped across the street where they faced a modest stone structure affirming Tulane University. Starting up a long walkway toward the entrance, Bobby stopped and took a pint bottle from his coat pocket, taking a stiff drink before passing the vodka to Byron. The men were dressed for the occasion, Bobby in a dark blue winter suit, a wide club tie; Byron wearing a seersucker suit with a standard striped tie with a Windsor knot. With the back of his hand, Bobby wiped his mouth. "How do I look?" he asked.

"Not all that bad," said Byron. "What about me?" Bobby licked his fingers to straighten Byron's hair before walking on, entering the administration building.

"Good morning," the receptionist said.

"And a good morning to you," said Bobby while Byron glanced round at the dignified, elaborately framed portraits of past university presidents and distinguished benefactors.

"May we speak to someone in admissions?" Bobby asked the well-dressed young woman, who led them inside a windowed, mahogany door. Byron watched her walk back to her desk.

A middle-aged woman with glasses hanging from a chain round her neck and a white blouse and black skirt led them into her office, where they sat before her desk. After several pleasantries and talk about the school's prestigious reputation, Bobby mentioned his association with Auburn University, then explained their reason for being there.

"Of course you realize the deadline for admission for the fall semester has passed. The cut-off date was February.

"I see," said Bobby. "I don't guess there are any exceptions to that," he said with a grin.

"I'm afraid not. Most high school seniors started their applications this time last year. Is the young lady considering other schools?"

"She has chosen Tulane. We've been through a great deal of information from other schools, and she wants to go here."

Has she taken the SAT?"

"Recently," said Byron.

"Are you sure there are no exceptions for this fall?" Bobby flirtatiously asked.

"I'm sorry," the woman said as she excused herself, returning shortly with an application packet, brochures and pamphlets for them to take. Bobby made one more futile attempt to keep the dialogue open as the woman subtly led them out of her office.

On the streetcar, on their way to Tiny's Bar, they looked over the admission papers. "Goddamn, Byron, that place is expensive."

"One of the most," said Byron. "It's a private school."

"Well, fuck, we can forget Tulane University."

When they got back to the house Dede's car was parked out front. Hanna and Dede were sitting on the porch steps. "Where ya'll been?" Hanna asked. Without acknowledging Dede's surprising presence—Bobby saying, "None a ya'll's bidness," Byron saying, "Drinking"— they left the girls to go inside.

They were sitting in the kitchen eating from cans of baked beans when Hanna came in, after Dede promised to be by the next morning to give her a ride to school and left.

"You want some beans?" Bobby mumbled.

"No," said Hanna. "I ate a sandwich at Dede's."

"What kind was it?"

"Roast beef."

"Roast beef. Oou hoo," Bobby proclaimed.

"On croissants, no doubt," said Byron.

Hanna poured herself a glass of orange juice, leaned against the refrigerator, then said, "Ya'll should see their house. I mean, shit, just the kitchen...the dishes. Her mother served us with these embroidery napkins on these nice China plates, just for a sandwich."

"You want a beer?"

"No, thank you."

Hanna followed Bobby back to the living room and sat on the floor in front of the lawn chairs. "Dede said you wanted to go to college," Byron said.

"She told ya'll that? I've thought about it. The guidance counselor said she thought I would do well in college. I thought about maybe going back to Florida after school, and go to some two-year college—just to see how I'd do. There's one where my grandmother lived. I've been talking to Dede about it. I could work and just take a couple of courses at a time. She said I could probably get some government aid. What do ya'll think? That is, if I did well enough on the SAT. Do ya'll think my fake transcript will work?"

"Bobby, do you have any cigarettes?" Byron yelled to the kitchen. Bobby leaned toward the door to throw a pack to him. Hanna went on talking about college. "Do ya'll honestly think I could pass college?"

"I think you're rushing things," said Byron. "You haven't finished high school yet."

"Ya'll think it's stupid, don't you?" said Hanna, stepping toward the kitchen where she saw Bobby shrug his shoulders. She turned back toward Byron. "Ya'll don't think I can pass college, do ya'll?"

***

The next morning Byron said, "Bobby, let's go talk to that guidance counselor at Hanna's school."

"For what?"

"I don't know. Just to see if she can suggest something."

"Did you hear her say she was going back to Florida?"

"Yes, well, it hasn't happened yet."

"Byron, I think we're wasting our time. That girl doesn't need us anymore. She couldn't care less about us now."

"I don't know," said Byron, "I don't think she really wants to go back to Florida. I think she's just saying that because she doesn't feel she has any other choices. Bobby, that girl is brilliant. She can do so much better than a junior college somewhere."

"Byron."

"What?"

"Do my teeth look like they hurt?"

"What?"

Bobby gritted and exposed his stained teeth to Byron. "I don't know, they feel sick or something."

"Have you brushed them lately?"

"That's it, I forgot to brush my teeth," said Bobby as he went to the bathroom, moments later stepping out the door, toothpaste in his mouth, mumbling, "ooy-outankshiscure?"

"What?" Byron yelled.

Bobby spat in the sink, then repeated himself loudly, "Do you think she is queer?"

* * *

Hanna was at school; Bobby was soaking in the Mr. Turtle pool while Byron sat in the living room going over the pamphlets and brochures from Tulane. One of the pamphlets presented smiling faces of the pretty coeds sitting round on grass pretending to be studying, one blond with obvious breasts beneath a dark green Tulane sweatshirt.

Bobby walked into the room drinking beer mixed with tomato juice. He went to the window and looked out. "Summer's coming!" he shouted. "And I'm still here. Byron, let's go out and do something. Let's get a bottle of wine and go sit on the riverbank. Let's take a short story book and read to each other. We haven't done that in a long time."

Byron said nothing.

Bobby turned away from the window. "Byron, remember that…what was her name…the girl who whined when you fucked her."

"Um huh."

"Remember how we thought she was crying? And I started feeling sorry for her?"

"Bobby, look at this."

"What?"

Byron was speaking of something he had just read. "Listen to this:

Federal entitlement awards are available to undergraduates pursuing a first baccalaureate degree that demonstrate exceptional financial need. Each eligible undergraduate must apply for the grant and submit a valid Student Aid Report prior to being considered for other aid."

"Will you forget that shit and let's go to the river? So, she can get financial aid. Good. Even if she qualifies, she can't get into college until next winter. By that time I will be back in a veterans' hospital and you will probably be dead. This might be the last spring of my life. I want to go to the river."

"Bobby, that girl could go to college scott fucking free!" said Byron.

"Good. Now, let's go to the river. Let's go get Earl and take him down to the river and read him 'Big Boy Leaves Home.'"

"You know something else, private schools like Tulane are required by the government, I believe, to have special funds set aside for deserving students who can't afford the costs. Needy kids. I remember helping this brilliant young black student along this line years ago. I don't imagine things have changed that much. Grants, loans. Pell grants, I used to know what those were. Something—"

"Needy my ass. With that body and face like hers,

you call that needy. It is you and I who are needy. Hell, we're fucking desperate."

Byron drifted from academics. "I've been thinking about something, Bobby. Do you know why she has been turning us down all this time?"

"She's queer."

"It's her age. It's the role she sees us in. When she gets out of school, everything will be different. She'll start thinking of us as…she'll feel like she's a woman instead of a girl. She'll be a fucking coed. You do remember coeds, don't you?"

"Dream on little dreamer."

"Well, it's possible, goddamnit. If she left us, and went out there in the cold world, by herself, she'd start appreciating us."

"She's been out in the cold world, all her life."

"But it's different now. I'm telling you, she'll miss us when she leaves."

"When she leaves, she'll be gone—that is all. Now, let's go to the river."

* * *

That afternoon Dede came in with Hanna. While they sat on the floor and complained about school, Byron tried to guess what kind of nipples Dede had beneath her Loyola sweatshirt, while Bobby convinced himself that Hanna had warned Dede about wearing more revealing outfits around him and Byron.

"Dede," Bobby finally interrupted her talk to say. She looked up at him sitting in one of the lawn chairs with the respect of a well-mannered adolescent toward a considerably older adult. "May I ask you something?"

"Sure," she said with a smile.

Bobby chose his words carefully and spoke meticulously. "Are you a virgin?"

Dede continued to smile as Bobby's grin grew and his mouth went crooked. "That's none of your fucking business."

Hanna looked at Dede. Both let an "ahuh," drop from their exaggeratedly opened mouths.

"You aren't, are you?" Bobby said.

"Bobby," said Hanna, "No wonder you and Byron have no women in your lives, God!"

"That's a perfectly respectable question," said Bobby.

Hanna started to get up, saying, "We've got to study."

"No, wait," said Byron. "Don't go yet. Bobby and I are lonesome. Talk to us. I promise you I'll make sure Bobby doesn't say anything nasty."

"Oh, ho," said Hanna. "Listen to the Reverend Burns."

"We have an English test tomorrow," said Dede.

"No problem," said Bobby. "Byron and I know more English than your teacher does."

"Yes, but ya'll are drunk," said Hanna.

However, the men did charm them into sitting with them longer. "But just a little while," said Hanna, "then we have to study." Soon however, after Bobby made some comment about wishing the girls would show him and Byron their breasts, the girls went to Hanna's room and shut the door.

Later, when they came out, Dede needing to go, Byron said, "Hanna, we looked at some information about financial aid for college today. I think it might be possible for you to go to school free."

"You mean welfare?"

"Hell, yes, he means welfare," said Bobby. "What's wrong with that?"

"It's not costing me anything to go to Newcomb," said Dede.

They all three looked at her. "There's this program where if one of your parents teaches full-time in these certain colleges, you get free tuition. Loyola is one of them."

"Dede's dad teaches at Loyola," said Hanna.

"I think Hanna can go totally free," said Byron.

After Dede left, Hanna sat on the floor to read a financial aid application. "Tulane?" Hanna said.

"If you are going to college it might as well be a good one," said Bobby.

"But, ya'll, that place cost a fortune, aid or no fucking aid. Everybody that goes there is rich."

"And poor people with good grades," said Bobby.

"Not with fake transcripts," said Hanna.

"Tulane," said Hanna reflectively. Then she said, "Ya'll stop it now. I'm gonna get my hopes up and just mess myself up. Anyway, it says here that the deadline for sending this is April the first." She dropped the application to the floor.

"It won't matter," said Byron, "You couldn't start until next winter semester anyhow."

"Then that settles it, I'm going back to Florida. I can get in a junior college over there without all this."

Nobody said anything for more than a minute, then Bobby said, "I think she should go to beauty college."

"I could," said Hanna.

"Aw, fuck, Hanna, cut out the bullshit," said Byron.

On his way to the kitchen to fix another drink, Bobby said, "I think you should go back to Florida and learn to make permanents for blue-headed women."

* * *

The next morning, when Bobby opened his eyes it took him several seconds to recognize what lay on the pillow before his face. It was a piece of silky, lacy, light yellow cloth—a pair of panties. As soon as he recognized what it was, he sat up on the mattress and shouted, "Byron!" A moment later Byron came to the door. "Look!" said Bobby, pointing to his pillow.

"What is it?"

"Look!"

Byron stepped over to the mattress. "Where did those come from?"

"That's what I want to know."

Byron knelt down and the two men looked at the panties as if they were looking at a sick bird or exactly what they were. Finally Byron picked them up and held them out at arm's length. "What are you doing with them?"

"Nothing," said Bobby.

"What are they doing here?"

"I don't know. I woke up and there they were."

They looked at one another with blank expressions. Then Bobby said, "Are you thinking what I'm thinking?"

"I don't know. What are you thinking?"

"That Miss Pretty Ass is growing up."

"She wants to go to college."

Bobby reached for the panties and crushed them in his hand, then opened them up again. "The little bitch is teasing us."

"That's alright with me. Tease me!"

Bobby looked deeply into the crotch of the panties. "What's she up to, Byron?"

"I don't know. But I know one thing, she's never done anything like this before. Have you thought of that?"

"What's she after, Byron?"

"I don't know."

They walked around the house all morning in a daze. And every once in a while, one, and then the other, would go to the door of the bedroom to take another look at the panties. It was almost noon when Byron said, "There's not but one thing to do."

"What's that?"

"We have to get her in Tulane."

NINETEEN

The weather that weekend was no less than wonderful. The sky was blue, the sun was bright, and Byron opened all the windows and doors of the house. Soon the dankness that had accumulated all winter was gone, and in its place was a nice sense of outdoors. Even the derelicts moved about more than they had since last fall. Byron and Bobby were in unusually good spirits, which called for lots of drinking. Hanna spent most of Saturday afternoon with Dede; they went off together in the Audi. But the men didn't mind. They were learning the discipline of patience. They said nothing about the panties, and Hanna had offered no more than that.

Saturday afternoon Byron and Bobby took the streetcar downtown, wandered about the French Quarter, sat in an open-front bar and watched the tourists—with their cameras, new white sneakers and souvenir Hurricane glasses—and after failing to pick up a couple of women wearing matching cowboy boots and hats, stopped off at the outdoor living room as two of the derelicts were dragging up a new old worn-out sofa.

When they got back to the house, Byron was the first to step into the kitchen, where before him on the table stood a typewriter, an electric Royal. "Bobby, look here."

"Son of a bitch," said Bobby standing beside Byron. "Where did that come from?"

Byron plugged the cord in a wall socket, sat down and turned on the typewriter as Bobby leaned over to examine it. "Get me a sheet of paper," said Byron.

Bobby brought him a sheet of paper, and he went to the bathroom, took his penis out of his pants, dropped his flip-flop, propped his foot on the commode rim, pissed on his fingers and rubbed his rotting toe while vaguely considering having his prescription for antibiotics filled. He yelled to the kitchen, "Boy you have no fucking excuse now."

When he returned to the kitchen, zipping his pants, he said, "Byron, don't you think we're overdue a party?"

"What excuse will we need?" Byron asked as he typed.

"Well," said Bobby, "What about a party to celebrate not needing an excuse?"

* * *

It was Byron who came up with the idea of inviting the derelicts and Georgianna over for a fish fry. And being the big spenders they were, they walked down

Magazine to a fish market, bought five pounds of mullet for forty-nine cents a pound, a half gallon of Popov, a sack of potatoes, three envelopes of Kool-Aid and ice. After stopping by to invite Georgianna, who was regretfully busy with something else, then going by the outdoor living room, they returned to the house, with several derelicts in tow. When Hanna saw them coming up the front steps, she went in her room and closed the door.

"Well, go get her!" Bobby told Byron as he started unwrapping the fish.

But before he did, Byron washed out the sink, somewhat, before emptying the Kool-Aid, most of the vodka, ice, adding water and stirring. "Punch!" proclaimed Byron before knocking on Hanna's door. She opened it with her purse over her shoulder.

"Where are you going?" Byron wanted to know.

"Out."

"But you can't, we're going to have a fish fry."

"I'm not staying here with a bunch of drunk men."

Byron's disappointment showed as Hanna spoke to the derelicts on her way out. No one else inside the house knew that she walked across the street to wait for Dede, while Bobby was looking for something to fry fish in.

By then, the derelicts had begun to take advantage of the Kool-Aid punch. Cecil said, "This is good. Who made it?" after dipping a plastic cup full.

"I got a skillet," Nip told Bobby.

"He shore does," said Cecil.

"We're going to need some cooking oil, too," said Bobby.

"If you give Cecil some money he can go get some lard," Earl suggested.

"Byron, where is the little pussy?"

When he told him Hanna had gone out with Dede, he too felt a drop in enthusiasm.

When Cecil returned with the lard and they melted it in the skillet, Old Fleetwood asked, "Ain'tchu gone meal 'em?" after Bobby had laid a slice of mullet in the grease.

"What?" asked Bobby.

"Meal 'em. I ain't never had fried mullet without meal."

Bobby stood before the skillet, considering Fleetwood's request, and said, "I like mine without meal. And I'm the host, Fleetwood," pointing a fork at him.

"I like 'em without meal, too," said Old Fleetwood.

* * *

The radio in Dede's Audi was tuned to an easy blues station. After Hanna flagged her down from the street corner, Dede wanted to know why she had been standing on the corner.

"They call it a party," said Hanna. "Bobby and Byron know these…these winos. These bums live, stay, screw off down the other way in this vacant lot. They all call it the outdoor living room."

"The what?"

"It's this place where these men drink and mostly live when the weather is okay. I'll show it to you sometime."

"But what's an outdoor living room?"

Hanna laughed. "They call it that cause they have these old couches with the springs sticking out under these trees, and these chairs and this old barrel they build fires in and all. They live there."

"You mean homeless people."

"Yeah. Homeless, street people, alcoholics, destitutes."

"And you know them?"

"Not me. Byron and Bobby."

"They're weird is what they are. Do Byron and Bobby drink all the time?" asked Dede.

"Just about."

"I can't believe they're still alive." Dede drove by a sports bar and glanced at the cars.

"Tell me about it," said Hanna. "But you know something, most of the time you wouldn't know it, except for Bobby's eyes and red face, and Byron's high stepping. After he drinks so much he starts walking like a giant duck or something." Both girls laughed. Dede wanted to know more about their drinking habits, and Hanna spent a while trying to explain part of their routine. "They average about a fifth of vodka a day—more some days. They don't buy it by the fifth though—half gallon. The cheapest they can find. They drink wine only if they don't have enough money for vodka. And beer, beer to them is like a coke or something."

"They're pickled," said Dede.

Dede drove round another bar looking for the car her boyfriend drove. Afterwards the girls drove to a park on the levee as a barge was drifting by in the night. They sat in the car, lit cigarettes and watched silently for a moment.

"Are they crazy or what?" Dede asked as they watched one of the barges go up the river.

Stuffing her feet beneath her, Hanna said, "I wish I could explain them to you, Dede. They're not just alcoholics." Hanna held her foot as she talked. She chose her words carefully. She wanted so much for someone to understand what she did about Bobby and Byron. "Their minds are working twenty-four hours a day." Hanna leaned her head toward Dede. "It's like they can't turn them off or something. I don't mean just thinking; they're going a hundred miles an hour. Like sometimes...Bobby...Bobby is like this little boy. I mean, this little boy that's got a million thoughts in his head, but he's still this little boy—and this man, too. He can be one and then the other, and then both. He can't do anything. He really can't. You oughta see him changing a lightbulb. He can't. I swear. It's like he can't breathe or something when he tries to do anything with his hands. It's like his mind gets ahead of his hands or something. I mean, he's smart as shit, but he can't do anything practical. I can't explain it."

"Really?"

"The best way I know to explain them is they're perfectly...perfectly...imperfect. I mean, they make every mistake known to the human race. But it's sort of like they do it on purpose. Like they're pretending to be...And that doesn't mean they aren't serious—they are, lots of the time. They can be more serious than anybody you'll ever know. God, can they be serious." Hanna ran her fingers through her hair. "Like one minute they make more sense than anybody, and then the next you'd think they were these total imbeciles, like they just stopped being what they really are...and I know I'm not making any sense. It's just that you can't explain them to anybody. Does that make any sense?"

"Sorta, I guess."

"I wish I could explain it." Hanna stared toward the lights across the river. "It's like they live the way they do because they don't believe living one way is that much different from living another, or something. Like they don't think anything is wrong. And they don't think anything is right. Things just are. It's like they've figured something out. Like, they like everything. And then they don't like anything. Sometimes you oughta hear them talking. I've seen them sit for hours talking about things nobody in the world could talk about that long—drinking, smoking, and talking. About all this weird stuff. It's like they have their own language and nobody else in the world would ever know what they were saying—like they know this something nobody else does."

"Don't you think maybe they're just crazy?" Dede asked.

Hanna nearly chuckled. "Like these two foxes or something maybe. Byron, he's a walking encyclopedia. Bobby is too. No, they aren't crazy—not unless I am too. God, Dede, they've taught me more things in a year than I've learned in the rest of my life put together. Shit, sometimes I think they could probably teach a...a blind person to run through a jungle. You know what they did one time? They read *Moby-Dick* out loud to each other—the whole book. *Moby-Dick*. Do you know how long *Moby-Dick* is? It took them something like a week to do it, but they sat in those lawn chairs day in and day out, drinking, smoking, and reading. I mean, sometimes from early in the morning till late at night— drunk as skunks. Have you ever read *Moby-Dick*?"

"Have you?"

"I tried. It's bor—ing. I mean, bor—ing."

Dede started blowing smoke rings. "But Hanna, they're fucked up."

Hanna told her more, about their childhoods, how they came from respectable families, how they had been expected to set the world on fire, then a story Bobby once told her about Byron.

"One time I got mad with Byron, and Bobby, I guess, wanting me to see him in a different way told me about this time when Byron was teaching school. Dede, this will tell you a lot about what I mean. I mean, they're...well. Byron taught school, high school in this town, and one time there was this boy, this black boy, this was back when the schools in Alabama were first integrated. This boy, his father came to the school one day while a lot of the students were sitting on the grass, during lunch or something. This boy's father was like retarded, and people were always making fun of him and getting him to do things so they could laugh at him. Well, this day, the boy's father came up to the school, where these students were outside, and they got him to do something like dance or something, egging him on and stuff. And that boy was out there too. I mean, you can imagine. Then this boy's daddy got to going and got tickled so much that he peed in his pants. Bobby said it ran down his pants and it was so obvious because of the pants the man was wearing, just wet his whole front.

"Well, Byron saw it happen, and the kids laughing and making fun of him, right there in front of his boy. Can you just imagine? And you know what Byron did? He went out there, walked over to where the boy's father was standing, laughing along with all the kids. Byron went up beside the man and put his arms around him and Byron pissed in his pants. I swear that's what Bobby told me. Byron pissed on himself and let it run

down his legs and pants right there in front of his fucking students. Can you believe that?" Dede only stared
across the river. "I mean, who else would do something
like that? Bobby said Byron then walked over to where
the boy was standing, over by the school, away from the
others, and put his arm around him and walked back
inside the school with him."

"That is really something," said Dede.

"I swear Bobby told me that."

Dede stared toward the river for several moments
without either girl saying anything. Then they talked
for a while about the ramifications of Hanna's story,
about the possible virtues of true virtue, whether or not
they were capable of destroying reputation for a noble
cause, as they drifted into talk about college, how Dede
felt she was starting to feel older, more mature. Hanna
wanted to know if Dede believed she could really make
it in college. She laughed thinking that just months ago
nothing like that ever seriously entered her mind. She
said she envied Dede for having a real family and nice
furniture. Dede said she envied Hanna for the unusual
experiences in her own life, reminding Hanna of something. "Oh, Dede," she said, "I feel terrible about something I told you earlier. You know what I said about
those men at the house, those—wine—those people
you asked me about. Well, I lied. They ARE friends of
mine. I love them. I feel so shitty about being ashamed
to claim I know them. They're some of the best...what-

ever-you-want-to-call-thems I know."

"Cool," said Dede.

"Dede," said Hanna, "Let's go back to the house and let me introduce you to them. Especially Earl and Cecil. And old Fleetwood...and Nip..."

However, when Dede cranked the car to back up, another automobile pulled in beside them and immediately two boys got out. One was Dede's boyfriend, the other was a fellow who had asked Hanna out several times. He was a clean-cut boy with closely trimmed blond hair. Both boys seemed shy as they stood outside Dede's Audi and talked about nothing in particular. A while later Dede got out and walked down the rock slope to the edge of the river with her boyfriend. Hanna got out, too. The four of them sat on the gray rocks for more than an hour talking about things high school seniors talk about, and laughed the way they do when things aren't settled between them. It was a fine night, a vague chill in the air, but not unpleasantly cool. The river was active with barges and tugboats moving up and down. The water slapped at the rocks and the moon shone brightly right above a little tree just to the young people's left. As time passed and the moon got higher in the sky, Dede and the boy with her started to talk between themselves. For a while Hanna and the blond-haired boy talked too, but theirs was interrupted often with intervals of silence. Then Dede and her boyfriend got up and went back to Dede's car. Another half an hour went by before the blond-haired boy stood up, brushed off the seat of his pants, and held his hand out for Hanna. They went back to the other car and the boy got them both cold beers out of an ice chest, then led Hanna on a walk down along the edge of the river. There were more trees and shadows down that way, and soon the boy picked a spot underneath a tree and Hanna sat down on the grass with him. They talked some more, laughed a little, then talked some more. The laughter grew more and more strained and contrived, until the boy picked up Hanna's hand and very gently kissed it. It was the first time Hanna had been touched that way by a boy since leaving Florida. It felt nice, and soon she could smell the faint scent of some male cologne as the boy put his face to her neck. That was nice, too. She could feel her hand trembling as she turned to face him, as she felt the breath from his mouth on her cheek. She tried to tell herself the trembling was because of the chill in the night air. They kissed and touched each other and said nothing. And soon Hanna was on her back, on the damp grass. She could feel the weight of the boy's shoulder on her breast. That too felt nice. She could feel her hands on his taut back, the way his neck felt with its whiskerlike hair, the smell of that cologne again, the way his mouth felt, and the dew that had penetrated the back of her blouse. She was not aware of the exact moment at which the boy's leg moved between hers. Too many things were starting to happen at once. The moon was now straight above them, the water still lapped at the river's edge, the boy's neck was perspiring, and it was warm on her lips, and everything still felt nice. Hanna's eyes were closed, and they would remain that way until it was all over.

* * *

It was early morning when she got back to the house, all the lights were on and both Byron and Bobby were on their mattresses snoring. The place smelled awful. Plastic glasses sat all about the living room floor, several filled with cigarette butts and others turned to their sides. The ukulele lay on the floor beside one of the lawn chairs. Hanna walked to the kitchen. It was worse. There was a puddle of water on the floor; the stove had streams of grease all over it. An iron skillet was filled with grease-soaked half-fried sticks of potatoes that barely resembled French fries. On the table, on a grocery sack that had been torn open, lay awful pieces of something that could or could not have been fried fish. Then, as she was about to turn out the light and go to her room, she noticed the typewriter, set on the cabinet by the sink, with a piece of paper attached to the roll bar. Stepping closer, she read, "Dear Hanna, I don't know where you got it, but you shouldn't have. I think I love you. Byron. P.S. Where'd you get it?"

TWENTY

When they got to the top gray-granite step, Bobby adjusted Byron's tie before they went inside. The receptionist who greeted them from her desk was not the same young woman they had seen before. This one looked bored. After the two men dressed in out-of-date suits explained that they wanted to see someone associated with admissions, the woman disappeared into the room behind her. She returned a moment later and invited Byron and Bobby to go on in. There behind her desk was the middle-aged lady they saw the time before. She recognized them.

"It's certainly a lovely day," Bobby said as he sat in the straight chair beside the one Byron took. The woman looked impatient and said that she only had a few minutes to spend with them. It had something to do with a meeting she had to attend.

"Oh, we understand," said Bobby. "And we won't take up much of your time. The pressures of your position I'm sure are overwhelming."

The woman smiled the smile of a woman who indeed had an abundance of pressures and was proud of it.

Byron did not give her a chance to finish that smile. "We want to enroll the girl we told you about before in Tulane."

"You mean, Sophie Newcomb," said the woman.

"That'll be okay," said Byron. "But we want to get her in this fall."

The woman leaned forward and picked up a pencil. "If I remember correctly, the young lady has not yet applied for admission."

"That's right," said Byron. "What we want to know is how we can get around the rules."

"I'm afraid that's impossible," the woman said.

Bobby grinned and Byron said, "She's very intelligent."

"I'm sure she is," the woman said.

"No you aren't," said Bobby.

The woman said, "I beg your pardon."

"Your apology is accepted," said Bobby. "But you aren't sure that she's intelligent. But she is."

Byron leaned forward. "Ma'am, this girl is a special case. She's very poor, but very smart. We've helped raise her, and we've just got to get her in school—in this school. This fall. All we are asking is how we may go about doing that. We'll do anything that is necessary. We'll talk to anybody and everybody. This is the most important thing in our lives. She has no money, no sources of any money, and no family of her own, but she's brilliant. Now, we've read the brochure you gave us before, and according to those, there are plans available for people like that."

"Yes there are," said the woman. "And here at Tulane—"

"Sophie Newcomb," Bobby reminded her.

She only gave him an impatient look and went on talking to Byron. "—We want to help such students, but we still have a cutoff date for admission. If I recall, the young lady has not even taken her SAT. And as for financial aid, that is a rather complicated process."

"Were you a cheerleader?" Bobby asked.

"A cheerleader?" repeated the woman as if she could not believe what she had been asked.

"In high school. Were you a cheerleader or a majorette? Doesn't she look like a cheerleader, Byron?"

"No, I can't say that I was."

"I can't believe that," said Bobby. "I told Byron after we were here before that I bet you were a cheerleader, and that you won first place in the Miss Crawfish Beauty Contest. It's your cheek structure."

"Well, I'm flattered, I'm sure," said the woman. "But no, I'm sorry to say I—"

"Where are you from?" asked Bobby.

"Where am I from?"

"Yes, where are you from?"

"She has taken the SAT," said Byron. "And she's already completed and sent in the forms requesting financial aid."

The woman turned back to Byron.

"Miss Watermelon," said Bobby.

The woman glanced back at him and smiled briefly before saying in Byron's direction, "That's a step in the right direction, certainly. But still, I'm afraid the earliest she could be admitted would be next winter semester, and that's if her grades, SAT and recommendations all qualify. Has she considered a state school, possibly a junior college? Many of the trade schools today are offering courses and curriculums she may be interested in. Louisiana has a fine vocational program, I understand."

"We're getting off the subject and rambling," said Byron. "What we need to do is get the specifics. For instance, whom must we talk to in order to get the ball rolling?"

The woman sat back in her high-back chair and said, "You may talk to the dean of admissions, I guess. But, as I've already said, it's all spelled out in the material I gave you before. I understand how frustrating it must seem, but most all universities have similar requirements. Some, I must admit, are more strenuous than others. But all have their deadlines."

"May we see the dean?" asked Byron.

"Surely, you may." The woman's eyes began to blink rapidly. "You will need an appointment though."

"Where do we get that?"

The woman stood up and stepped to the door. "Kathy," she said to the young woman at the outer desk, "would you show these gentlemen to the dean's office?"

"And you're sure you were never a cheerleader?" Bobby asked again before they left. The woman did not even bother to smile this time.

The dean of admissions' office was on the same floor, but down the far end of the dark oak hall. On the way there, Bobby and Byron talked about the feeling of academia the place gave them. It had a scent of pencil shavings and age, like an old library. They stopped halfway down the hall to light cigarettes, but when they went inside the dean's reception office, the fat black woman behind the first desk explained that smoking was not allowed. "Is that constitutional?" Bobby wanted to know, and the lady laughed. She seemed genuinely friendly. They stubbed their cigarettes out in a trash can and Byron began to explain to her what they wanted.

"The dean's not in his office right now."

"When will he be back?" asked Byron.

"The assistant dean is in, I believe."

"Then may we see him?"

"It's a her."

"Well, that's alright, I guess," said Byron. "If she's not anything like the woman down the hall."

They had to wait almost half an hour before they were led into the assistant dean's office. Bobby spent most of that time trying to talk Byron into leaving and coming back another day. And they had almost made that decision before the woman ushered them into a plush office. A rather handsome woman stood to shake their hands before offering the chairs.

"Are you a graduate of Tulane?" Bobby asked her as he took his seat.

"Smith," she said.

"Smith. I once courted a girl from Smith," said Bobby.

"No you didn't," said Byron in his gutteral voice.

Bobby chuckled with surprise. "Byron, I sure did."

"He did not," said Byron.

The woman was amused and more than a little bit thrown off her professional guard.

"Byron, that's embarrassing. I tell this lady something and you call me a liar, right in front of her."

"He had one date with a girl who went to Smith for a year and dropped out," said Byron

The assistant dean smiled her way back into as much of a professional face as she could for the moment. "May I help you gentlemen?"

"Yes, you may," said Bobby. "We want to enroll a girl in your school."

"It's gotten complicated," said Byron. The two of them spent several minutes explaining the dilemma, and several more pleading Hanna's case.

"I see," the woman finally said. "But those are the rules, I'm sorry to say."

"And I believe you mean that," said Bobby. "Byron,

this woman is one of us."

The assistant dean did not know what to make of them, but she was amused, and eventually she gave up trying to maintain her professional standoffishness. Bobby asked her several questions about herself, and told her some things about him and Byron. One of her dear friends happened to be from Montgomery, and Bobby tried to place her as being someone he might have some connections with. "May I smoke?" Byron finally asked, and the woman opened a desk drawer and passed him an ashtray.

"You were overweight as a child, weren't you?" Bobby then asked the woman.

"I sure was. But I can't believe I'm sitting here talking to you two like this."

"Oh, don't say that," said Bobby, "People don't talk to one another enough. We're all just children when everything is said and done. Did you ever play doctor when you were little?"

"Now that's where I draw the line," the woman said. "You gentlemen obviously mean well. I certainly admire your trying to help Hanna. But I'm going to have to stick with my initial explanation. I doubt even the president's daughter would be admitted without a complete application."

"That is a marvelous suit you are wearing," said Bobby, "Isn't it, Byron?"

"Now, Mr. Long, that will do you absolutely no good

at all. And I really do have things to do."

"I understand," said Bobby. "And you have been kind to listen to us. It's nice to see that behind that academic facade is a very delightful human being—and I mean that."

"May I ask you one more thing?" said Byron as Bobby had already gotten up from his chair. "What should we do—honestly? I mean, if you were in our position, what would you do?"

The woman stood up too. "I would gather up all the necessary information and application papers and submit them. Then I would think in terms of next January."

"Are you married?" Bobby asked.

"I sure am," said the assistant dean.

"You don't run around, I don't suppose?" said Bobby.

"I'm sorry I couldn't be more help," the woman said as she offered her hand to Byron, then Bobby. She then saw them to the door and managed to resume her role.

They left the old granite building from the back entrance, which faced a quadrangle that was enclosed by similar old structures. Several students sat about the grounds while others were walking on the sidewalks beneath the old live oak trees. When they got down the steps and started on one of the sidewalks, Byron took a bottle from his coat pocket and Bobby lit them both cigarettes. "There's only one thing to do," said Byron.

"Byron," said Bobby, "look at that one." He nodded

at a girl in leotards and a T-shirt walking toward one of the buildings. Neither man said anything else until she went inside the building, then Byron said, "We have to go straight to the president." It was just then a young fellow was coming toward them on a bicycle. Byron flagged him down and the young man used his sneakers for brakes and stopped just as he reached them. "Are you a student here?" Byron asked. The young man was. "Where is the president's office?" The student pointed to the building they had just left.

"Second floor, I think."

"What do you study?" Bobby asked him.

"I'm a pre-med student," the boy said.

"A very good curriculum," said Bobby before the fellow went on his way, and he and Byron walked on. Then in a minute he said, "Byron, what time is it?"

"How should I know?"

"We should find out."

"Why?"

Just then they approached a woman who looked to be in her late twenties sitting on a bench writing on a legal pad. Bobby asked her for the time, told her she was a very pretty lady, and they walked on.

"Why did you want to know the time?" Byron asked him.

"Because, in about ten minutes some of the classes will probably be letting out. We can see what today's coed looks like."

They sat on a bench halfway down the quadrangle, took another sip of vodka, and waited while they discussed seeing the college president about Hanna. "You have to go to the source for things like this," said Byron.

"I don't think we should go to his office. We should go to his home. Catch him out of his position. Maybe meet his children, his wife. Win the wife, win the president is what I always say."

"Win the president, get some pussy, is what I always say," said Byron.

"We need to find out where he lives. Byron, don't most college presidents live near their campus?"

"Bobby?"

"What?"

"Did you ever go on a panty raid?"

"Hell no. I was too busy fucking."

Just then Bobby caught sight of a man walking toward them. He looked like he could be a professor. Bobby stood up. "Let's ask this gentleman," he said. And when the man came close enough, Bobby said, "Pardon me. My friend and I are looking for the president's home. Do you know where we could find it?"

"You mean the university president?" the man said in a voice that sounded North Carolinian.

Bobby nearly chuckled. "Are you a professor?"

"I am," the man told him.

"English," said Bobby.

"Economics," the man told him.

"Well you certainly don't look like it," said Bobby. "Byron, doesn't he look like a literature man? You aren't a communist, are you?"

The man looked at him with something like a kind smirk.

"Well it's alright if you are. Marx had his heart in the right place, I think. Even if he did let one of his children starve to death." Bobby leaned his head to one side and looked the professor in the eyes. "Did he really do that?"

The professor turned and looked off across the quadrangle. "Let's see, the president's home…"

It turned out the president's home was just off the main campus, not very far from where they stood. So Bobby thanked the man, shook his hand, then, as he started to walk away, said, "Adam Smith was a nice man, too, don't you think?"

The professor raised his hand and walked on.

Bobby and Byron did not immediately go to the president's house. They had to wait for the classes to change so they could watch the young women coming out of the various buildings. It wasn't long before they started pouring out, darting here and there. "Look at that one," Byron would say.

"Look at that one," Bobby would say.

"The blond," said Byron.

"The one in the blue shorts, Byron."

"Goddamn!"

"Byron, we should come here every day."

"Bobby."

"What?"

"These girls aren't going to let you fuck them."

"And why do you say that?"

"Because you have nothing to offer them."

"Neither do you."

"Neither do you."

Bobby stuck his hands in his pockets. "I don't want to talk about it anymore." Then he looked Byron's way. "Sometimes you irritate the hell out of me, Byron."

***

They followed a pathway between two of the oldest stone buildings and came out on a sidewalk on St. Charles Avenue. The professor had told them to go right until they came to a booth where a sentinel would be posted; that would be Audubon Place. Inside the huge iron gates would be two rows of houses on opposite sides of a boulevard-like street. The sentinel could point out the president's home.

When Byron and Bobby reached the entranceway to Audubon Place they stood along the outside of the gate and looked down the street inside. On both sides were mansions, not houses, close enough together to be considered a neighborhood. It was just a very fine neighborhood of modest mansions. And as the man in the quadrangle had explained, a uniformed guard, an elderly man, sat inside the stone booth, reading a newspaper.

"You know he isn't home this time of day," Bobby told Byron.

"I know. But we just need to study the situation."

Bobby stepped up to the little guardhouse and said, "Good morning," to the sentinel. "Is this where we would find the home of Tulane's president?"

"Yep, shore is," said the guard.

"Which one is it?"

"That one." The old man pointed to the left of the gates to an immaculately kept, high-columned place painted off-white.

"I wouldn't think the president would be home right now," said Bobby.

"Not unless he's sick."

"I wouldn't imagine you know when he comes and goes, would you? This is my friend, Byron, and I'm Bobby Long."

"Pleased to meet you," said the old man.

"We would like to speak with him. When do you guess the best time for that would be?"

"Hard to say. You'd be better off to go to his office and make an appointment."

"I don't guess just anybody can go in and knock at the front door of his home."

"Not unless you have an appointment or invitation. Students you know."

"Oh, I can understand that," said Bobby. "I don't

suppose there are exceptions to that?"

"Family and friends," said the old man.

"Well thanks for the information," Byron told him as they walked off down the sidewalk.

They decided not to take the streetcar back to the house yet. It was such a fine warm and sunshiny day, they decided to go out into Audubon Park and sit on a bench, to watch the people and drink.

"How's your face?" Byron asked as they both watched a woman who was walking unnaturally fast go by, wearing a powder blue sweatsuit. The part of her they both focused upon was the lines where her panties were. The elastic went high up her hips.

"It still hurts," said Bobby as he turned to face Byron. "How does it look?"

"It's still warped."

Bobby felt his cheek and the bone that still felt detached from something inside his face. "But am I still handsome?"

"Bobby?"

"What?"

"You know those panties on your pillow?"

"Yes. And I know where they came from."

"You do?"

"Yes. You put them there."

"You knew that all along, didn't you?"

"Yep. After I thought about it."

TWENTY-ONE

The next Saturday morning Byron and Bobby were up early. Hanna had explained the typewriter. She and Dede stole it from the high school. "It was no fucking big deal," she told Byron. "It was one of a pile of them in this room nobody uses since they started using computers."

"Compliments of Bonnie and Clydette," said Bobby.

They took beer and tomato juice out to the front porch to enjoy the pretty weather. "I want to go to the beach," said Bobby. "Byron, let's get Hanna to call Dede and get her to take us to the beach."

The men still had not made an appointment to see the president of Tulane. They had talked about it, but it had gone no further than that; there were other things on their minds since summer was on its way. They had begun to leave the windows open all the time and Hanna had another week of school before graduation. The men had never seen her so excited. She was busy and happy, and she looked better than ever. The men were spending lots more time outdoors, occasionally shirtless, wallowing in the Mr. Turtle pool. Down at the outdoor living room somebody had found a new old sofa someplace, and Cecil and some of the others put one of the other ones out for trash. The old woman across the street who had given Byron and Bobby the cinder blocks for Hanna's bed had survived the winter, and Georgianna had started back to letting Bobby go all the way again.

The men were in the best of spirits this morning. "Let's go wake her up and get started," said Bobby.

So they went back inside and stood outside Hanna's door, and tapped on it lightly. "Hanna," said Bobby softly and gruffly. "Hannnnnnnah."

Byron tried it, "Hannnnah, Sugar."

"Whut?"

"May we come in?" asked Bobby.

"I don't care," she mumbled, still half asleep.

Byron tried to open the door, but as usual, it was locked. "It's locked," said Bobby.

"What do ya'll want?"

"We want to talk to you, Sugar Baby," said Bobby.

"'Sugar Baby' yourself. What about?"

"We could talk better if you opened the door."

"What time is it?" Hanna asked.

"Time to be nice to old people," said Byron.

"Go away," Hanna said in her sleepy voice.

The men waited for a moment, then Bobby started all over again, "Hannnnah."

"What, Bobby?"

"May we come in?"

"Oh, shit, alright then." They heard her get off her bed and quickly Bobby tapped Byron and motioned for him to get down on his knees like he was doing. When Hanna, wearing a long T-shirt, opened the door, they were in that position, with their hands clasped together like the beggars they were. Hanna couldn't help but smile. She shoved her hair back and went back to bed, climbed in and covered herself up. Byron and Bobby did not move until she acknowledged them. "Ya'll are so stupid."

"Hanna," Bobby began once more.

She opened her eyes and looked across her pillow at them. "What, Bobby?" she mumbled.

"Take us to the beach."

"Christ," said Hanna. "And how do you expect me to do that?"

"Call Dede, and ask her to go with us, and take her car."

"You call Dede."

"Alright, what's her number?"

Hanna chuckled hoarsely, "You wish."

"Hanna," said Byron.

"Whut?"

"Please."

"No. I'm sleepy. Now, ya'll get off that floor and stop acting like Chihuahuas."

They went right on pleading with her, saying one

ridiculous thing after another, until finally Hanna threw off the cover and said, "Alright, I'll call her. I'll call her. But she's not going."

"Yeah!" shouted both Bobby and Byron as they came to their feet.

While she was gone to the phone booth, Byron and Bobby fried her an egg, made some toast and fixed themselves Bloody Marys.

When Hanna got back they heard her speak to the old woman across the street before she came into the house.

"What did she say?"

"She said okay."

In their excitement, the men had to add some extra vodka to their drinks. And by the time Dede got there they were giddy with anticipation. Byron had on a pair of old pleated shorts he bought some years back in an Army-Navy surplus store. Bobby wore stark white shorts. They were both barefoot, and wore long-sleeved shirts rolled to the elbows. Bobby tied a knot at the bottom of his to take care of a couple missing buttons.

"Whooo hoo!" said Hanna. "For two old men, ya'll have cute legs. Chalky, Bobby, but cute."

Dede arrived in light green shorts, a man's oxford dress shirt, and canvas shoes. Carrying a rolled plastic bag, she spoke briefly to the men before she and Hanna went to Hanna's room while Bobby and Byron thought to themselves the shorts should be tighter round the ass.

When they came out, Hanna was wearing white shorts, sandals and a dark green T-shirt with "Tulane" written in bold white letters across her chest.

"Where are your swimsuits?" Byron wanted to know.

The girls glanced at each other. "I have mine on," said Dede.

"Me, too," said Hanna.

"Shotgun," said Bobby when they got to Dede's car.

Hanna opened the front door. "Ya'll sit in the back," said Hanna.

"Then I'm not going," said Bobby.

As Byron sat in the backseat, he poured himself a drink from the orange juice bottle they had half filled with vodka and finished filling with orange juice and ice.

"Then, don't go," said Hanna.

"I won't," said Bobby, and he started back to the house.

"Oh, Hanna, let him sit up here," said Dede.

Hanna got out reluctantly and said, "Alright, baby, have your little way."

Bobby started back to the car, grinning. "I swear," said Hanna as Dede started to drive away.

"Where are we going?" Hanna wanted to know.

"It's up to them," said Dede.

"Let's go to that place we went last summer," said Bobby. "That place on Lake Pontchartrain. What's it called, Byron? You know."

"I do not."

"Yes you do."

"I know a place," said Dede.

Hanna glanced at Byron and mumbled.

"Wait!" shouted Bobby. Dede slammed on the brakes. "We forgot the ukulele."

"Too late now," said Hanna. Dede stopped the car in the middle of the street until a decision could be made.

"Pa-lease!" said Bobby. "You can't go to the beach without a ukulele."

Byron passed him a plastic cup of vodka and orange juice and Dede looked at Hanna. They knew they were going back for the ukulele—sooner or later—so Dede backed up.

Afterwards, when they were back on the street, the girls lit cigarettes. Bobby reprimanded Dede for driving too carelessly, and leaned across the seat to help her. She zipped in and out of traffic like the native of New Orleans she was, while Byron plucked and picked the ukulele. "Dede, do you think my legs are chalky?" Bobby asked.

When they got on a ramp for the interstate, headed toward Lake Pontchartrain, Bobby leaned back, saying, "Byron, let's sing Dede 'My Gal.'"

Bobby turned to his side, leaned as much as he could toward Byron:

"My gal, she lives in a big brick house,

Her sistern does the same…" ("Sistern," Hanna chuckled.)

Bobby sang.

Then, Byron, "My gal, she lives in Conecuh County jail,

But it's a brick house just the same."

In harmony, "It's a brick house just the saammme,

A brick house just the same.

She'll be comin' round the mountain Charming Betsy,

She'll be comin' round the mountain Coralee…"

Dede, zipping in and out of traffic.

Bobby, "…My gal, she wears them old cotton drawers,

Her sistern does the same."

Byron, "My gal, she wears silky underwear,

But they come down just the same."

In harmony, "They come down just the saammme,

Oh, they come down just the same,

She'll be…"

"Ya'll dirty little boys," said Dede.

"Sex maniacs," said Hanna before reaching and saying, "Hand it to me."

"What?" said Byron.

"The ukulele," said Hanna. "Just hand it to me."

"What are you going to do?" Byron wanted to know.

When she got the ukulele, Hanna said, "Ya'll close your windows."

"Can you play that thing?" asked Dede.

"Can you?" asked Byron.

"A little bit. Close ya'lls windows—tight."

Dede was still darting in and out of traffic.

"Close your window, Bobby," said Hanna.

"Mine's closed," said Dede, her eyes glancing from the rearview mirror at Hanna, to the highway.

As Hanna began to strum, Bobby, his arm across the seat, said, "Okay, so you know some chords. Sing." Hanna kept plucking C, D and F and looked up with pride in her accomplishment.

"When did you learn to do that?" Byron wanted to know.

"Wait," said Hanna. Suddenly she started to sing:

"Way out west they have a name,

For rain and wind and fi-re…"

Bobby looked at Byron, Byron looked at Bobby, and Dede barely missed a pickup truck.

"…the rain is Tess, the fire is Joe,

With a fancy strum, They callll the wind, Mariah…

Miri-ah, Miri-ah,

They call the wind, Miriah…"

No one said a word as Hanna sang the entire song. She made a couple of mistakes and said, "Wait a minute," on both occasions, but otherwise she finished the last line, tapped the ukulele like it was a bongo drum once, then ended:

"…Blow my love to me."

When she was through, and looked up at Byron and Bobby, they neither one said anything until Bobby nearly climbed over the seat, the same time Byron reached to hug their little pussy. Had they not nearly choked her to death, she would have cried.

"Goddamn," said Byron. "Girl, when did you learn to do that?"

"That was so pretty, Hanna," said Dede, who just missed the back corner of a Chevrolet by no more than a yard.

"Aren't ya'll proud of me?" said Hanna.

"Shoot fire, yes," said Bobby.

Hanna was beaming, even though she tried not to show it. Byron was staring out the window, going back over the last several minutes with a flutter somewhere inside his chest. He could see the way Hanna's mouth turned as she sang, the way her eyes showed some confident yet innocent quality that had become so much a part of her over the months since that day she stood outside the hotel room.

"Hanna, where did you learn to do that?" Bobby asked.

"Bobby, you don't know everything about me. You think you do, but you don't." Hanna realized that he was trying to give her a compliment, and very quickly said, "I've been practicing." She turned to Dede, "Byron taught me the chords last year. You remember that, Byron?"

Byron nodded and went on looking out the window, while Bobby kept trying to get Hanna to play something else, something he could sing along with.

"Bobby, I've got to practice more. I don't know all the chords." Bobby's disappointment was indicated when he sat back and crossed his arms.

It was not long before Dede turned off to the left and was heading west alongside Lake Pontchartrain, on a two-lane highway. The lake was not in view, but there were signs that they were near water, recreation homes set back among woods, sail and motorboats here and there, oyster shell driveways, an occasional lot of boats for sale and the passing of windsurfers atop Hondas and Toyotas. For several miles, Dede drove behind a slow Jeep pulling a fishing boat.

There was not a cloud in the baby blue sky. It was a day for the beach and being outdoors, the kind of day on which Byron and Bobby were at their best. And they were with two of what they considered to be the most precious things in life. The liquor tasted good, the women were fine, and the song was, to their minds, as good as could be. And they had a little money in their pockets. And it was still morning; the rest of the day was ahead of them.

Dede took a right at an intersection alive with folks fueling up motorboats and buying up ice and beer and other spring leisure paraphernalia. They were going toward the lake. Byron started to sing "Won't You Come Home, Bill Bailey." Hanna knew the words from having listened to them sing it so many times. She and Bobby joined in, and Dede sang along on the more familiar parts. And after that, Bobby kept saying, "Oh! Oh! I have one. I have one." Then when he got everybody's attention he said, "Byron, give me a chord." He sang "Barbara Allen" by himself and was almost finished when Dede got to the place.

They parked the Audi underneath a cypress tree, before a narrow beach where some children played and at the edge of the calm water while young parents and young couples sprawled along the shore. Far out in the lake were several small fishing boats and an occasional pleasure boat. Light breezes came and went.

No one was allowed to leave the car until Bobby finished his song, then he and Byron made new drinks while the girls rounded up their things for a day at the beach. Byron took the ukulele, Bobby the container of vodka, orange juice and rapidly melting ice. Hanna carried the cooler with an ice pack. As they reached the sand, Bobby said, "Now you women remember to look out for anybody weird. You never know what kinds of people you're going to meet at a place like this."

"The pot calling..." Hanna mumbled.

"Woman, you're starting to sound more like your mother every day," said Bobby.

Dede glanced at Hanna, curious about any response she might have. The men were walking behind them as Bobby babbled on about any foolishness that came to his mind before they decided on a spot to spread towels. Bobby stepped out of his flip-flops and shirt, to expose an increasing crimson belly, flexing his dilapidated muscles as a kid might do for an admired uncle. "What do you think?" he said as he jerked his shorts up and grinned. The girls never looked up, as they were involved with tanning lotion and lip balm. "Hey!" he demanded.

"About what?" said Hanna.

"Me!"

"Cute as an oyster," said Hanna.

Byron was looking at a woman in a dark brown swimsuit with long slender legs he imagined wrapped round his, having to take off his sunglasses to enhance the fantasy, while Bobby noticed a woman in a pregnancy one-piece. "I love pregnant women," he said, while Dede and Hanna spread a blanket brought along for the men to keep them some distance away from their tanning chores. "Why are we sitting so far away from everybody else?" Bobby wanted to know as he rolled onto the blanket.

"Tell him, Hanna," said Dede.

Hanna, sitting on a beach towel, touched Bobby's more decent foot with her toe. "So that if ya'll got to talking dirty nobody else could hear."

Finished spreading lotion on her legs, Dede passed the tube to Hanna as Bobby noticed a mildly hefty woman walking by. "Young lady," spoke Bobby as the woman stepped up her pace with no other response.

"Oh Lord," said Hanna.

Byron lit a cigarette, sat on the blanket and stared toward the water.

Bobby said, "Dede, may I ask you something?" Bobby was stretched out, half on the blanket half on the sand, using his propped hand to rest his head on.

"I don't know," said Dede.

"You know you won't be able to stop him," said Hanna.

"Have you ever…"

"Bobby, don't start," said Hanna.

"Woman! I was just going to ask her if she had ever read Chaucer."

Even Byron laughed.

Then suddenly Bobby softly began an off-subject recitation:

"As I listened from a beach-chair in the shade
To all the noises that my garden made,
It seemed to me only proper that words
Should be withheld from vegetables and birds.

A robin with no Christian name ran through
The Robin-Anthem which was all it knew,
And rustling flowers for some third party-waited
To say which pairs, if any, should get mated.

No one of them was capable of lying,
There was not one which knew that it was dying
Or could have with a rhythm or a rhyme
Assumed responsibility for time.

Let them leave language to their lonely betters
Who count some days and long for certain letters;
We, too, make noises when we laugh or weep,
Words are for those with promises to keep."

Nothing was said for several moments. "May I ask you something?" Dede enquired.

"I don't know," said Bobby. "Is it dirty?"

"Is there anybody you would not try to screw?"

"Byron," said Bobby. "Now, may I ask you a question?"

"Sure," Dede said.

"When are you and Hanna going to take off your clothes?"

"We aren't," said Dede.

"Well, then how do you expect to get a tan in those other places?" Bobby said.

"Bobby," said Hanna, "we lied. We didn't wear swimsuits."

Byron spoke. "Bobby, we might as well leave."

"I agree," said Bobby, "no hairlets, no nothing."

"Shit for sense," mumbled Hanna.

"How can you stand them?" said Dede.

"I keep them out of jail," said Hanna.

"God, can you imagine them teaching school?" said Dede. "Can you imagine being in one of their classes?"

"Byron," said Bobby, "look over there," referring to a young lady who just stood from her beach towel.

"They should be in jail," said Dede.

"Dede," said Bobby, "what is Hanna like at school? Are we raising her right?"

Dede sat up, crossed her legs, reached for a cigarette, saying, "Oh, what is Hanna like at school? Well, for one thing, she's cool. I mean, really cool." As she smiled, with enthusiasm in her voice, Dede went on. "Annnnd-ah, she's…" Squirming slightly, to get her thoughts together, she said, "I can remember the first time I ever saw Hanna." Hanna had started scooping up sand and letting it drain through the bottom of her fist. "I thought she was pretty," Dede continued. "I mean, not conventionally, but I thought she was pretty. I mean, like she…first of all, the guys…the girls thought she was shit. I did too, at first. Before that…But…" Dede nudged Hanna on the back with her foot. "Should I tell them this?"

"What are you going to say?"

Dede leaned over and whispered in Hanna's ear. Hanna got a serious look on her face and said, "I reckon so."

Dede told them about the slut panties incident. "Girl," said Byron, "You never told us about that. Damn."

Bobby said, "Me and Byron would have kicked

some ass."

"Did that really happen?" asked Byron.

"Byron, Dede is very popular," said Hanna.

"Yeah, I am," said Dede. "And I didn't even speak to Hanna for the longest—not until after Christmas. I mean, I thought about it, just because she looked so pitiful."

"It watn't that bad," said Hanna. "Was it?"

"It was bad," Dede said with a frown.

"Why did you finally have anything to do with her?" asked Bobby.

"Oh!" said Dede. "The slut thing was one thing. And after that speech she made, the one about that streetcar down in the French Quarter. You know that Tennessee Williams thing. It was that day I knew I would like her. I mean, ya'll should've seen her that day." Dede tossed some fallen hair back with a flip of her head. "She had on this real neat beret, this burgundy beret, and this outfit that made her look, I mean, great! It was sort of sleazy, but not really. Sort of Frenchy looking or some-thing. And she was so cute giving that speech. She had everybody in stitches, this really dry sense of humor. I mean, God, I thought she was the smartest person I'd ever seen. I thought to myself, this girl is nobody's fool. She was great. It was like she wasn't anything I thought she was." Dede started fumbling with a near empty cig-arette pack. "...It was like she had changed since...or that is, my feelings about her had changed.

"And she was funny, too. Hanna has the best sense of humor…I mean, like…like when a teacher will start to jump her ass, somebody—say, a group of girls. Hanna is the one who always makes it seem like she's innocent, like she had nothing to do with whatever was going on. And what's funny is she's usually the one who starts it. And everybody thinks she's so quiet—God!"

Byron and Bobby were both looking at Hanna, who would glance at them, then shift her eyes quickly away. She was pleased with the things Dede was saying, but it all made her a little uncomfortable.

"Oh, you know what she did one day?" Dede went on.

"What are you fixing to tell?" Hanna wanted to know.

Dede shifted her shoulder, giggled and said, "There's this psychology teacher…"

Hanna gave Dede a vicious look that turned into a plea, "Don't tell them that."

"Tell it," said Byron.

"Dede, if you do…"

"Tell it. Goddamn," said Byron.

Hanna only tilted her head to her sympathetic hand.

"…One time…" Dede started. "…He's this teacher that thinks every girl at our school just falls all over herself to get to have anything to do with him. So, one day Hanna and I got this idea…it was Hanna's idea."

Hanna started piling and packing sand over her feet. Dede peeked round to see her expression before continuing. "What we were going to do, see, is…Hanna was going to sit up front of his classroom, so that…uh, so he could look up her dress."

Byron and Bobby jerked their heads around in Hanna's direction. "And while she was doing it, I was supposed to watch Mr. White to see what he did. It was great. He got to stumbling around and trying to act normal. But it was real obvious what he had on his mind. He was all goggly-eyed, and while he was talking, he kept moving back and forth from where he could get a good look."

"And, I swear," said Dede, "that man lost his place on his notes at least twice."

"Girl, did you do that?" Bobby asked Hanna, who barely nodded.

"How much did you show him?" Bobby wanted to know.

"It watn't nothing," said Hanna. "I just pulled my skirt up some."

"It was enough," said Dede.

"Dede did it, too," said Hanna.

"You nasty little things," said Byron.

"Us nasty? What about him? You should've seen his face. He looked like this old lecher. I mean, God. I thought he was gonna start slobbering."

"Did you get wet between the legs?" asked Bobby.

"Lord, Bobby," said Hanna. "It was just this stupid joke. He asked for it. I can't stand him."

"Me either," said Dede.

"Not even a little bit damp?" Bobby persisted.

Dede looked at Hanna and both girls rolled their eyes at one another. "Bobby, you have the nicest way of saying everything," said Dede.

"And you two are vulgar," said Bobby.

The men were rapidly getting drunk on warm vodka and orange juice.

"When are you two going to take off your clothes?" Byron wanted to know.

Dede and Hanna looked at one another. "Byron, we've already been through that."

"What?" asked Byron.

"Never mind," said Hanna.

"What?" Byron repeated, his eyes growing red.

Most of the remaining afternoon the men talked. They moved from one subject to another, often with no apparent reason. And the girls were content to lie there and listen to them while soaking up sun. Once Bobby started talking about his younger years, one summer when he had been a lifeguard and discovered a way to see into the girl's dressing room at the municipal pool. Then he and Byron got to reminiscing about their lost innocence, and Byron told the girls about a time when he and a friend saved their money and went to Atlanta and bought a prostitute. Then Bobby had to tell about the first time he had sex and all the intimate details while complaining about the hot vodka they continued to drink. Several times toward the latter part of the afternoon the girls tried to talk them into leaving, to no avail as Bobby was telling about a romance he once had with an Italian girl while he was a Marine Corps officer stationed in Naples, about the two of them wandering about a mountainside meadow naked, sipping wine and making love in a field of bright red flowers.

"You amaze me, Bobby," said Dede, "how you can tell such a graphic story so romantically and make it seem almost clean. You know, I can imagine both of you as the... the fair-haired boys you say you were."

"Lord, Dede, have they conned you," said Hanna.

"Woman," said Bobby, "Listen to your more intelligent friend. Dede, that girl never gives us an inch."

People had started to gather up their belongings and drift away as the sun dropped closer to the water. It was a lazy time of the afternoon and finally the men agreed to go.

The drive back to New Orleans was quiet; everyone had been drained of energy by the sun and alcohol. While they were listening to jazz on the radio, Byron and Bobby dozed off to sleep for a short while, then woke up abruptly when Dede stopped to get gasoline. The men used the occasion to urinate and buy a pint of vodka and cold juice.

It was almost dark when they reached Carrollton

Avenue, and Byron needed to stop again. After this the men started to come back to life. Hanna had switched the radio back to a rock station, and something about the song struck a chord in Bobby, and by the time they had gone another few miles, the silent late afternoon had been replaced with talk about going somewhere else.

"I have to go home," said Dede.

Bobby pleaded with her for a while, then gave up and started in on Hanna. Then, when she said she was tired and only wanted to go take a bath and go to sleep, Bobby said, "Well then, do you girls want to see my peter?"

And it was just after Hanna said, "Will shit never cease," that Dede turned onto the upper end of St. Charles Avenue, just as Bobby unzipped his pants, only wanting them to hear the sound of the zipper, just as Dede accelerated. Then all of a sudden Byron realized where they were and shouted, "Stop the car!" and Dede slammed on the brakes.

"Bobby, look!" said Byron.

"What?" said Bobby.

"Fuck!" shouted Dede.

Hanna turned around and reached over the seat and slapped Bobby's face so hard he thought for a moment he was sober.

"What'd you do that for?" Bobby wanted to know when everything stopped.

"I don't know," said Hanna with her hand over her

mouth. "Did I hurt you?"

Byron opened the door on his side and climbed out.

"Byron, what are you doing?" Dede shouted. She was concerned about getting her Audi further off the street.

"Byron!" yelled Bobby.

"Look, Bobby," said Byron, "Audubon Place." He bent down and stuck his head through the backdoor window. "You want to go now?"

Possibly, had he waited another second, or had he made the suggestion a moment earlier, Bobby's reaction might have been different. But he had made it at the exact moment he did, and it struck Bobby as the best idea of the day, so he opened the door and got out, too.

"What in the world are ya'll doing?" Hanna yelled.

Dede rolled down her window. "Byron, get your ass back in this car. What do you think you're doing?"

Byron leaned through her window and gave her a peck on the forehead before she could move. Then he ran across the street along with Bobby. The girls were hysterical. "What are they doing?" Dede wanted to know.

"I don't know," said Hanna, "and I don't care. Leave them."

"We can't do that," said Dede.

"Then what do you suggest?"

"I don't know."

Automobiles had to slow down in order to get around the Audi, and occasionally a horn would blow. "I know one thing," said Dede, "I've got to move this fucking car. What are they up to? Where did they go?"

"There!" said Hanna. She could see them standing out front of an entranceway, next to a booth talking to what she guessed was a guard of some kind.

"Let's just see what happens," Dede said and just then saw a parking space up ahead.

"You aren't staying here I hope," said Hanna.

Across the street Byron was trying to explain to the sentinel, who happened to be the same old man they had met before, how important it was that he and Bobby got to see Tulane's president. "I can call the house and ask," the old man offered.

"Don't do that," said Byron. "What we really want to do is get to the door. If we could just get him to see us…" The old man knew he was talking to, at the very least, strange characters, not just because of their physical appearance, either. "I'd better call," the guard persisted.

Bobby threw up his hands, then let them fall to his sides. "Give me a cigarette, Byron." Byron fumbled in his shirt pocket and finally took out a crumpled pack. The old man was dialing the number. Byron and Bobby could not hear what he said. They walked around with their heads down and waited. "Did you bring the vodka?" Bobby wanted to know. In a minute the old man stepped out of the booth scratching the back of his head. "The president's not at home."

"Are you sure?" Bobby asked.

"Oh, I'm sure."

Bobby looked at Byron with his hands on his hips. "What do we do?"

Byron looked at the old sentinel. "May we just go up to his house and knock?"

"I'm not allowed to letchu do that. It would be my job for sure."

"I understand that," said Byron. "But may I ask you something, Mister...uh..."

"Portwood," the old man told him.

"Mister Portwood, is it possible that he is really in, and that sometimes you're told he is not, just to protect his privacy?"

The old man took his cap off and scratched the back of his head. "It's possible, I expect. But it don't matter. I'm just doing my job, you understand."

"We certainly do," said Bobby. "But let me ask you this, what would happen if we were to just walk over there and knock on his door? Would you mind if we did that? It's really important. A young girl's life is at stake here."

"It wouldn't matter to me personally."

Across the street Hanna and Dede were watching. "What are they doing?" Hanna wanted to know.

"I have no idea," said Dede. Then all of a sudden they saw Bobby and Byron walking away from the little guardhouse just as the man they had been talking to stepped back inside his booth.

"I'll have to report this," the old man said as Bobby

and Byron, both barefoot and in their short pants, had started up the walk to the porch of the president's home. "We've got to hurry," said Bobby. A moment later they were standing before the double-door entrance, where Byron rapped loudly with the elaborate brass knocker. "I've got to pee," said Byron.

"Me too," said Bobby just as one of the doors opened and a woman who appeared to be a maid stood before them. Several things happened at once. While Bobby was trying to explain to the maid what they wanted, taking too long to do so, a police car turned into Audubon Place, the old sentinel met them, and just then the president of Tulane, himself, stepped to the front door. Two policemen were walking toward the house. Byron knew he had to talk fast. "Sir, my name is Byron Burns, and I know this is a very unorthodox meeting. But I need to talk to you about something that my friend here and I must talk to you about." By then the policemen were on their way up the walkway. "Please, sir, I know we aren't presentable, we've just come from the beach, and we've been drinking, and I know it appears awfully strange, us standing here like this."

"Doctor, is everything alright?" one of the policemen asked while he held a transmitter to his side.

"Sir," said Byron, "if we could have just five minutes of your time. Just five minutes..." Byron held his opened hand out to help with his plea. "Just five minutes. Then if you don't think...what we're here about is worth your time—your concern—then…" He put his hand on his hip. "Then so be it. We'll go peacefully with these good gentlemen here."

The president of Tulane glanced from one of them to the other, then smiled, looked at the policemen, and finally said, "I think it's alright." Then to Bobby and Byron, he said, "Would you men like to come inside?"

Bobby smiled back at the rather distinguished-looking president. "We certainly do appreciate this. And we will not take up any more of your time than is absolutely necessary."

Across the street Hanna and Dede could see the entire thing. "They're going to jail," said Hanna. "God, what are they doing?"

"Wait! Look! They're going inside," said Dede. They could see Bobby and Byron disappear inside the fine old house, as the president stepped to a policeman standing near the porch, said something, then went back into the house. The policemen stood on the well-lighted porch for several minutes before going back to their car where they stood talking to the old sentinel.

Inside the mansion Byron and Bobby were graciously led into one of the front-most rooms and offered a sofa where they sat like grade school children in the headmaster's office.

"May I offer you something to drink?" the president of the university asked as he took a seat in a wingback chair across from them.

"That's very kind of you, sir, but we don't want to impose on you that way," said Bobby. A moment later the maid disappeared and did not return.

"Doctor," Byron began, "we have a problem that only you can help us solve. May I begin by giving you a little background? I promise you, we'll be as brief as possible."

"Sure," said the president with downcast eyes and a kind face.

"We want to be as honest as we know how to be," Byron continued. "As hard as it may be for you to believe, Bobby here, and I, are rather well-educated men. Bobby has a Ph.D. from Auburn University. And I graduated from the University of Alabama with a master's in English. Sir, I tell you this only to assure you of some credibility in our intruding on you as we have."

"What my friend is trying to say," interrupted Bobby, who thought Byron was going too slow, "is that we both fell from grace. We're both bad to drink. We think you should know that right up front, so that when we finish, you will see that we have been as honest as we know how to be."

"I understand," said the president.

"There's a girl," Byron continued. "Her name is Hanna."

"She's graduating from high school next month," Bobby added. "She's an A student."

"Brilliant," added Byron. And for most of the next

half hour they told the president all that they felt they could about Hanna. They left out only those things concerning the truth about Hanna's earlier schooling and the trumped-up transcript. They told him as much as they could about her mother, the way she had died, how Hanna came to stay with them because she had nowhere else to go, how they had tried to give her as much as they could under the circumstances, elaborating about how well she had done in school. They were excellent, as if they had rehearsed for months, and when one would lose his intensity for a moment, the other was there to take up and go on with the drama. And what a drama it was. They leaned, and frowned, blinked their eyes, waved their hands, looked at each other, looked directly into the eyes of the president, and spoke eloquently. That they had consumed more than two fifths of vodka since the early morning did not at all interfere with their coherence. They were pleading for Hanna, and they gave it all they had. They used humor appropriately and refrained from it just at the right moments. They read the president's face, and took every advantage they could find to use whatever hints he offered to maneuver him into understanding what they so desperately wanted him to understand. They did not smoke and they did not ask for drinks. They humbled themselves every way they knew how without being downright dishonest.

And then it was over. They brought their plea to a

crescendo and then very quietly resolved it. They had only to wait for the president's reply. Until now he had said very little. He got out of his chair and stood with his hands in his pockets and walked the floor for a few moments. Then he turned to Byron and Bobby, and with a smile simply said, "Why not? I don't see why we can't make an exception in a case like this."

Byron and Bobby looked at each other, but did not dare move. This was far more than they could have expected. They had only meant to establish something that would leave the door open. Neither man believed what he had just heard. It was just that simple. The man had spoken—the president.

"Did you say she hasn't gotten her results from the SAT?" he said to Byron.

"No," said Byron. "But we'd bet our lives she will score more than enough…"

"Our lives," said Bobby.

The president smiled and nodded. "I'll tell you what. Get the SAT score and the transcript to us as soon as possible…As far as the financial aid material… you say she's already mailed it in?"

"Nearly a month ago," said Byron.

The president nodded several more times as he looked down at the floor. "I'm eager to meet Hanna." Then he looked up and smiled once more and said, "Are you sure you wouldn't like a drink?" This time Byron and Bobby decided it was time to have some whiskey.

And while the president was gone from the room, Byron discovered that Bobby's fly was still open.

TWENTY-TWO

Hanna participated in only one of the senior class activities before graduation. She did not want to ask Byron and Bobby for any more money, for one thing. For another, she just was not interested in most of them. She was so excited about going to Tulane that anything short of an absolute catastrophe would make no difference in the least. Still, at night, when she went to bed, she could not believe who she was. "College! God!" she often said aloud. She started looking at herself in the mirror as if she was somebody she didn't even know. She made twelve hundred and forty-two on the SAT, which was over a hundred points more than was required to be accepted to Sophie Newcomb. And her transcript showed an A-minus average. Even Hanna was starting to believe she had brains. "College! God!" And Sophie Newcomb too, which, according to Dede, was one of the best girls' schools in America. Girls from all over the country came to Sophie Newcomb—rich girls. Girls who had chosen her school—her school—over all the others they had considered. An expensive school that Hanna was going to scot-free. Everything was going to be paid for—everything. She was going to have to work. Work-study, whatever that meant. Something to do with a part-time job on campus. She was as poor as a person could be, and for the first time in her life she was so proud to be. All she had to do was keep her grades up and for the next four years her life was so grandly laid out for her. And Bobby and Byron had convinced her, for the present at least, that she was more than capable.

If Ray could see her now. That all seemed like another life, and yet it had only been a year and a half that she was...Well, it wasn't even worth thinking about. And then again, it was. Bobby and Byron had taught her to accept all her life—all of it. "Girl," Byron once told her, "you are always a culmination of all that came before, and your visions of those things that you imagine will come down the road. It's all part of the same thing." And Hanna had thought about that, lots. Ray was just as much a part of Hanna James as Sophie Newcomb would become. It was all part of the same thing. It wasn't ugly anymore. It just was.

When it finally, still guardedly occurred to her that it was true she was going to college—in New Orleans, Sophie Newcomb—Hanna started to panic. "What'll I major in?"

"Nothing," Byron and Bobby told her.

"Whatah you mean, nothing?"

"Liberal arts," they told her.

"But my guidance counselor said…"

"Fuck your guidance counselor. We got you this far, didn't we?"

"But…"

"But nothing. Liberal arts, and relax. Somewhere down the line you'll decide something. And no doubt you'll change your mind a hundred times, and life will go on, and love will come, and Hanna will come too—hopefully."

"God! Ya'll are so fucking SICK!"

"Hanna?"

"What, Bobby?"

"Give Byron and me a piece of pussy."

Hanna could only smile as tears made her blink. "Ya'll. God, ya'll mean so much more to me than that."

Byron needed to break the sentiment. "What means more than pussy?"

"Are ya'll coming to my graduation?"

"Do you want us to?"

"Of course."

"Are you going to be ashamed of us?"

Hanna stepped out of the lawn chair, over to Byron, then Bobby, gave them both warm kisses on their lips with lasting hugs.

Afterwards, Bobby said, "Fucking A, we'll be there."

***

Hanna made two Cs on her final report card, but that didn't matter, Tulane was only interested in the grades up to her last semester. She could have done better, but she had been so busy. Taking care of all the details for college had kept her running. She had to meet with the president of Tulane. She had to talk with deans and aides and secretaries. She had to fill out, it seemed, a thousand forms—more financial forms, housing forms, boarding forms, not-interested-in-sorority forms, trial schedules…Then she would have to show them to Byron and Bobby, to assure them she had made no mistakes—they were all the time harping on "No mistakes, Hanna. None! This isn't Loblolly J.C. you're going to."

And then there were graduation things—class day practice, graduation practice, cap and gown pickup, class photographs, an awards ceremony (Hanna was given an award for most outstanding English student.)

And then there was the matter of a white dress for class day.

"Hell no," said Bobby. "We've done enough for your precious little pussy."

"But, Bobby…"

"Go talk to Byron."

Byron was out back soaking in the Mr. Turtle pool and reading J.D. Salinger's "Teddy." His hair was dripping, as he had just gone under the water to cool his face. Hanna came down the porch steps and wandered toward him as if she had no particular purpose in mind, not sure just how she was going to approach the matter. "Byron," she finally began.

"What is it, Sugar Baby?" he said, without looking up from his book.

Hanna sat down on the ground in front of him, picked up a twig and started punching holes in the dirt. "I…" she began and stopped.

Byron took the book away from his face and laid it to the ground. "What's the matter?"

"I have another problem." Her head was down and she started digging out a little hole with the twig. Then she sighed and said, "I have to have a white dress for that stupid class day thing."

Byron didn't say anything for a moment as he stared at the top of her head. Then finally he said, "It's been a tough year, hasn't it?"

Hanna looked up at him and smiled weakly. "Oh, Byron," she said, then broke down crying. Through the sobs she said, "I feel so stupid."

"Why?"

"Asking ya'll to keep on—I feel like…"

Byron gave her time to stop crying. And when she began to whimper and wipe at her eyes with her fingertips, he said, "Hanna."

"Whut?"

"Everything takes time."

"I know. But…"

"You're an amazing girl."

Hanna looked at him. She could not believe what she had just heard. Byron had never said anything quite like that before. She started crying again, and once more Byron waited until she was about finished. He leaned over the side of the pool and picked up his glass of vodka and juice and took a sip.

Then all of a sudden Hanna looked up at him again, still whimpering, and abruptly shouted. "Why do you keep drinking that goddamn stuff, Byron? Don't you know it's gonna kill YOU?" Her lips were quivering and the tears were rolling down her face. "GODDAMN YA'LL! Sometimes ya'll make me so goddamn fucking sick! You just go on and on and on…" Hanna brushed away the tears with her forearm.

Byron knew not to speak until she settled down. He lit a cigarette, took another sip of vodka and waited for her.

"Why, Byron? Why?"

Byron continued to say nothing as she went on crying. Then when she began to whimper this time, he said, "Wipe away your tears, girl. Everything is all right. Bobby and I just haven't gotten it right yet."

"Oh, Byron, you always say things like that when I'm trying to be serious."

"I know. But everything is happening the way it should. That's hard for you to understand, isn't it?"

"Yes sir," said Hanna. She had not meant to say

"sir." It just tumbled out of her mouth along with a snif-
fle. Byron said nothing about it.

"You will one day," he told her. "Do you remember
once, I told you about the secret people—the ones…"

"I remember," said Hanna. She had almost stopped
crying.

"Then dry your eyes, Girl, and…and get on with it."

"But, Byron…" Hanna did not know what she was
feeling all of a sudden. Something inside her started to
stir, something that felt almost like nausea, but overwhelming and confusing. It almost felt like it would
choke her. It was strange, and confusing and strong and
good. It made her want to climb over into the little wading pool and crawl into Byron's arms. It startled and
frightened her. She just wanted to bury herself inside
his old chest and feel him wrap his old emaciated arms
around her, to feel his old vodka-soaked heart bounce
against her ear—the way she knew it must bounce
sometimes. She wanted to tell him that everything was
all right for once. Hanna did not move. She knew she
couldn't. She could feel the tears coming back. Oh,
Byron. Oh, Byron. Oh, both of you, was all the thought
that she could think to think.

"Now, what's this about a white dress?"

"Nothing."

***

That night Hanna went off with Dede to a gathering of some of the seniors on the riverbank. Byron and Bobby went down to the outdoor living room. Earl and the others were feeling down. One of the derelicts had been hauled off to a TB sanitarium somewhere in Texas. It was an old fellow named Morley who had hardly said a word since Byron and Bobby had known him. He had always seemed to like them though, and smiled a lot when Bobby got to telling some of their tales about women.

For a while the derelicts talked about their old, nearly toothless companion. Then Bobby stood up from the sofa, and shouted, "Gentlemen, enough of this! Old Morley wouldn't want this! If Morley were here, right now, he'd want to hear about good pussy and good times." Bobby stood with his hands on his hips for a moment, then one of his wicked grins spread across his face as he said, "Now, take Byron and me. We now have more pussy than we can stand." Heads came up all around the place. "Tell them, Byron. Tell these people about the beauty of red pussy hair—a mountain of it."

"Whoa shit!" said Earl.

Bobby's throat could not contain a chuckle. "Tell them, Byron."

"Like a strawberry patch," said Byron.

"You boys ain't gettin' no pussy," said Earl, as if he was not certain he was telling the truth.

"No?" Bobby pointed straight at Earl's face and

looked the derelict in his eyes and grinned again. "No, you're exactly right. Not unless this taste that stays on my tongue all the time is my imagination. Tell them, Byron."

"Liquid heaven," said Byron.

Bobby stuck out his tongue and turned around to the group for everybody to see.

"Look like tobaccer slime to me," said one wino.

Byron leaned back and put his hands on top of his head. "Bobby, tell them about the other night on the beach."

"Beach?" said Earl.

"Oh, hell, Byron, these people don't want to hear about things like that. Cecil will have a heart attack."

"What about the beach?" said Cecil.

Bobby threw up his hands. "What's the use? They won't believe us anyhow."

"I will," said one derelict. "Hell, you boys convinced me a long time ago. Anybody who can get two precious womens like them you two have, I call the masters. I say 'sir' to people like that."

Everybody laughed and Bobby started a tale about two nymphets and two hungry aging men on a beach.

It was past midnight when Hanna got in from the senior gathering. Byron and Bobby were asleep on their mattresses. She stopped at the door to their room and stood and looked at them for several moments before going on to her room. What was going to become of them, she thought as she tossed her purse into one of the lawn chairs and turned out the light. Inside her room she flicked the light on, closed the door and started unbuttoning her blouse. Then something caught her eye and she stepped closer to her bed to see if what she thought she had seen was real. There, lying on her bed, was a row of one hundred dollar bills—ten in all. Hanna stood there with a hand on one of the buttons of her blouse staring at the money. She did not move. She felt a strange feeling that someone was watching her, and finally managed to turn around and go out the door back to where Byron and Bobby still lay the way she had seen them just a minute or so earlier. She went back to her room; the money was still there. And she knew that she knew where it came from— Byron's house trailer. She sat on the bed and started to cry. The whole year flashed before her in darting episodes, all the way back to that cold winter morning when she woke up to the sight of Bobby's limp penis and her unbuttoned shirt, even here and now knowing in her heart of hearts she had not unbuttoned it.

After a while Hanna lifted herself off the bed and finished taking off her clothes. But when she got into bed she did not go to sleep. She had a talk with herself. She was more confused than she had ever been in her life. What was she feeling? Pity for them, gratitude, respect, admiration—even worship. It was all too close to her. She had to get away from them. They had stolen her life, it seemed, raped her in the worst way possible. What in God's name did they want from her—did all she have to do was open up her legs and let them finish the job—just lie down and give the only thing she had left to give? Would it take that and nothing more—nothing less? Then could they give herself back to her? Hanna buried her head in her pillow and cried so much that she wondered if she could ever stop. It wasn't right, they were two old men, old enough to be her fathers, old enough to…to…just these two stupid old drunks who had done everything there was to do in their stupid lives, and now they wanted to devour her or something. She went on crying, keeping her head in the pillow so no one could hear her, and trying desperately to make sense out of what she felt. The sense did not come.

* * *

Along with starting to school at Newcomb in the fall semester, Hanna was one of several students who were given special permission to live on campus for the summer while she worked for room, board, and a small salary as a library aid. She would be moving to the campus and staying in one of the dorms soon after her high school graduation.

She bought a white dress for class day, but it was not a new one. She found it in one of the French Quarter thrift stores for ten dollars. Dede had a fit over it.

The weather was growing hotter, Bobby and Byron spent lots of time in the Mr. Turtle pool, and Hanna stayed frantic most of the time with all the changes she was about to make. The men offered her very little help; they stayed drunker than usual most of the time, and kept out of her way. They went more frequently to Georgianna's place, slept more, and talked a lot about taking a trip one day.

Hanna's graduation ceremony was on a Friday night. She left the house early that morning for a final rehearsal at the high school. Afterwards she planned to go over to Dede's house. Dede wanted her to do something to her hair. Bobby and Byron did not get out of bed until the middle of the morning. Bobby wandered to the kitchen first and got himself a glass of plain orange juice. Then Byron came in and reached for the vodka bottle.

"What do you think you're doing?" said Bobby.

"What?"

"No drinking today."

"Fuck that."

Bobby laughed. "It was your idea."

"I changed my mind," said Byron as he took the bottle over to where the plastic cups were. Bobby jumped over to him and snatched the bottle out of his hand. "If I can do it, so can you."

"Well I can't do it. Now give me that bottle."

"Yes you can." Bobby put the bottle behind him.

"Come on, Bobby, Goddamn."

Bobby's grin grew bigger. "No. Drink a beer—a light beer."

"I want that vodka."

"Nope. Remember now, we're going to not drink today."

"Oh hell, one drink did not a drunk make," said Byron turning to open the refrigerator. He found two beers inside and took one.

"Water it down," said Bobby. "Mix it with water."

"Fuck you," said Byron as he broke the top and took a swallow.

"You weak son-of-a-bitch," said Bobby as Byron smiled at him and went to the living room. A minute later Bobby came in with the other beer and his glass of orange juice. He took one sip out of the juice, then a swallow from the beer. "When do we start getting dressed?" he asked.

"What do we do all day is what I want to know."

"We could...we could...we could go...you want to play some gin rummy?"

They tried to play cards but it was no fun and Byron finally got up and went to take a bath. Bobby took the opportunity to get a swig of vodka, then went in the bathroom and sat on the floor while smoking and talking, mostly about how to have a few drinks without getting drunk before nightfall. "I'll tell you what," suggested Bobby. "One swallow an hour."

"No now," said Byron. "It won't work."

"Then half a swallow an hour."

"No. I'll tell you what. Let's wait till three o'clock. There's no way we can drink too much in that short a time."

"Two."

"Three!"

Eventually Byron got out of the bathtub, and Bobby got in. Byron took the opportunity to get a drink of vodka.

The morning was miserable. Smoking was no fun without something to hold and drink, and nothing they did could get their minds off the vodka they knew was just a short distance away. They tried to play gin rummy again, but that too reminded them of drinking, so they wandered about the house until nearly noon when Byron went out to the Mr. Turtle pool. Bobby joined him after sneaking one more shot of vodka.

"Bobby, did you take another drink just then?"

"What do you mean another? I haven't had the first one yet."

"You've had at least two."

Bobby chuckled. "I have not."

"At least two."

"And how many have you had? Takes one motherfucker to know another."

"None," said Byron.

"In the history of mankind, no one will ever know if

that is a lie or not."

They had decided that when three o'clock came they would have a legitimate drink, then start getting dressed, although the graduation was not until seven, deciding if they were dressed, feeling more dignified, maybe, they could compete with their urges.

They actually made it until two-thirty-five and then started reasoning away all the reasons why they might be able to wait until exactly three—since they had nearly proven they might be able to wait. So at two-forty they had their first drinks.

It was just after four when Dede brought Hanna back to the house. They sat in the car and talked for a while about trying to room together fall semester. Hanna would be moving into one of the dorms the next week to start her work program. She had already told the men she would like to go ahead and start making the transition—that it was time.

Dede told Hanna as she shut the door she would be by to pick her up for the graduation around six. Hanna reminded Dede that Byron and Bobby wanted to ride with them, waved at Cecil down the street headed for the outdoor living room, and ran into the house. But once she opened the door she stopped in her tracks and her mouth dropped open. For there stood the men, side by side, clean-shaven, well-groomed hair, grinning, and wearing tuxedos. They looked absolutely impressive.

* * *

The day Hanna moved out Byron and Bobby offered to go with her to the campus, help her get organized, but Hanna told them she would rather they did not do that. She said she wanted to say good-bye at the house, that she might start acting stupid. "Besides," she said, "I'll be seeing ya'll. It's not like I'm going around to the other side of the world."

"Yes, but in some other ways that's exactly how far you're going," Byron told her.

The good-bye was nothing special, they had been in the process of sending her off all that weekend. Dede came by for Hanna, they loaded her things in the trunk and backseat of the Audi. Byron and Bobby sat on the front porch steps, both in short pants and shirts with sleeves rolled up to the elbows, and watched. Then, when it was finally time to go, Dede stood alongside the car while Hanna timidly stepped up to the men. Then suddenly her lips started to quiver, and she slowly shook her head and said, "You fucking shit for senses," then burst into tears. Both stood up and wrapped themselves around her. Bobby wanted to whisper something in her ear, but the crying kept her from hearing it to start with. Then finally she stopped crying enough to say, "What, Bobby?"

Bobby put his mouth over her ear and said, "When are you going to give us some pussy?"

Hanna slipped out of their grip and stepped a little away from them, then reached out and smacked Bobby on the mouth with a kiss, smiled, and said, "Probably never." Bobby laughed. Then Hanna looked at Byron and started crying again. She wrapped her arms around him and sobbed until he pushed her away and said, "Go on, woman. Go to college." Hanna saw moisture in his eyes before she turned and ran to the car and jumped in. The men said good-bye to Dede and stood and watched the girls drive away. They neither one could think of anything funny to say, so they just stood there.

* * *

The month of June went by slowly for Byron and Bobby. Hanna had written to them twice. She was excited and looking forward to fall and getting started. Her work was easy, she had met a couple of people she really liked, and the food was "pretty fucking good, but I miss balogna." She told them she loved the campus late in the afternoon when she could look out her window, where she played with the future.

As for Byron and Bobby, they started spending more time with Georgianna and the derelicts. Earl and Cecil had walked to the river with them one day, and they had read to them from a Mark Twain collection of stories, Earl later telling the derelicts, "Them boys can make a story come to life."

Byron and Bobby talked little about Hanna, except to say occasionally, "Our little pussy" this or that. Byron started sleeping on Hanna's bed, and Bobby stayed on the mattress in the other room. They played gin rummy for Hanna's bed.

Life for them certainly was different. There was a lot more freedom, but it was not the kind of freedom they cared that much about. The house was no longer so well kept up. It was quieter around the place— except when the derelicts came over, and they did so more often now that Hanna was gone.

They talked about taking the streetcar up St. Charles to see her, surprise her, but they did not. They just continued to miss the smells of a girl in the house. They talked about taking a trip somewhere and actually did after buying an old pink Plymouth for three hundred dollars that used about as much oil as gasoline, that had to be entered from the passenger's side because the driver's door was stuck.

Mostly they just drank, and talked with each other, told each other stories they had already told more than once. "Did I ever tell you about that time" was the way it often went, and the other would lie so that the one telling the story would not get his feelings hurt. But there was always a new twist, and the one listening would add things and ask questions for new interest's sake. They did not quarrel nearly as much now that Hanna was gone, and all of a sudden there was more money for liquor and other necessities. Byron still had a little more than a thousand dollars left out of the house trailer money, and was about to reach a last draft of his novel.

Dede dropped Hanna off one day in late July, saying she'd come back for her. Hanna opened the front door. "Ya'll." she said before going to the kitchen where she could see Bobby and Byron out back in lawn chairs with their feet in the Mr. Turtle pool. Before going outside, she stepped into the room that had been hers. Byron's typewriter was on the cinderblock and plywood table, alongside a two-inch-thick stack of paper. The bed, in disarray, had not been moved; otherwise the room was a mess. As she started to walk out, something occurred to her. She put one knee on the bed, leaned over and picked up the sheet of notebook paper she had so long ago taped against a jagged hole in the wall, folded it and stuck it in her pocket before going out back to the Mr. Turtle Pool to see her...her...

One autumn day Hanna stepped off a streetcar out front of Tiny's Bar to say hello to Nick. To her surprise, Earl was sitting at the bar. The two men gave her a hug before she asked about Bobby and Byron. "Child," said Earl, "I gotta tell you this story. A while back, those boys took off in that old pink Plymouth. They said they was going up to Memphis for a vacation. Oh, by the way, Byron sent his book off to some place out in California. But, anyway, they got lost on their way to Memphis, took a wrong road, talking, and ended up in Birmingham, Alabama, and it was at night. So here them crazy sonsofbitches were, driving down a street in downtown Birmingham, Byron driving and Bobby, you know Bobby, well, he was telling Byron one of his long-winded stories, drinking, drunk, rambling on, and the front door on Byron's side fell off. I mean, fell off, right there in downtown Birmingham, just dropped off the car. Well, sir, those boys didn't do nothing but keep right on driving while Bobby kept telling his story. They never looked back."